Praise for

BLUE in the FACE

"Filled with delightful characters, witty remarks, and jokes aplenty, this book is a delightful tale and loads of fun. Fans of the Sisters Grimm [and] Lemony Snicket . . . will find much to like and chuckle over." —*School Library Connection*

"Fans of wordplay, puns, and fractured fairy tales should be right at home." —*Publishers Weekly*

"Familiar nursery-rhyme characters assume arresting new personas in this witty, clever story of personal transformation. . . . A surprising heroine fulfills her destiny in this rollicking version of Mother Goose." —*Kirkus Reviews*

BOOKS BY GERRY SWALLOW
(AKA DR. CUTHBERT SOUP)

A Whole Nother Story
Another Whole Nother Story
No Other Story

MAGNIFICENT TALES OF MISADVENTURE
Blue in the Face
Long Live the Queen

Magnificent Tales of Misadventure

BLUE in the FACE

Gerry Swallow

illustrations by Valerio Fabbretti

BLOOMSBURY
NEW YORK   LONDON   OXFORD   NEW DELHI   SYDNEY

First published in the United States of America in January 2016
by Bloomsbury Children's Books
Paperback edition first published in January 2017
www.bloomsbury.com

Bloomsbury is a registered trademark of Bloomsbury Publishing Plc

For information about permission to reproduce selections from this book, write to
Permissions, Bloomsbury Children's Books, 1385 Broadway, New York, New York 10018
Bloomsbury books may be purchased for business or promotional use. For information
on bulk purchases please contact Macmillan Corporate and Premium Sales Department at
specialmarkets@macmillan.com

The Library of Congress has cataloged the hardcover edition as follows:
Names: Swallow, Gerry, author. | Fabbretti, Valerio, illustrator.
Title: Blue in the face : a story of risk, rhyme, and rebellion /
by Gerry Swallow ; illustrated by Valerio Fabbretti.
Description: New York : Bloomsbury Children's Books, 2016.
Summary: When ill-mannered, eleven-year-old Elspeth Pule awakens in a strange
forest where nursery rhyme characters dwell, she must both learn compassion
and teach the merits of a good temper tantrum in order to return home.
Identifiers: LCCN 2015021235
ISBN 978-1-61963-487-9 (hardcover) • ISBN 978-1-61963-488-6 (e-book)
Subjects: | CYAC: Behavior—Fiction. | Characters in literature—Fiction. |
Fantasy. | Humorous stories. | BISAC: JUVENILE FICTION/Fantasy & Magic. |
JUVENILE FICTION/Humorous Stories. | JUVENILE FICTION/Nursery Rhymes.
Classification: LCC PZ7.1.S925 Blu 2016 | DDC [Fic]—dc23
LC record available at http://lccn.loc.gov/2015021235

ISBN: 978-1-61963-489-3 (paperback)

Book design by Yelena Safronova
Typeset by Newgen Knowledge Works (P) Ltd., Chennai, India
Printed and bound in the U.S.A. by Berryville Graphics Inc., Berryville, Virginia
2 4 6 8 10 9 7 5 3 1

All papers used by Bloomsbury Publishing, Inc., are natural, recyclable products
made from wood grown in well-managed forests. The manufacturing processes
conform to the environmental regulations of the country of origin.

For Phoebe, my little giant

BLUE in the FACE

Chapter 1

The following is a partial list of things that fly: airplanes, helicopters, kites, UFOs, birds (excluding emus, penguins, and a few others that just aren't into it), certain squirrels that are very much into it, bees, bats, butterflies, and blimps.

The following is a list of additional things that fly at 1841 Briarwood Place, Suite 207, home of the Pule family: books, toys, cups, plates (commemorative and otherwise), spoons, forks, small electronic appliances, and shoes. Especially shoes. In fact, there goes one now.

"Look out, Delores!" shouted Sheldon Pule as a wooden-soled clog sailed toward his wife's perfectly groomed, cotton-candy-like head of hair. As it turns out, being regularly assaulted by flying objects may not be much fun, but it is very good for the upper thighs. Delores Pule was, as a result, in very sound shape, and she deftly avoided the shoe as it whizzed past her left ear and took out a vase on the mantel. This was not just any vase. It was a cremation urn, housing the powdered remains of Mrs. Pule's mother, Wanda, a woman so mean and nasty that she had it put in writing that upon her death she wished to be cremated and have her ashes scattered over people who had annoyed her.

Only the cremation half of her wish had been carried out. The remaining stipulation had not been honored for two reasons. First, there were too many people Wanda had found annoying and not nearly enough remains to go around. Second, her daughter was not nearly so cruel as to go dumping ashes on people. The meanness had apparently skipped a generation and been passed down to Mrs. Pule's eleven-year-old, shoe-throwing daughter, Elspeth.

Mrs. Pule shrieked at the sight of the urn falling toward the tiled floor below. The vase shattered with a dull crunch while a small mushroom cloud of Mrs. Pule's mother wafted into the air, partially covering Mr. Comfy, the formerly all-black family cat—an animal that had, during Wanda's lifetime, annoyed her a great many times.

Meanwhile, Elspeth was reloading. This time, she was winding up to hurl one of Mr. Pule's golf clubs like a javelin. Elspeth despised those golf clubs as much as one person can despise an inanimate object. When her father was not busy working, gallivanting all about the country doing his silly job, he should have been spending time with his daughter, she thought. Not chasing a tiny ball around a park full of holes.

"No, no," pleaded Sheldon Pule, taking refuge behind an easy chair. "Those clubs are brand-new."

"I don't care!" shouted Elspeth. Her chubby face, already the shape of a pomegranate, was beginning to resemble one in color as well.

The golf club soared across the room, hit the cushioned back of the easy chair, ricocheted off, and knocked a wooden rack holding Mrs. Pule's collection of miniature souvenir spoons off the wall. On its way down, the rack nearly struck Mr. Comfy, who, by now, was feeling none too comfortable about any of this.

The small spoons scattered across the floor with a deafening clang, the one from Mount Rushmore falling presidents first into the heating vent. Elspeth was happy with the result. She detested those spoons as much as the golf clubs. Each spoon was a special gift to her mother from her father, brought back from his travels. For Elspeth, he brought tiny soaps and shampoos from all the hotels at which he stayed. While she might have been quite excited to receive them when she was three, eight years later the novelty had worn off.

"You told me I could have a pet!" Elspeth wailed. "And now you're going back on your word. How can you even live with yourselves?" This time she picked up the entire bag of golf clubs, raised it above her head, and heaved it onto the coffee table with a racket that resulted in much

3

banging on the ceiling by the young couple living in the apartment below.

"We were thinking something like a goldfish," said Mrs. Pule. "Or a parakeet, perhaps."

"That's the dumbest thing I've ever heard," Elspeth shot back. "You can't ride a goldfish. And you can't get wool from a parakeet. I . . . WANT . . . A . . . LLAMA!"

"Sweetheart," Mr. Pule reasoned. "We live in an apartment. We can't possibly keep a llama. For starters, where would it sleep?"

"I will get bunk beds. He will sleep on the bottom, and I on the top."

"But what about your night fits?" reminded Mrs. Pule. Elspeth's angst often failed to leave her body even while in slumber, and she spent most nights thrashing around in her sleep, which would result in her falling out of bed on a regular basis. Frequently she woke with the feeling that she was being watched by some unknown presence. Whether it was a ghost, an intruder, or merely a product of her very active imagination, she could never be certain.

"Then I will sleep on the bottom and he will sleep on the top," said Elspeth.

"You can't train a llama to climb a ladder," said Mr. Pule.

"How do you know?" Elspeth shot back. "Have you ever tried?"

Mr. Pule, forced to admit that indeed he had no experience in the field of llama wrangling, changed his approach.

"Even if you could teach a llama to climb a ladder, I'm pretty sure keeping such animals within the city limits is against the law. I'm sorry, but it's just not possible."

"Fine," shouted Elspeth, which in no way should be taken to mean that things were fine. She folded her arms across her chest, drew in a deep breath, and held it. And held it. And held it some more. Then she waited for that look—the one her parents always gave each other just as they were about to cave in to her demands. Her face reddened further, then purpled. Her eyes bulged from their sockets. And then it came. That sweet, wonderful look of concern.

"Okay, okay." Mr. Pule was the first to give in. "You can have a llama. We'll just have to . . . find a way to make it work."

Elspeth drew in a deep breath. She smiled and ran to her father. Still a little dizzy from the lack of oxygen, she took a zigzag path getting there.

"Thank you, Daddy," she said, falling into his arms. "You're the best father in the whole wide world."

"Yes," said Mr. Pule with a nervous chuckle, thinking that perhaps the exact opposite might be true. As Sheldon hugged his daughter, he was looking over her shoulder at Delores, whose face bore the same look as his own—a look that said, "What have we gotten ourselves into this time?"

"My friends at school are going to be so jealous." Elspeth beamed. This statement was wrong on two counts. As you might imagine of a person in possession of such poor manners, Elspeth had no friends at school.

In addition, as of earlier that week she had no school. She had been suspended for having yet another tantrum in class, which included throwing the globe at her teacher, its raised surface leaving a Greenland-shaped bruise on poor Mrs. Weed's forehead. Elspeth was told not to return to school until she was ready to apologize to her teacher and to her class for the disruption. In the days following, she had not found herself ready and, in fact, had stated that she would never apologize to "that ridiculous cow."

To make matters worse—if there is anything worse than hitting your teacher in the head with Greenland—this was the seventh school from which Elspeth had been expelled. In the entire city, there was only one school that had not banned her from admittance, and that was the very prestigious and very expensive private school known as the Waldorf Academy, which was in no way related to that salad with the walnuts in it. It was a school that boasted graduates who had gone on to become Nobel Prize winners, presidents of major corporations, and that guy who made millions by inventing the trap door on the bottom of the toaster to let out all the crumbs.

Elspeth's parents had arranged a meeting on the following Tuesday with the school's principal. If he were to find their ill-tempered daughter lacking, the only other option would be homeschooling, and Mr. and Mrs. Pule were not prepared to subject themselves to such round-the-clock terror.

"Okay, dear," said Mrs. Pule. "It's way past your bed-time, so off you go."

"Yes, Mother," cooed Elspeth, suddenly the most agreeable person on the planet. "And you know, now that I think about it, maybe you're right. Maybe a llama is not the right way to go."

Mr. and Mrs. Pule looked at each other with utter shock and surprise and breathed a simultaneous sigh of relief. "Oh," said Mr. Pule. "I'm so glad you've come to your senses, my dear."

"Yes," said Elspeth. "I don't know what I was thinking. After all, why would anyone want a llama for a pet when for the same price you can get an alpaca? Good night now."

As Elspeth skipped off to her bedroom, her exhausted parents just stood and watched. "Well, I'm glad that worked out," said Mr. Pule, wiping perspiration from his forehead. "By the way, what's an alpaca?"

"Not sure," admitted Mrs. Pule. "But I'm hoping it's a member of the goldfish family."

And with that, she found the broom and dustpan and began the task of sweeping up what remained of her mean, dead mother.

There was a little girl,
Who had a little curl,
Right in the middle of her forehead.
When she was bad, she was very, very bad.
When she was worse, she was horrid.

Chapter 2

Sitting alone in her room, Elspeth listened to the sounds to which she'd become all too accustomed. Still, they made her heart sink a little each time she heard them: the sharp snaps and long, wide zippers as her father packed his bags for yet another extended road trip away from the family, all in the name of commerce.

Sheldon Pule worked as a door-to-door hearing-aid salesman. In addition to its potential for severe knuckle damage (you have to knock very loudly when selling hearing aids door-to-door), it was also a job full of pressure and uncertainty. One never knew, month to month, how many hearing aids one might be lucky enough to sell. And now Sheldon felt more pressure than ever before, knowing that he would have to make enough extra money to send his daughter to private school, while at the same time housing and feeding a full-grown alpaca, which is not even a distant relative of the goldfish.

Mr. Pule kissed his wife on the cheek, then stopped by Elspeth's room long enough to give her a quick pat on the head. Then he toted his bags out the door, climbed into his well-traveled car, and drove off.

The next morning, a hundred miles away, Mr. Pule had been out on the job, already desperately knocking for two hours (at one house, no less), when there came a forceful knock at his own door at 1841 Briarwood Place, Suite 207. Mrs. Pule, who worked from home part-time as a tax accountant, opened the door to reveal the Pules' landlord, the short, red-faced Mr. Droughns, standing on the other side.

"Oh, hello, Mr. Droughns," said Delores. "How are you today?"

"Not well, I'm afraid," grumbled Mr. Droughns. The redder his face became, the more his new hair plugs stood out, giving the top of his head the look of a lawn sprinkler. "We've had more complaints. About the noise."

"Yes," said Mrs. Pule. "We had a little . . . family mis-understanding last night. I'm happy to say it's all been worked out. You needn't worry. It won't happen again; you have my word."

"I had your word last time as well," Mr. Droughns said with a sneer. "And the time before that. I'm sorry to say that if there's a next time, I'll have no choice but to issue an eviction notice."

"I completely understand," said Mrs. Pule, with a smile meant to charm. "Oh, and while you're here, remind me once more about the pet policy."

"One cat or one small dog, neither weighing more than twenty-five pounds." His eyes narrowed with suspicion. "Why do you ask?"

"Oh, no reason, really," Mrs. Pule lied. "It's just that our Mr. Comfy has put on a few pounds lately and I just wanted to make sure he hadn't exceeded the weight limitation. You know how it is with cats. One day you turn around and they're as big as an alpaca."

"What the devil is an alpaca?" asked Mr. Droughns.

Since the previous night, Mrs. Pule had taken time to look up some information about alpacas online and found that, as it pertained to Mr. Droughns's pet policy, they are virtually no different than llamas.

"You don't know what an alpaca is?" asked Mrs. Pule hopefully. "Uh . . . it's a member of the goldfish family, I believe. All right then, have a nice day." With that, she shut the door, leaned back against it, and wondered what would get them evicted sooner: their tempestuous daughter or the sudden appearance of a large domesticated pack animal indigenous to the foothills of South America.

All that day, because she had no school, Elspeth sat in her room and searched the Internet for images of alpacas, trying to decide just which color she would pre-fer. White with reddish-brown spots would be nice. But that would clash with the bright lavender walls in her bedroom. Of course she was certain that, with some sim-ple pleading or caustic threats, she could get her parents to paint the room. Perhaps a bright yellow. It would cer-tainly complement her sunny personality, she thought.

"What's your opinion?" she asked Dolly Dew Eyes, who sat on the desk and stared at the computer screen with eyes that never blinked and a vacant smile that always shone. The fashion doll's golden locks had long ago been scissored away, leaving its head looking very much like Mr. Droughns with his silly hair plugs. A gift from her parents on her third birthday, Dolly Dew Eyes had remained Elspeth's best friend and closest confi-dante, most likely because the doll, made of plastic and paint, was unwaveringly agreeable.

For instance, never was there a better chess oppo-nent. Dolly was a very cheerful and gracious loser. This allowed Elspeth to hone her skills in all facets of the game while at the same time developing the confidence that comes with winning one hundred percent of the time.

"That's exactly what I was thinking," said Elspeth. She was beyond pleased that Dolly Dew Eyes also consid-ered a nice canary yellow to be most suiting. "We should begin as soon as possible so that when the alpaca arrives it won't be subjected to any nasty paint fumes. It's bad enough in here as it is with that mildew."

She was referring to a patch on the carpet that was frequently wet and had soured since it first showed up several months before. Her parents had made numerous complaints to Mr. Droughns about a possible plumbing problem in the apartment upstairs, but he steadfastly maintained that he could find nothing that would cause water to puddle on Elspeth's bedroom floor.

"The good news is," said Elspeth, "that once we paint the room yellow, the carpet will have to be changed too. I'm thinking light blue."

Dolly Dew Eyes seemed to agree with this as well. "That's what I love most about you, Dolly Dew Eyes," Elspeth said, giving the doll a warm, cheek-to-tiny-cheek embrace. "We like all the same things. So then, when Daddy returns this weekend, he will take me to the paint store to pick out the most perfect shade of yellow."

By the time Mr. Pule lumbered in late Friday night dragging his suitcases, Elspeth was already asleep, making this the perfect time for Mrs. Pule to bring up the subject of eviction with her husband.

"While you were gone, we had a little visit from the landlord," she said, speaking in hushed tones. "We cannot bring an alpaca into the apartment. Droughns will have us out on the street in no time."

"Well," said Mr. Pule, "the wool would keep us warm."

"This is nothing to joke about, Sheldon."

"I wasn't joking," Sheldon replied dryly. "I don't think we have much of a choice here. If we say no, she's bound to throw a fit and get us evicted anyway. Furthermore, she's quite liable to deliberately sabotage her meeting at Waldorf next week. Then what will we do?"

"I think we need help," said Mrs. Pule. "Professional help."

"What professional help?" said Mr. Pule, throwing up his frustrated hands and running them through his similarly frustrated and steadily graying hair. "We've tried everyone."

This was very nearly true. Over the years, Mr. and Mrs. Pule had read just about every book on parenting they could find, all to no avail. In addition, they had met with almost every expert within driving distance, and none of the advice they were given ended up having any effect at all.

"We haven't tried *everyone*," said Mrs. Pule.

"Oh no," said Mr. Pule. "No way. Not that quack."

"He's quite respected."

The person to whom Mrs. Pule was referring was a gentleman by the name of Dr. Tobias Fell, a family therapist famous for his tough-love approach to child rearing. His latest book, *Quit Your Whining*, had just broken into the top ten of the bestseller list and was now available in twelve languages. In addition, *Quit Your Whining* (or, in German, *Hör auf zu heulen*) had made Dr. Fell one of the most sought-after family therapists in the country, and getting an appointment with him on such short notice would not be easy.

"I don't know," said Mr. Pule, staring at the blank space on the wall where the spoon collection had once hung. "I just have a bad feeling about him."

"What could it hurt?" asked Mrs. Pule. "We don't have to take his advice. Besides, at this point we've really got nothing to lose."

"And what if we do take his advice and it still doesn't work?" asked Mr. Pule.

"Then the wool will keep us warm."

I do not like thee, Dr. Fell,
With pop advice and books to sell.
Though you may make our daughter well
I do not like thee, Dr. Fell.

Chapter 3

Finding a babysitter for their daughter was never easy for Mr. and Mrs. Pule. It had to be someone new to the area, a person unfamiliar with Elspeth's temperament. It also had to be someone with very good medical insurance.

Luckily, the teenage daughter of one of Mrs. Pule's new accounting clients was in need of some extra cash, so the Pules were able to sneak off to see the celebrated Dr. Fell, telling Elspeth only that they had a medical appointment.

When Mr. and Mrs. Pule were called into the office by Dr. Fell's assistant, the doctor directed them to sit in a pair of matching chairs that were as uncomfortable as they were stylish. Fell sat opposite them in a chair that looked to have three or four times the padding. On the wall behind him hung several diplomas, certificates, and awards, along with framed photographs of himself standing next to celebrities. His chin sported a goatee, and a small diamond stud adorned his left earlobe.

"Now," he said, flipping a tablet of paper over to a blank page. "I understand you're having some trouble with your four-year-old son."

"Uh . . . eleven-year-old daughter," Mr. Pule corrected.

"They grow up so fast, don't they?" Dr. Fell replied. "Now, why don't you tell me a little bit about what's going on?"

Mrs. Pule took the lead, explaining to the doctor that their daughter, despite the fact that they had tried to be the best parents possible, had become an insufferable tyrant. As she spoke, Dr. Fell did a great deal of scribbling on his pad.

"And so you see," Mr. Pule said in summation, "we really have no choice but to give in to her demands."

Dr. Fell scoffed at this, partly because when it came to scoffing, he was one of the best. "Of course you have a choice," he said.

"You don't understand," Mr. Pule interjected. "If she doesn't get her way, she holds her breath."

"And?" said Dr. Fell, entirely unimpressed.

"And she keeps holding her breath," added Mrs. Pule. "If we don't give her what she wants, we're afraid she could die."

Dr. Fell flipped the notebook to a fresh page and wrote something, then tore it out. "The next time your

daughter threatens you by holding her breath, try this."
He handed the paper to Mr. Pule, who read it aloud.

"Ignore her?"

"Yes," said Dr. Fell. "Ignore her and let her hold her breath for as long as she likes."

"That's the most ridiculous thing I've ever heard," said Mr. Pule, rising to his feet. "And what happens when she dies from lack of oxygen?"

"She won't die," said Dr. Fell with a condescending chuckle. "The worst that will happen is that she will pass out, and when she does, her body will naturally start breathing again. The important thing is to make sure she doesn't hit her head on anything on the way to the floor."

By the time the elevator reached the lobby of the building, Mr. Pule was still fuming. "'Make sure she doesn't hit her head on the way to the floor'? How could someone be so callous toward a mere child?"

"I know you're upset, dear," said Mrs. Pule, walking out into the parking lot.

"Upset?" Mr. Pule practically shouted. "We just paid that idiot four hundred dollars to tell us that we should just sit back and watch our daughter hold her breath until she passes out. You're darned right I'm upset."

While Mrs. Pule muttered some words of support, Dr. Fell's words were playing over and over in her head.

The important thing is to make sure she doesn't hit her head on anything on the way to the floor.

Mrs. Pule took advantage of the twenty-minute ride home to convince her husband that giving Dr. Fell's advice a shot was really their only choice.

"Okay, okay," he finally agreed. "We'll try it. Once. But I just want to go on record as saying I am deeply opposed to it."

When they arrived back home, where Elspeth and the babysitter had been alone together for almost two hours, they found her locked in the closet. Not Elspeth—the babysitter.

"I had no choice," said Elspeth, once the babysitter had been paid, consoled, and sent on her way. "Her behavior was atrocious. She had the nerve to try to deny Dolly Dew Eyes a second bowl of ice cream. Have you ever heard of such rudeness?"

Mr. and Mrs. Pule were indeed familiar with rudeness on that level and beyond.

"Elspeth, dear," her mother said. "Your father and I need to have a little talk with you. Perhaps you'd like to have a seat on the sofa. The nice, soft sofa."

"What is it?" asked Elspeth, picking up on the concern in her mother's voice. She knew they had just returned from a doctor's appointment. Perhaps one of them was gravely ill. Or was it something worse? Maybe her mother was pregnant. The thought of some wrinkly, screaming baby getting spit all over her belongings was something Elspeth could not bear to consider. And if she thought that her parents ignored her now, just how little attention would she get once a newborn arrived? "Is something wrong?"

"Good question," said Mr. Pule, chuckling nervously as Elspeth lowered herself cautiously to the sofa while clutching Dolly Dew Eyes tightly to her chest. "It seems that we do have a slight . . . situation, I'm afraid."

As someone who had been placed in both advanced English and math, Elspeth was certainly smart enough to know that when someone said they had a situation, it was never a positive thing.

"We had a visit from Mr. Droughns the other day," said Mrs. Pule.

"Does he still have those horrible hair plugs?" asked Elspeth with pantomimed vomiting for effect.

"Yes, dear," said Mrs. Pule.

"I hope you told him how ridiculous they look."

While other hairless dolls might have taken offense to this, Dolly Dew Eyes said nothing and stared off into space with those expressionless blue-gray eyes.

"I was really in no position to insult the man," said Mrs. Pule. "He was quite angry as it was. In fact, he threatened us with eviction over the noise complaints."

"I haven't made any noise complaints," Elspeth protested.

"No," said Mrs. Pule. "Complaints made by the neighbors about noise coming from our place."

"I see," said Elspeth. "I guess you'll just have to learn to go about your chores more quietly."

Mr. and Mrs. Pule gave each other a look. "It's not the chores," said Mrs. Pule, exhaling deeply. She rubbed her hands together and realized her palms were wet with nervous perspiration. "It's . . . you."

The confusion on Elspeth's face was absolutely sincere. "Me? What do you mean, me?"

"Your tantrums have disturbed the other tenants to the point that they have asked the landlord to kick us out."

"Ha! Good luck with that," said Elspeth with a laugh of disdain. "I'm sure they'll forget all about their little threats once I sic my alpaca on them."

And there it was: the perfect segue into the next topic at hand. "Yes, about that," began Mrs. Pule. "I'm sorry to say that, upon further reflection, we can't let you bring an alpaca into the apartment."

Elspeth sprang to her feet and punched at the air with an accusatory finger. "I knew it! I knew you'd go back on your promise! You are the worst parents in the entire world!"

Then, for a solid three minutes, Elspeth tossed out every nasty word she could think of toward her loving mother and father, and she could think of nearly all of them. Then she moved on from hurling words to hurling solid objects. With Dolly Dew Eyes in her left hand, she used her right to throw toys, books, shoes, the phone, and Mr. Comfy, who did not, it seemed, fully appreciate the convenience of air travel. He yowled as he was tossed across the room and did not stop yowling even when he came to rest on Mrs. Pule's head.

Mrs. Pule screamed and tore the terrified animal away, losing a good deal of her cotton-candy hair in the process. Still, Elspeth's parents did not waver from their anti-alpaca position.

When throwing the family cat at one's mother proves ineffective, it's time to pull out the big guns. Elspeth spouted her famous line. "Fine!" she said, folding her arms across her chest with Dolly Dew Eyes clutched between her arms and her aquamarine T-shirt. Elspeth then drew in a deep breath—deeper than usual, for she sensed that this time it wouldn't be easy.

Then she waited. And waited. For that look. Her eyes darted back and forth between her father and her mother, searching for a sign that one or both of them were about to crack. Then something strange happened—something that had never occurred before. Mr. and Mrs. Pule calmly settled back into their chairs and began what appeared to be a casual conversation, though Elspeth could not hear what they were saying. By now so much blood was rushing to her brain in an attempt to deliver oxygen that it thundered past her eardrums, drowning out every sound in the room.

If it wasn't infuriating enough that her parents would ignore her in this time of severe oxygen deprivation, they now had the audacity to become blurry. How dare they mock her by distorting their own images, thought Elspeth. And now, what was this? Were they dimming the lights? Of all the nerve. And was the room spinning, or had the rug beneath Elspeth's feet become a swirling eddy of doom with the power to pull her under? It certainly sounded like a cyclone, as the pressure in her head built until it felt as though her ears might go shooting off in opposite directions.

And then, just like that, the room went completely dark.

Roses are red,
Violets are blue,
Eggplants are purple,
And Elspeth is too.

Chapter 4

Elspeth found herself immersed in complete blackness and utter confusion. The only thing she knew for certain was that she was lying flat on her back. When she opened her eyes, the first thing she noticed was that her parents were nowhere to be found. Had they been so callous as to walk away, leaving her alone on the living room floor? The second thing she noticed was that the living room was also nowhere to be found. The ceiling had been replaced by a soft light, twinkling through a canopy of translucent green leaves, shuddering in a soft breeze.

For a moment, she was afraid to move. Her hands at her sides, her fingers probed what she would have expected to be the shag carpeting but felt a lot more like moss and dirt. Bringing her fingers close to her face, she noticed the rich, dark soil beneath her nails.

Slowly, she sat up to find herself in the middle of a thick forest. She wanted to call out but was fearful of who or what her cries might summon. Elspeth had grown up in the city, and other than a handful of trips to visit mean old Grandma Wanda in the country, she had never been outside it. A forest was something she had seen only in movies, and she'd never had the desire to visit one in person. It was her understanding that the so-called great outdoors generally lacked things like indoor plumbing, television, and Internet access. This might be acceptable to wild animals and bugs, but for humans it seemed a barbaric place at best.

Still, she had to admit it smelled rather nice. It was the unfamiliar sounds that gave her discomfort—the squawking and chirping of what she assumed (and hoped) were birds and the rustling of trees in the wind.

"What is this?" Elspeth whispered. "Where am I?"

"I think you mean," came a strong voice from very nearby, "where are *we*?"

With the quickness of Mr. Comfy dodging a commemorative plate, Elspeth rolled to her hands and knees and scanned the area with nervous eyes. "Who said that?" she demanded in a shaky voice. "Who's there?"

"Why it's me, of course," the voice answered.

When Elspeth looked down she saw Dolly Dew Eyes with eyes no longer absent and plastic body no longer stiff and motionless. The doll was standing and, with very real and supple palms, brushing dirt and pine

27

needles from her fashionable but badly frayed blue cocktail dress.

"Look at this mess. I hope the next time you decide to keel over you'll have the courtesy to put me down first."

"You . . . you can talk," gasped Elspeth.

"Yes, I can," agreed Dolly Dew Eyes, almost as surprised as Elspeth at her newfound vocal abilities. "Well, what do you know?"

"But . . . I don't understand. Why are you talking like that? In that voice?"

"What's wrong with my voice?" asked the doll while smacking her dirty palms together.

"Well," said Elspeth, "for one thing, you sound so much older than you are."

"And how old do you think I am?" asked the doll.

"I got you for my third birthday," Elspeth replied. "And I'm almost twelve, which means you couldn't be more than nine in toy years."

"You assume," said the doll, "that I was brand-new at the time. Fact is that I'm twenty-seven."

Elspeth was thankful to still be sitting on the ground, otherwise these words might have knocked her right off her feet. "You mean . . . are you saying . . . my parents bought you . . . used?"

"Garage sale," said the doll. "Fifty cents, if you can believe that. Imagine what that did for my self-esteem. And then, on top of that, you go and cut off all my hair. Thanks a lot."

"You know, I think I liked you better when you couldn't talk, Dolly Dew Eyes," said Elspeth.

"Oh, I'm sure you did," said the doll. "That way you could go on, day after day, convinced that I actually like you. And by the way, please do not refer to me by the awful name Dolly Dew Eyes. Good grief."

"I was only three when I named you," Elspeth reminded the doll.

"The other girl was three when she got me and still had the good taste to call me Fashion Farrah, which is the name on the box and is what I prefer to be called."

Elspeth suddenly realized something. "Wait a minute," she said. "I'm sure it's probably a simple misunderstanding, but did you just imply that you don't like me?"

"Let's face it, you're not a very likeable person, are you?" the doll answered. "Always putting words in my mouth. Not to mention all the yelling and throwing whenever you don't get your way. It's embarrassing, really."

Elspeth was unaware that her mouth now hung wide open and her bottom lip had started to quiver. The very idea that her beloved doll could have such negative feelings toward her was too much for Elspeth to bear, and she began to do something she had not done in a very long time. She began to cry. It started out as a whimper then quickly morphed into that type of full-on crying you see in the movies when someone is trying very hard to win an Academy Award.

The blubbering went on for a very uncomfortable few minutes and might have continued much longer had Elspeth not made a very determined effort to force those sobs and her sorrow back from where they had come.

"No," she said, mopping up the tears with her shirtsleeve. She stood and wiped her nose with that same sleeve and then stamped her foot. "This is nothing to cry about. You're just a stupid old doll."

"Excuse me," said Farrah. "I am not stupid."

"You are if you think you're going to find your way back home without my help, so I suggest you start being nicer to me."

"Home?" said the doll. "Why would I want to go back there? All I do is sit in your silly purple room all day. I never get to leave the house because you're too embarrassed to be seen with me."

"That's not true," Elspeth protested. "It's lavender, not purple."

"Aha! So you *are* ashamed of me." The doll jabbed its tiny finger in Elspeth's direction. "Just admit it already."

"Well," said Elspeth, stalling while trying to think of how to put it diplomatically. "Just . . . look at your hair. I mean, seriously."

"There you go," said the doll, her hands on her hips and her painted-on eyebrows turned downward in a fierce scowl. "If I had any doubt that you were a horrible person before, I certainly don't now."

"You listen to me, you little plastic runt," said Elspeth, while fighting off the urge to punt the doll into the surrounding greenery. "I will not stand here and be lectured by some two-bit garage sale item."

"First of all, fifty cents is four bits," said the doll. "And I may be a garage sale item but I have something you'll never have: self-respect. I'll bet your parents are sorry they ever . . ." The doll cut herself off in midsentence.

"What?" Elspeth demanded. "Sorry they ever did what?"

"Nothing," the doll insisted. "I started to say something, but . . . it's none of my business. It's between you and them, and I'll leave it at that. Have a nice life."

The doll turned on her plastic heel and huffed off into the shadows of the trees.

"Wait!" Elspeth called out. "Don't leave me here alone." The girl's plea went unanswered. Elspeth thought of what might make Dolly Dew Eyes change her mind. "I could get you a wig!" she shouted through cupped hands.

Elspeth stood and watched as her once favorite toy disappeared behind a large fern. She was now all alone, officially friendless and miserable, in a strange forest, far from home.

A tisket, a tasket,
A doll that's made of plastic.
I held it tightly in my arms
And on the way I dropped it.
I dropped it,
I dropped it,
And on the way I dropped it.
It wandered off into the woods
And now I fear I've lost it.

Chapter 5

Elspeth cautioned herself not to panic. There must be a simple explanation for how she ended up in this forest and an equally simple way of getting home. When she turned a slow and complete circle, it was what she didn't see that confused her most. Other than a set of tiny ones made by Dolly Dew Eyes on her way into the forest, there were no footprints. Nor were there any tire tracks. So how did she get here if not by foot or by car? Though it seemed an extreme improbability, Elspeth quickly checked to see whether she might be wearing a parachute. Nope. No parachute, so she hadn't been dropped from an airplane.

Several feet away, she saw a narrow path, and she decided that, at this point, there was very little to lose by taking it. She walked lightly at first, painfully aware of the snap of every little twig, though in time her fear began to subside in favor of fatigue and irritation.

With each step, things looked more and more the same. Also consistent were the sounds of the forest, and they remained that way for some time until Elspeth heard a very loud thud directly behind her, followed by a high-pitched shriek and a groan.

She turned to see a roundish bush beneath a tall tree. The bush was moving about violently, making both rustling and grunting noises as if a human and a shrub were engaged in a wrestling match. Elspeth, despite her all-around rotten attitude, had never before fought with a shrub, though she did once tackle the Christmas tree after discovering that Santa had failed to bring her a real live unicorn.

The fight finally ended when out of the bush came a mess of flailing arms and legs attached to a large, oval body.

"And stay out!" yelled the shrub at the oddly shaped man, who had risen to his feet and was now brushing leaves and dirt from a well-worn black tuxedo. He appeared to be missing both neck and shoulders, his head and body one continuous thing. What drew Elspeth's attention next were the cracks running down the left side of the man's face. Not lines of age, but actual cracks in the surface of his leathery skin.

"I beg your pardon, madam," the man said to the shrub in the most suave British accent one could imagine. "It's my vertigo come to call once more. I must, henceforth, eschew any and all desire to sit in trees and upon walls. Please accept my humble apology."

He bowed slightly toward the talking shrub, and the shrub seemed to think about it for a moment before saying, "Don't worry about it. No harm done. Just don't let it happen again."

"Rest assured, I shan't," replied the man.

Being in the presence of a talking bush, Elspeth's first instinct was to take off running. But considering that she had no idea where she was, she decided to go with her second instinct, which was to ask for directions and then take off running.

She put her hands on her hips and thrust her chin forward to convince the man and the shrub, but mostly to convince herself, that she was not afraid. "Hey! Mister," she said in her most polite voice, which by anyone else's standards would be considered quite rude.

"Yes?" he said in that delightfully smooth accent, his right eyebrow arching up just slightly. "May I be of some assistance?"

"I hope so. I need you to tell me where I am, and I need you to tell me right this instant."

"Where you are right now, my child, is in the forest."

Elspeth rolled her eyes and puffed out a sharp exhale of frustration. "Uh, hello? I know it's a forest. What I need to know is where I am in relation to my apartment so that I can get home again."

The man arched his eyebrow once more, a bit surprised by Elspeth's extreme lack of manners. He looked back at the shrub, and the shrub seemed to shrug. Of all the things Elspeth had never expected to see during her lifetime, a shrugging shrub was very near the top of the list.

"How utterly rude," said the bush.

"You want rude? I'll show you rude," said Elspeth. She kicked a small rock, and when she did, the rock hollered, "Hey! Watch it!"

Elspeth jumped nearly a foot off the ground and let out an ear-piercing shriek. "This is ridiculous," she snarled. "Is everything alive around here?"

"But of course," said the man. "You mean to say that things aren't alive where you come from?"

"Not rocks," said Elspeth. "Or bushes, or dolls, for that matter."

"Ahh," said the man. "You're from the Deadlands."

"I'm from the greater Seattle area," Elspeth retorted.

"Yes," the man said. "I've never been to the Deadlands, but we have had the occasional emigrant."

He stepped toward Elspeth, then, upon closer examination of her face, he abruptly froze. His eyes widened and his jaw slackened. "Oh my goodness," he gasped. "Could it be? Is it really you?"

"If it's not me, then it's someone doing a very good impression," said Elspeth. "Of course it's me."

"I know what you're thinking," said the shrub to the man. "But it's not her. Slight resemblance, but too chubby."

36

"I am not chubby," said Elspeth, folding her chubby arms across her chest.

"And too obnoxious," the shrub added.

"Yes," said the man with a nod. "Not the stuff of heroes."

"Quit talking about me as though I'm not here," spat Elspeth. "Especially when I don't want to be here. I want to go home. Now."

"Yes," said the man. "However, I'm afraid any attempt to leave is strictly against the law."

"I'm an American citizen," Elspeth said in the way that most people do while uttering those exact words. "I know my rights."

When the man responded with a slow shake of his head, she took a moment to study him more closely. "You look familiar. Have we met before?"

"Not to my knowledge," said the man. "The name is Dumpty. Humpty Dumpty."

"You're Humpty Dumpty?" said Elspeth flatly. "Right. And I'm Little Bo-Peep."

Mr. Dumpty snickered as he replied, "I mean no offense by this, but I know Little Bo-Peep. She happens to be a very good friend of mine. And you, young lady, from what I have thus far observed, are no Bo-Peep."

With this, Elspeth let out her own little snort. "I should hope not. She couldn't even keep track of a herd of sheep. Exactly how dense do you have to be to lose an entire herd of sheep?"

"Flock," said Dumpty. "Sheep travel in flocks."

"Whatever," Elspeth snapped back. "The point is, what on earth was she thinking? For starters, everyone knows that alpacas are a far better investment."

"Financial considerations aside, the first thing you should know is that Miss Bo-Peep did not lose her sheep, as you suggest," said Dumpty. "They were taken from her."

By now, Elspeth had heard quite enough from this condescending ellipse. "I am well aware of the story of Bo-Peep—of how she lost her sheep and didn't know where to find them."

"If that's what you've been told, then I'm afraid you've been duped," Dumpty replied.

"That's right," said the shrub. "Duped."

"Excuse me?" barked Elspeth. "I wasn't talking to you, so maybe you should mind your own business there, Shrubby McHedge."

"My name is not Shrubby McHedge," the shrub protested with a haughty rustling of its leaves. "It's Tanya."

"I don't care if your name is Florence Nightingale. I'm quite familiar with the story of Little Bo-Peep, and you're not about to convince me that she did not lose her sheep."

"If we can't convince you," said Dumpty. "Then perhaps Bo-Peep herself can." He focused his gaze on an area somewhere behind Elspeth, and when she turned around she was surprised to find a very plain woman, perhaps the age of her own mother, wearing a soiled and tattered calico dress. In one hand was a long stick, nearly as tall as the woman herself, and, draped around her shoulders, a large canvas satchel. Her deep, sad eyes stared at Elspeth in astonishment. "Is that . . . ?"

"No," said Tanya. "I thought so at first too. But too chubby."

Elspeth spun around and glared at the shrub. "Say that again and I'll pull you out of the ground like a common weed."

"And obnoxious."

"You know what's obnoxious?" asked Elspeth. "Grown-ups going around pretending to be nursery rhyme characters. Humpty Dumpty and Little Bo-Peep? Give me a break."

"I assure you, no one is pretending anything," said Dumpty. He nodded to Bo-Peep. "The Book. Show it to her."

Bo-Peep unbuckled the satchel and removed a large, leather-bound book. She then walked over to Elspeth and held out the book, which Elspeth accepted with reluctance.

"Careful with that, please," said Dumpty. "It's one of only two in existence. The remaining copies were burned."

"Burned?" said Elspeth. "By who?"

"Whom," came a deep voice from above.

Elspeth glanced up to see, sitting on the branch of a maple tree, a large gray owl. "An owl who says *whom*? Seriously?"

"Only when it's appropriate," said the owl.

Dumpty huffed and shook his head. "Pay no attention to him," he said. "That's Fergus, our resident know-it-all."

"*Whom* is the correct usage," said Fergus. "Excuse me for insisting on proper grammar."

"It's just not important right now," said Dumpty. "The important thing is the stories. All rewritten, white-washed, and somehow smuggled into the Deadlands by Old King Krool himself."

"I think you mean Old King Cole," Elspeth countered. "Who, as I understand, was quite a merry old soul."

"Merry old soul indeed," Bo-Peep retorted. "Take a look at page seventy-one, then tell me if you still think so."

Elspeth thumbed through the pages until she found the right one. It was titled "Little Bo-Peep" and featured a black-and-white ink drawing that bore a very strong like-ness to the woman standing in front of her.

"Go ahead," said Tanya. "Read it."

Elspeth did not like being told what to do, especially by foliage. And though she was an avid reader, she abso-lutely loathed having to do so aloud. When she was younger, a sizeable gap between her two front teeth caused her to speak with a slight lisp, which some of the other children seized as the perfect opportunity to make fun of her. The lisp had long faded, with the arrival of her adult teeth and the narrowing of the gap to the width of a nickel, but her dislike of public oration lived on.

Despite her lingering self-doubt, Elspeth cleared her throat and started in. *"Little Bo-Peep has lost her sheep.* Aha!" she said with a smug grin. "I told you she lost them."

"Read the entire passage," said Dumpty.

Elspeth sighed, shook her head as if this were the biggest waste of time, and began again. *"Little Bo-Peep has lost her sheep to the king and his grumbling belly. The miserable glutton turned the sheep into mutton and gobbled them up with mint jelly."* Elspeth lowered the book, not sure what to make of what she had just read. "So wait a minute," she said to Bo-Peep. "You're saying you didn't lose your sheep; they were stolen from you and eaten?"

"That's right," Bo-Peep confirmed. By the glassy nature of her eyes, it was clear that hearing the story still caused her a great deal of sadness.

"That is pretty terrible, I suppose," said Elspeth. "You must have screamed your head off."

"Not really," said Bo-Peep. "I did cry for two weeks."

"Yes, I suppose crying could be effective too," Elspeth said. "But I've found screaming to be more empowering. You should try it next time."

"What would be the point?" said Bo-Peep. "First of all, there won't be a next time. I have no more sheep. Second of all, it wouldn't do any good anyway. King Krool is a very wealthy and powerful man."

"True," said Dumpty. "He can do pretty much whatever he likes. After all, look what happened to Little Miss Muffet."

41

Elspeth took the bait. "Okay, what happened to Little Miss Muffet?"

"Page twenty-four," said Dumpty as he took a seat on a mossy log. The log, being accustomed to such familiarity, said nothing.

Elspeth flipped through the book to the page in question, which featured an ink drawing of a funny-looking girl running from a large spider flashing an evil grin. Once more, Elspeth read aloud. *"Little Miss Muffet told the king he could stuff it, when he came for her curds and whey. So Krool sent a spider to frighten and bite her—she went bald and now wears a toupee."* Elspeth snorted at the thought of Little Miss Muffet in an ill-fitting hairpiece.

"I'm glad you find it humorous," said Dumpty, rising to his feet. He took the book from Elspeth and handed it to Bo-Peep, who secured it once more in the satchel. "The poor woman has not been the same since. I'm sure you'll find it equally funny to hear that the three little kittens lost their mittens in a house fire started by Krool's nephew Dave. And, that when Little Jack Horner refused to hand over a Christmas pie, Krool sent his goons around to teach the boy a lesson."

"What kind of lesson?" asked Elspeth.

"Let's just say he won't be sticking in his thumb to pull out a plum anytime soon," said Dumpty.

"I don't understand," said Elspeth. "If these are the original stories, why would anyone want to change them?"

"Krool is no different than any other dictator when it comes to image control," said Dumpty. "He's done quite an excellent job of erasing any written record of the stories of his many victims, of which I am one."

"Don't tell me," said Elspeth. "Let me guess. You didn't fall off the wall, you were pushed."

For a moment, Dumpty's self-confidence seemed to droop slightly along with his posture. "No," he said quietly. "I regret to say that I did indeed fall off the wall."

"At least the king's men and his horses tried to put you together again," Elspeth replied.

"Ha! Lies, all of it," sneered Dumpty. "Not only did they make no effort to put me back together again, but they attacked so viciously that I consider myself quite lucky to be alive." As a matter of habit, Dumpty ran his hand down the side of his cracked face.

"Why did they attack you?" asked Elspeth. An oddly foreign emotion stirred inside her. Though she couldn't be certain, she thought that perhaps she was beginning to feel sorry for Dumpty.

"They accused me of spying on Old King Krool."

"And why would they do such a thing?"

"Because I was spying on him," said Dumpty, the brightness returning to his eyes and the rigidity to his posture. "After all, it's my profession."

Elspeth's eyelids drooped slightly, revealing her skepticism. "You're a spy?"

"Indeed," said Dumpty. "Or at least I was. Difficult business when you're frequently off balance. It's stress, I suppose. First came on when Krool took over and hasn't left me since."

"This is all very interesting," said Elspeth, who normally took very little interest in the problems of others. "But I really have to be going, so if you could point me in the direction out of this place, I'll be on my way."

Dumpty looked to Bo-Peep, then back at Elspeth, who waited for a response until impatience got the better of her. "Hello?"

"As I mentioned before," said Dumpty, "any attempt to leave will result in your immediate arrest."

"If the alternative is spending the rest of my life here, I'll take my chances," said Elspeth. "Now, which way?"

"As far as anyone knows," said Dumpty, "there's only one way back to the Deadlands."

"Seattle. I'm from Seattle," said Elspeth.

"Right," said Dumpty. "Only one way back. And, as I understand, it's at the bottom of a well."

Elspeth scrunched up her face as if it were a wet rag in need of wringing out. "Are you saying I have to go to the bottom of a well just to get home?"

"Afraid so," said Dumpty.

Elspeth looked all around her, assuming the well in question should somehow be in plain sight. "Okay, where is this stupid well?"

"Don't know," said Dumpty. "There are hundreds of them throughout the kingdom. For the location of the precise one you'd have to ask the only two people who know: Jack and Jill. And it just so happens that, at this moment, they are being held prisoner in the castle dungeon."

"So you're saying the only way for me to get home is to climb down into a well, but before I do that, I have to go to some castle and ask Jack and Jill for directions?"

"Yes," said Dumpty. "But to do that you'd have to be out of your mind."

Jack and Jill, with courage and will,
Went looking for their daughter.
While searching they found a way out of town,
Hidden down deep in the water.

Chapter 6

Wh hile it is true that Jack Sprat could eat no fat and his wife could eat no lean, contrary to popular belief this had less to do with personal taste than with simple economics. Since Krool ascended to the throne, rising inflation had resulted in prices for food, both fat and lean, skyrocketing out of control. For example, whereas hot cross buns used to be one a penny (two a penny with a coupon), they now ran in the neighborhood of six or seven dollars apiece.

It was assumed by some that this lack of affordable food was what had led Jack and Jill to venture onto the king's land in search of something to fill their empty bellies. But Dumpty knew the full truth of the matter, for they had confided in him, making him promise not to tell a soul. This was a promise he was about to break.

"They were searching for their daughter," he said, his eyes cast downward. "Or her remains, more precisely."

Elspeth was not sure she wanted any further details of this story, but she got them nonetheless.

"When she was but a year old, Krool stole her away and reportedly threw her down a well."

Elspeth was positively horrified. "He threw a child down a well? Why would someone do such a thing?"

"Fear," said Dumpty.

"Fear of what?"

"Of the prophecy. That a young girl matching her description would one day rise up and lead the people in revolt."

Elspeth needed no more convincing that this Krool fellow was a nasty piece of work and now wanted more than ever to find her way out of this dreadful place.

"Going to the castle would be foolhardy," said Dumpty. "Of course, you're more than welcome to stay with us until Jack and Jill are released from prison."

"And when will that be?" asked Elspeth.

Dumpty rubbed his chin and looked at Bo-Peep. "The word on the street from Little Robin Redbreast is that they've been given life sentences. But with good behavior, you never know."

Elspeth screamed and drew her foot back with the intention of kicking a small rock but pulled up just short, being that she was in no mood to be yelled at by gravel just now. "This is ridiculous. If the only way for me to get

48

home is to go to the castle, then I insist I be taken there this minute."

Dumpty sighed, and Bo-Peep shrugged. "Follow me," he said.

With Bo-Peep trailing behind them, her stick upon her shoulder, and Fergus the grammar owl keeping pace from above, Dumpty escorted Elspeth down the same path Elspeth had been on but in the opposite direction.

"Is this the way to the castle?" asked Elspeth suspiciously after about ten minutes of walking. "It doesn't look like a road that would lead to a castle."

"Patience, child," said Dumpty.

Elspeth tried her best to muster up some of this thing called patience, and the group trudged on in silence until Dumpty stopped abruptly and turned to address a large willow tree. "Good morning, Manuel," said Dumpty.

"*Hola*, Señor Dumpty," the willow tree acknowledged in a slow, sleepy voice.

"If you don't mind," said Dumpty. He made a sweeping motion with his hand, from left to right.

"*No problemo*," replied Manuel.

Manuel pulled back his branches to reveal a large clearing in the forest. Peering in through the newly created passageway, Elspeth was surprised to find an encampment. Set up around the perimeter of the glade were rows and rows of tents, all of different sizes and in varying states of disrepair, patched with swatches of mismatched cloth. In the middle of the clearing was a

49

campfire and, hanging above that fire, an iron pot, giving off a thick steam, which mingled with smoke from the fire, the mixture thinning as it wafted up above the treetops.

"You said you were taking me to the castle," Elspeth sniped.

"I said no such thing," Dumpty replied. "I merely said, 'Follow me,' and you did. And here we are."

"And where's here?" Elspeth demanded.

"We call it the suburbs," said Bo-Peep.

"Boy, that's a stretch," said Elspeth. "Why would anyone choose to live here?"

"We're not here by choice, I assure you," said Dumpty. "We were forced here years ago when we were banished from our former home of Banbury Cross." He then motioned with his hand again. "Ladies?"

Elspeth stepped into the glade, and Bo-Peep followed. Never before had Elspeth been witness to such poverty and misery, and for a moment she just stood and stared at the downtrodden residents of the encampment. There were hundreds of them wandering about listlessly or sitting on large rocks or tree stumps, their heads in their hands, their faces drawn and despondent.

But what Elspeth noticed most was not the look of any one thing or of any one person, but the smell of everything. "What is that awful stench?" she asked.

Dumpty sniffed at the air. He looked at Bo-Peep, and the two exchanged a quizzical shrug. Though Elspeth found it unbearable, apparently Dumpty and Bo-Peep had become used to it, like people who live near a paper mill or downwind of an egg salad factory. "Could be the peas porridge, I suppose," said Dumpty.

For the record, he was partially correct. The smell was a putrid combination of peas porridge in the pot, nine days old, and the odor one might expect from a large group of people who, for a week and a half, have eaten nothing but legumes. Though food had been in short supply for years, a recent drought had taken the problem to an increasingly desperate level.

"Would you care for a bowl?" asked Dumpty, as required by his fine English upbringing.

"Goodness, no," said Elspeth with a scornful sneer.

Turning her nose away from the smell, she spied to her right, sitting on a log and rocking rhythmically back and forth, an oversize dinner plate staring off into nowhere while making a steady humming noise from deep down in its throat.

Elspeth put her hand to the side of her mouth, leaned toward Bo-Peep, and whispered, "Is that . . . ?"

"The Dish," Bo-Peep said with an empathetic shake of her head.

"What's wrong with him?" said Elspeth, still almost whispering.

"We're not sure, really," said Bo-Peep. "All we know is that he once resided in the castle and worked in the kitchen. One day last month, he ran away with the Spoon. As to why, he's far too traumatized to talk about it."

51

"And what did the Spoon have to say?"

"Don't know," said Dumpty. "The Spoon speaks only Portuguese. When he speaks at all, that is. He's been equally affected, I'm afraid. It's likely we may never find out what happened to those poor chaps. And that's why I've brought you here. To show you what might become of you if you insist upon going to the castle."

"You're wasting your time, because I'm going to the castle irregardless," said Elspeth.

"Regardless," came that deep voice from above. "*Irregardless* is not a word."

Elspeth looked up to find Fergus sitting on a branch, a look of self-satisfaction on his flat face. "Fine," she said. "I'm going to the castle *regardless*. After all, I really don't have much of a choice, do I? If you think I'm going to hang out here with you pathetic losers for the rest of my life, you're sadly mistaken."

The sting of the insult registered briefly on Dumpty's scarred face. "We may be pathetic losers, as you so indelicately put it," he replied, "but at least we're all still alive, which is more than I can say for a certain four and twenty blackbirds, who refused to heed my warning about traveling to the castle and were, as a result, baked in a pie."

"Hey, what's that all about, anyway?" asked Elspeth. "Seriously, who bakes blackbirds in a pie?"

"Someone who really hates blackbirds, I suppose," offered Bo-Peep.

"Or someone who really loves blackbirds," said Dumpty, unaware that he was rubbing his empty belly as he spoke. "In a rich gravy, covered with a flaky crust." It took a very loud and very sharp and very gravelly voice calling his name to snap Dumpty out of his pie-themed fantasy.

"All right, Dumpty," said the middle-aged man, who had shuffled up with the aid of a gnarled walking stick. Equally gnarled was the man himself, his arms and legs seemingly double-, or perhaps triple- or quadruple-jointed, bending in ways and in places that human limbs normally refuse to. "When are we going to get some decent food around here?" In the man's non-walking-stick hand was a bowl of the same sloppy peas that bubbled away in the pot just a few yards away. The man's individual portion emitted no steam because, after all, though some like it hot, and some like it in the pot nine days old, there are also those who prefer it cold.

"My cat won't even eat this garbage," he said and hurled the bowl to the ground. A cat with arms and legs every bit as crooked as the man's proved him quite wrong by quickly running over and scarfing it down, because down is the direction in which things are generally scarfed.

"I'm sorry," said Dumpty. "But I'm not sure what you would expect me to do about it."

"I expect you to do whatever it takes to get us something decent to eat," groused the Crooked Man. "After all, you are the mayor of this dump."

"Only because no one else would take the job," Dumpty snapped back. "And I'm doing the best I can. These are difficult times for all of us."

The Crooked Man's eyes narrowed, and a sneer revealed yellowing teeth. "For all of us? I notice that you don't appear to have lost any weight."

"Just what are you implying?" said Dumpty with barely restrained outrage.

"You know exactly what I'm implying," snapped the Crooked Man. "Good day, sir!" With an abbreviated snort and a quick and aggressive tip of his hat, the man and his crooked cat shuffled away.

"So that's the Crooked Man who walked a crooked mile," remarked Elspeth. "How did he get all . . . you know?" Elspeth contorted her limbs until she resembled an Egyptian hieroglyph.

"Little advice," said Dumpty. "When walking a crooked mile—or any other kind of mile, for that matter—never count on the king's carriage to stop at a crosswalk."

It appeared that the Crooked Man amounted to one more victim of Krool's complete disregard for others. He was also, as Elspeth would soon discover, not the only resident of the suburbs to take issue with the dwindling food supply. There was one to whom the lack of quantity and variety was not only of nutritional concern, but was also, as he saw it, a matter of life and death.

"Yo, Dumpty!"

Elspeth was surprised (but not as surprised as she might have expected) to see what appeared to be an enormous wheel of cheese standing nearly the height of her chin and rolling in her direction.

"Hey, man, the Cheese needs to have a word with you," said the Cheese, rolling right past Elspeth and Bo-Peep as though they didn't exist and stopping just inches from Dumpty.

It probably goes without saying that never before had Elspeth encountered a talking dairy product, especially one with the habit of referring to itself in the third person (or in this case, the third cheese).

"I'm putting in an official request for a personal security detail," said the Cheese.

"Security detail?" said Dumpty.

"That's right. Bodyguards, man. You should see the way that Crooked dude looks at the Cheese. And every time I roll past Jack Sprat's wife, she starts drooling like a basset hound. I'm afraid to close my eyes. I haven't slept in days. Look at me, man. The Cheese is at the end of his rope."

"You're being paranoid, my good man," said Dumpty, placing a comforting hand on the Cheese, a gesture that became much less comforting when Dumpty removed the hand and casually licked it as if no one would notice.

"Hey, hey," said the Cheese. "Did you really just do that?"

"Do what?"

"You just touched the Cheese, then licked your hand."

"What?" said Dumpty, feigning ignorance. "Why, that's absurd. I was merely trying to determine which direction the wind was blowing." Dumpty raised a moistened index finger into the air.

"You see what I mean?" the Cheese said, turning to Elspeth as if the two had been previously acquainted. "People look at me, and do they see a wheel of the finest aged imported cheddar? No. They see food. I'm telling you, Dumpty, you have no idea what it's like."

"What do you mean I have no idea what it's like? Of course I do. After all, I'm half egg on my mother's side."

"Yeah, but nobody's gonna eat you. No offense, but look at you. You're all . . . you know, cracked up. Now, about that security detail."

"I'm sorry, but a private security detail is not in the budget," said Dumpty. "Besides, I've got more important business to tend to. At this moment, I'm doing my best to convince this young lady that she would be foolish to attempt a journey to the castle." He motioned toward Elspeth.

"Hey," he said. "You look just like . . . nah. Too chubby."

That was the closest in her life Elspeth had ever come to punching a wheel of cheese.

"I could really use your help in dissuading her," said Dumpty.

"Oh no. No way," said the Cheese. "I don't get involved in other people's business."

"Please," said Dumpty. "I think it's important that we . . ."

"You heard me. The Cheese stands alone. Now, if you'll excuse me, I need to stay downwind of old twisted mister and his zigzag cat before they come after me with a fork. In the meantime, if anything bad should happen to the Cheese, it'll be on your head."

As Elspeth watched the wheel of cheddar roll away, leaving the egg-shaped Dumpty to scratch his head, it occurred to her that if she ever found her way home again she would very much enjoy a cheese omelet.

Hey diddle diddle, Krool broke the cat's fiddle,
The cow was bumped off by his goons.
But still to this day, no one can say
Why the Dish ran away with the Spoon.

Chapter 7

Though the Cheese proved to be as uncooperative as he was high in cholesterol, there was still no shortage of others who were perfectly willing to provide Elspeth with examples of why a trip to the castle would be ill advised.

Standing in the middle of the encampment, she listened as patiently as she could while Little Jack Horner spoke in a quavering voice of the violent encounter with Krool's henchmen, the horror of the event still as much alive in his eyes as was the pain in his badly disfigured thumbs. It was difficult to tell which the boy found more difficult to bear: the brutal mangling of his opposable digits or the loss of that delicious Christmas pie that had to be, quite literally, torn from his hands.

"You got your thumbs broken over a stupid pie?" asked Elspeth, folding her arms across her chest. "Why didn't you just give it to them?"

"It was plum," said Jack, as if that should be all the explanation necessary. He gazed at the empty space before him with such longing that one might think the very pie in question was hovering in the air, just out of reach of his damaged hands. "Have you ever had freshly baked plum pie?"

"I'm much more of a cake person," Elspeth responded. "I don't really like fruit. Or vegetables. Especially vegetables. Though I am quite fond of candy corn."

All that talk of fruits, vegetables, and striped, triangular candy was beginning to draw a hungry crowd.

"If only we had fresh vegetables," said the Old Woman who lived in a shoe. "I would certainly see to it that my children did not turn their noses up at them."

Elspeth glared at the Old Woman. "I think you're the last person who should be bragging about parenting skills," she snapped.

"What do you mean by that?" asked the Old Woman, who took great pride in the fact that she had managed to raise an entire brood of well-mannered children, whose only noticeable fault was that they all smelled vaguely of leather.

"What I mean is, didn't you whip your children soundly and send them to bed? Which, I do believe, is against the law in most states."

The Old Woman's mouth dropped, and her face registered a look of absolute horror. "What?" she gasped. "And just where did you hear such an awful thing?"

"She's from the Deadlands," Dumpty explained. Then he turned to Bo-Peep and said, "Please. Enlighten the young lady."

Bo-Peep responded by opening the book and reading aloud.

"There was an old woman who lived in a house, with her twenty-six children and one tired spouse. But they all had to move to a big, smelly shoe, when Krool razed their house to make room for a zoo."

Bo-Peep clapped the book closed once more.

"That's all very tragic," Elspeth admitted. "But I don't see how this concerns me in any way. Now, I believe you've wasted enough of my time. I would like to go to the castle and speak with Jack and Jill, and I would like to go now!"

It was then that Dumpty realized there was no reasoning with the child, and, having officially given up on his efforts to discourage her, he agreed to escort her as far as the edge of the forest.

Elspeth offered little in the way of good-byes to those she had met because, as far as she was concerned, she would never see them again anyway, so what would be the point? Besides, she found them all to be a bunch of sniveling, whining crybabies. If there was one thing that irritated Elspeth more than not getting her own way, it was people who refused to stick up for themselves.

They set out on the long walk to the edge of the forest, with Dumpty leading and Elspeth following close behind. She might have walked beside him were the path wide enough to permit it. Of all the creatures she had so far met, Dumpty was the most tolerable of the bunch. In fact, Elspeth felt a sort of fondness for the man as well as a genuine concern when he abruptly stopped walking, wobbled a bit side to side, then reached out for a tree branch.

"What's wrong?" asked Elspeth, catching up to him. "Are you okay?'

"It's nothing," said Dumpty. "Just my vertigo. It tends to get worse when I'm feeling anxious. Which, with this horrible drought, seems to be all the time lately. Not to worry. I'll be fine."

"Okay," said Elspeth, her concern giving way to impatience. "So can we keep moving then?"

Dumpty took just a moment more before continuing on. When they arrived at a place where the path became two, Dumpty directed Elspeth to take the one on the right and cautioned her to be careful of the sinkholes.

"Sinkholes?" Elspeth replied. "You mean holes that sink? Into the ground?"

"Yes," said Dumpty. "Some of them are quite full of lava. Torcano Alley is teeming with them."

"What the heck is Torcano Alley?"

"It's a wide strip of dry, flat desert between the forest and the cliffs beyond," Dumpty explained.

"Okay. And what exactly is a torcano?"

Elspeth soon learned that a torcano was, as the name might imply, a combination of tornado and volcano—a rapidly swirling funnel cloud of ash, pumice, and lava. Reminding Elspeth that he was a spy by trade and not a geologist, Dumpty could provide no scientific explanation for these strange and randomly occurring events.

"It is the height of torcano season," Dumpty said, "so keep your wits about you and get across the alley as quickly as you can. Once you do, you'll find a switchback trail which will take you to the crest of the cliffs. From there, you'll be able to see the castle, sitting in the center of Banbury Cross, just off in the distance."

Elspeth craned her neck forward, trying to see what the path before her held in store, but its curvy design lent her a glimpse no more than fifteen or twenty feet ahead.

"You could come with me," she said. "That is to say, you *should* come with me. After all, I'm still eleven and technically in need of a guardian. It is the law, you know."

"I would if I could," said Dumpty. "But I've been declared an enemy of the Crown. Should I be captured, it would not go well for me."

With that, Dumpty shook Elspeth's hand and wished her luck in her quest to find her way home. As he turned and waddled back the way they had come, Elspeth just stood and watched, trying to keep sight of him for as long as she could. When the last bit of him had disappeared among the trees, Elspeth stood motionless and in complete silence. She thought of calling out for Dolly Dew Eyes and wondered what had become of her former best friend.

In the end, she decided that that would amount to a sign of weakness, and instead resigned herself to completing the journey alone. Elspeth picked up a long, thin stick that she felt would be good to have for protection. As she began to sharpen the end of the stick with a flat rock, the stick (Gene to his friends), felt compelled to voice his objection.

"Whoa," he shouted. This outburst caused Elspeth to drop the stick with a high-pitched shriek, having momentarily forgotten where she was. "What do you think you're doing?"

"I'm sharpening you," said Elspeth. With an angry huff, she plucked Gene from the ground and returned to the work at hand.

"Sharpening me?" said Gene. "I certainly hope you're not planning on using me as some sort of weapon." When his protest was met with only the sounds of Elspeth's determined honing, he continued. "You should know that I am a lifelong pacifist. And I strenuously object to any attempts to fashion me into a spear or some other pointy implement of war."

"Relax," Elspeth muttered. "I promise I'll only use you in self-defense."

Gene thought these terms reasonable. He agreed to allow the sharpening to continue, although he didn't have much say in the matter being that he was just a stick—and a pacifist stick at that.

When she had completed the task, Elspeth took Gene in hand and the two continued on together. By and by, the path grew wider and the trees thinner until finally, just up ahead, was the very edge of the forest. Standing at the border between forest and desert were three hand-painted signs, spaced about six feet apart, reading, in order from left to right: KEEP OUT!, DO NOT ENTER!, and DON'T EVEN THINK ABOUT IT!

Elspeth, a self-taught expert on the art of disobeying rules, chose to disregard the signs. But as she made a move to sidestep them, the sign on the left shouted, "Hey! Can't you read? I said, keep out!"

Elspeth leapt back. But her fear and surprise quickly turned to anger.

"Of course I can read," Elspeth shouted, while thrusting Gene the pacifist stick in the direction of the sign. "Better than you can, I'll bet. Besides, I couldn't care less what you say. You're just a boring old sign."

"Boring?" said Keep Out, while Do Not Enter and Don't Even Think About It snickered at his expense. "Quiet!" he said to them. "This isn't funny." Then Keep Out hopped, pole and all, several feet over until he stood directly in front of Elspeth, blocking her path.

"You obviously have no idea to whom you are speaking," the sign sputtered. "My father just happens to be . . ."

"Wait. Let me guess," said Elspeth. "Slippery When Wet? Duck Crossing? Employees Must Wash Hands Before Returning to Work?"

While her outburst absolutely enraged Keep Out, it had the other two signs doubled over with laughter. "Duck Crossing," said Do Not Enter. "Now that was a good one."

Keep Out hopped angrily back toward his fellow signs. "Go ahead, laugh it up. But just so you know, I'm putting you both on report."

"For what?" Don't Even Think About It scoffed.

Without warning, Keep Out lunged forward and head butted (or sign butted) Don't Even Think About It, striking with sufficient force as to knock the rival sign right off its stick, sending it clanging to the hard dirt. "For leaving your post," sneered Keep Out. "Now, does anyone else want a piece of this action?" He made a move toward Do Not Enter, who was no longer laughing. The smaller sign backed away quickly.

"Easy now," he said. "I don't want any trouble."

Satisfied that he had reestablished himself as the alpha sign, Keep Out turned his attention back to Elspeth, whom, he soon discovered, had seized upon the infighting as an opportunity to slip away unnoticed. All that remained of the girl was a sign of her own making, scratched in the dirt with her stick. It read: NO SIGNS ALLOWED!

"You think you're funny, do you?" shouted Keep Out. "You'll be sorry you disobeyed me!"

Elspeth heard the warning twice as it echoed off the steep, reddish cliffs rising up at the far end of Torcano Alley. When the words quickly faded into silence, Elspeth found her mind muddled with a new set of questions. Would she ever find her way home again? Were her parents out looking for her or happily going about their lives preparing taxes and peddling hearing aids door to door? Perhaps it was far worse than that, Elspeth thought. What if she came to find that her parents actually dumped her off here so as to be rid of her once and for all?

If that were the case, she vowed right then and there to call the police and have them thrown in jail just as soon as she could get to a phone. With the both of them firmly locked up, she could have as many alpacas as she desired. An entire herd perhaps. Or did alpacas travel in flocks? Regardless, Elspeth wished she had one at that moment on which to ride.

If wishes were horses, then beggars would ride,
Until they got hungry enough to eat those horses.
Then no more rides.

Chapter 8

With her father frequently out on the road, canvassing new territories for potential hearing-aid buyers, her mother busy preparing other people's taxes, and her friends nonexistent, Elspeth had spent a great deal of her young life in solitude. Still, she had never before felt quite so alone as she did now, plodding across the vast flatlands of this strange and eerily quiet place.

The earth here was littered with black rocks, varying in size from pebble to boulder. The ground was scarred with thin fissures and wide crevasses so deep that darkness hid the bottoms of them and made Elspeth wonder if there was any end to them at all. She could step or skip over the smaller ones, but the larger faults required her to alter her course time and time again, taking her along a zigzag path that would more than double the length of the hike.

Walking for nearly an hour now, she had long ago discarded Gene when it became apparent that the stick would never shut up.

"What do they always say about us?" said Gene. "*Sticks and stones will break your bones.* What kind of thing is that to tell a child? Sure, I've known some stones in my day, but sticks? It's just not in our nature. Still, they won't even let kids play with us. 'Put that stick down,' they say. 'It'll poke somebody's eye out.' As if I would ever do such a thing. It's ridiculous is what it is. And kindling? Don't even get me started on kindling. You want to know what I think?"

"No, I don't," said Elspeth. As lonely and in need of a weapon as she may have been, she'd finally had enough. She hurled the talking stick, end over end, into a patch of tall, dry grass.

"Hey," called out Gene. "That was not very nice at all. Come back here, you little brat."

"Sticks and stones," Elspeth muttered over her shoulder as she marched onward. Nearing the red cliffs at the far end of Torcano Alley, she felt as though she was finally getting close.

The directions thus far were impeccable, and there she was now, standing before the narrow trail that zigzagged its way to the top of the cliff. Still, she hadn't expected the way up to be quite so steep. It seemed better suited to a mountain goat or an alpaca than to an eleven-year-old girl who had just walked three miles across a fractured desert landscape. She decided that before going on, she would sit for a moment and rest her legs.

She found a large rock, and prior to taking a seat upon it she issued a preemptive warning. "I'm going to sit on you now. And I don't want to hear any back sass," she spouted, taking the tone often directed at her by her know-it-all teachers.

Elspeth lowered herself onto the rock and was both surprised and relieved when it said nothing. Perhaps the rock, like the Spoon, spoke only Portuguese. Or it could be that the rock, in awe of Elspeth's presence, found itself at a complete loss for words. Regardless, her time resting upon it was cut short by a whirring, crunching noise that grew louder by the second. It was as if someone had poured a handful of rocks into a blender and turned it on high. Although she had never before heard anything like it, somehow she found herself blurting out, "Torcano!"

She rose quickly and there it was—no more than a quarter mile away and coming toward her, swirling black and orange, two hundred feet in height, from slender foot to wide, hungry mouth. Elspeth stood, unable to move, mesmerized by its immense beauty and destructive power.

The torcano was sweeping along the face of the cliff, pelting it with rock in both solid and liquid form. Patches of sage and dry grass in its path evaporated like cotton candy in water, instantly and without remnant. Elspeth's

71

heart pumped so furiously she felt as though it might burst right through her sternum. The only safe place to be was at the top of the cliff, but it was clear that she would never make it in time. She'd get halfway up at best before being instantly cremated like her grandmother, her ashes taken by the breeze and perhaps scattered over the forest and those who had annoyed her.

The only other option was to try to outrun it. Without further hesitation, Elspeth took off, her pudgy arms pumping furiously, her weary feet pounding at the dusty ground. She didn't have to look back over her shoulder to realize she was losing the race. The whirring and crunching grew increasingly loud, and pebbles landed at her feet still smoking. One hit the back of her arm, and it felt like the sting of a hornet, sharp and deep. She knew there would be others and winced in anticipation. A second smoldering rock hit the back of her leg, singeing her calf and nearly knocking her to the ground.

Just when she thought she had taken her last step, she heard a voice calling out from above. "Hey, up here!" She stopped and frantically scanned the cliff side for the source, but in a world of talking sticks, rocks, and bushes, she wasn't sure what she was looking for. When the voice spoke again, saying, "This way," a quick flash caught her eye. About twenty feet up the face of the cliff, she spied the tiny figure of a man, no bigger than a ground-hog. The glint of light had been the sun's reflection off the man's shiny, dime-size belt buckle. Nattily dressed in colorful silk, he stood at the mouth of a small cave.

Elspeth wasted no time in scampering up the side of the cliff, clawing at the dry dirt as the torcano continued its violent pursuit, closing in with incredible speed.

"Hurry!" implored the tiny man. Of course she was hurrying, but with every two steps up, she slid back another on the steep and crumbly surface.

Finally, she lunged forward and, with the fingertips of her right hand, took hold of a small ledge jutting out from the floor of the cave. She managed to get her left hand upon the ledge as well but was still unable to pull herself up. The man tried to help by taking hold of her sleeve and tugging with all the might contained within his tiny frame. The small rocks that whizzed past Elspeth's head were like boulders to the man, yet he did not flee. Instead, he dug in and pulled harder.

Another smoldering rock zipped by Elspeth's ear as the torcano moved to within a hundred feet. She ground her toes into the side of the cliff. "Come on!" groaned the miniature man, his fancy shirt and hat by now soaked with perspiration. Another rock bounced off the back of Elspeth's hand with a searing pain and an unpleasant sizzle, yet she managed to keep her grip on the ledge. With her arms, she pulled harder. With her legs she pushed more forcefully until finally she was able to swing one knee and then the other up onto the protruding rock.

With the sound of thunder, the torcano swept across the opening to the cave just as the terrified girl and the man crawled frantically inside. As it passed, small rocks and showers of sparks flew into the cave. Elspeth and the man shielded their eyes and held their breath as the torcano moved beyond the cave opening and continued its menacing path down the side of the cliff. When the racket had faded and the dust had settled, the man stood up and wiped the ash from his eyes, unaware at that moment that one of the sparks had done him the extreme dishonor of lighting his pants on fire.

"That was the worst torcano I've ever seen," said the man.

"Your pants are on fire," said Elspeth.

"Oh, no lie," the man insisted. "That was a bad one."

"No, I mean your pants are literally on fire!"

The man let go with a squeaky scream and began running around the tiny cave while swatting furiously at his silk-covered backside. Elspeth reached out with her right hand and smacked the man to the ground then took a handful of dirt and threw it on him, dousing the flames.

It took several moments for the man to regain his breath, and when he did, he sat up and looked at Elspeth. "Thank you," he said. "I must say, unfortunate circumstances aside, it's nice to finally meet you. In fact, I was beginning to think you'd never come."

"What are you talking about?" Elspeth said, coughing up some dust with a dry hack. "Who are you?"

"Why, I am the king," said the man as he wiped a layer of ash from his charred pants seat. "Welcome to my castle away from home, as it were."

"You're King Krool?" asked Elspeth.

"King Krool?" the man scoffed. "I should hope not, that no-good phony. I am the real king, William the Umpteenth." He held out his right hand, which featured a ruby ring on the index finger. Though Elspeth couldn't be sure, she got that feeling that the man fully expected her to kiss the ring. She did not. Instead, she laughed.

"William the Umpteenth?"

"Yes," said the man, rather defensively. "The Winkie family has ruled this land for so long, we've more of less lost track of exact numbers."

"Winkie family? Wait. William Winkie?"

"King William, if you don't mind."

"You're Wee Willie Winkie?"

The man clenched his teeth and both fists. He may have been clenching other parts of his body as well, but those were the only ones visible. "Arrggghh," he growled. "I hate that name. It makes me sound ridiculous. Blast that Krool and his horrible lies." The man stomped at the dirt and threw a punch at an invisible target.

"I don't remember reading anything about you being king," Elspeth said suspiciously.

"Sure you do," Winkie insisted. *"Good King William, runs through the town, fleeing from those who would take his crown?"*

"Nope," said Elspeth. "Doesn't ring a bell."

Unfazed, Winkie continued. *"Who let them in without a knock? Why is the drawbridge open when it's past ten o'clock?"*

Elspeth shook her head. "Hmm, no. In the version I remember you were just running around putting everyone to sleep. You know, *Wee Willie Winkie runs through the town, upstairs and downstairs in his nightgown.*"

"Nonsense," said Winkie. "I readily admit I may not be the most dynamic public speaker, but I don't believe I've ever put anyone to sleep. In fact, I think I'm an excellent conversationalist. Or at least I used to be. I'm a bit out of practice. It's been quite lonely here, as you might imagine."

"Isn't there a Mrs. Winkie you can talk to?" asked Elspeth.

Winkie sighed. "Alas, no," he said. "And not for lack of trying on my part—you can be sure of that. However, it seems that women prefer a somewhat taller gentleman. Not to mention one with a bit more up top." He removed his hat and ran his right hand over the smooth shiny surface of his hairless head.

"If it's someone to talk to you're looking for, why don't you move to the suburbs?" asked Elspeth. "There are hundreds of people to talk to out there."

"As much as I'd like to," said Winkie, "I'm afraid it would put everyone in great danger. You see, Krool wants me dead, for reasons I'm sure you can imagine. As I live, so does the prophecy."

There it was again. That word. "What did you mean before?" Elspeth asked. "When you said you thought I'd never come?"

As he repositioned his hat upon his bald skull, the sadness instantly left his face, replaced by a sly grin. He leaned in like someone about to tell an off-color joke and said, "I know who you are. You're Elspeth Pule."

Of all the things Elspeth had thus far encountered, including talking sticks, bushes, and rocks, this was the one that confounded her most. "Where did you hear that?" she said. "I haven't told anyone my name since I got here."

"For many years I've waited," said William, becoming giddier by the second. "I'd almost given up hope that you'd find me, but here you are."

"I didn't find you," said Elspeth. "You found me, remember?"

"A mere technicality," said the wee former king. "Regardless, there's no doubt that you are the one."

"The one what?"

"The one about whom it is written, of course. The great warrior who will come and vanquish the evil Krool, and restore me to my rightful place upon the throne."

Winkie, Winkie, little tsar,
How Krool wonders where you are.
Sitting in his castle high,
Feasting on a blackbird pie.
Winkie, Winkie, little tsar,
How Krool wonders where you are.

Chapter 9

Either King William had always been this way, or years of living in exile, holed up in a dark cave on the edge of Torcano Alley, had made him a complete nut case. He paced about the dimly lit cavern, waving his hands and talking a mile a minute while his eyes darted about in their sockets like two flies trapped in a mason jar.

"And when I am king once more, we will have a parade. With banners and streamers and flowers." He delivered the words in a high-pitched shout. "And I'll declare the day a national holiday. It will be known as Winkie Wednesday, and it will be held on the first Wednesday of the month. What do you think?"

"Yes, excellent," said Elspeth in such a way that the sarcasm could be detected only by the expertly trained ear. "I think celebrating Winkie Wednesday on a Wednesday is probably the right call." She began crawling toward the cave entrance (or in this case, the exit). "Good luck with it."

"Oh, luck will have nothing to do with it," said William. "It will all be due to your skill and bravery."

Elspeth stopped, then sighed and spoke without bothering to turn her head. "Hey listen, Winkie . . ."

"King William, please," Winkie interrupted. He rushed around to once more place himself in Elspeth's line of sight.

"Whatever," she replied. "Either way, you have me confused with someone else. I'm a sixth grader, not a brigadier general, okay? And I have about as much intention of restoring you to the throne as I do of volunteering at a soup kitchen."

King William remained silent, still unsure and waiting for further clarification.

"Which would be none! As in no intention whatsoever!" Elspeth shouted while fighting off the urge to give the tiny man a good shake or a sound flick with her index finger. "Zero, nada, no chance at all. Got it? Good. Now, if you'll excuse me, I'm on my way to the castle."

"Great," beamed King William the Umpteenth. "Getting started right away. I like it." He rubbed his hands together as if warming them over a roaring bonfire of revenge. "That Krool won't know what hit him. I can't wait to see the look on his smug face when he's hauled off to the dungeon for the unspeakable crimes he's committed. Then perhaps I will finally find a queen with whom to share the glory."

Elspeth stared at the former king. He was either a very poor listener or a door-to-door hearing-aid salesman's dream come true.

"For the last time," she said, "I'm going to the castle to see Jack and Jill, apparently the only two people who know how to get out of this ghastly place. And as soon as they tell me where the well is, I'll be back home before you can say hickory dickory dock. Now, if you'll excuse me."

Elspeth resumed crawling toward the exit when William scampered in front of the girl, again blocking her way (as well as a way can be blocked by someone the size of a bowling pin). "But you can't just leave," he said in a voice that sounded demanding and plaintive in equal measure. "You absolutely must restore me to my throne. It is written in the Book. I'd show you, but there are only two copies in existence."

"Listen," said Elspeth. "A lot of things are written. Doesn't make them true. I once wrote that I wanted to be president of the chess club because I enjoy working with others."

King William once again looked unsure.

"I don't," said Elspeth. "At all. In fact, not only do I not enjoy working with others, I'm not that fond of others in general. Or of working, for that matter. And this is beginning to feel a lot like work." With the back of her hand, she nudged King William aside and then crawled out of the cave.

Lying on her belly, she shimmied backward until her legs fell over the side of the ledge.

"But if not you, then who?" William whimpered. "Who will rid the people of that evil despot?"

"Why don't you recruit some of your loyal subjects?" Elspeth grunted as she lowered herself from the ledge and dug her feet into the side of the cliff.

"Are you kidding?" said William. "Why do you think Krool banished them to begin with? Because they're all a bunch of sniveling, yellow-bellied cowards."

"On that much we agree," said Elspeth.

"Except for Dumpty, I suppose," said Winkie. "Shame about the vertigo."

"Yeah, real tragic," said Elspeth. She released her grip on the rock ledge and began a controlled slide down the sheer, powdery surface.

"But please," William shouted after her. "I did save your life, if you recall."

"Yes," said Elspeth. "I'll be sure to send you a thank-you card the minute I get home." She skidded down the remaining several feet and then walked toward the switchback trail.

A quick visual assessment showed that it had suffered some damage at the hands of the passing storm. Large chunks of the trail had been blasted away, while other sections were blocked by piles of simmering rocks. All of this would increase the degree of difficulty and add time to an already arduous climb. There was no use in complaining, but Elspeth didn't let that stop her. She muttered and cursed as she trudged up the trail. Meanwhile, Winkie continued to call out after her, his words coming through only in snippets.

"But it is written . . . saved your life . . . big parade . . . Winkie Wednesday."

When she came to those piles of rocks blocking the path, she managed to get beyond them by clinging to small outcroppings on the cliff side and shuffling over, being careful not to take so long as to be steamed alive by the heat rising off the newly formed stones. When she encountered those places where the path had been obliterated, she jumped across the expanse, giving little consideration to the fact that one misstep would send her sliding and tumbling back to the flatlands below. It wasn't that Elspeth was necessarily brave so much as she had become completely fed up. Her tenacity was fueled far more by outrage than by courage.

This is the way it had been for almost as long as she could remember. On her first day of school a small group of children, led by the always-catty Sofia Jean Fleener, began needling her about her pudgy arms and her overly round face. When she replied with a lispy "Thticks and thtones may break my bonth," Sofia Jean pounced upon that as well, and Elspeth did what many children might do in that situation. She cried.

The next day, the teasing began anew, but this time Elspeth did not cry. Instead, she made a split-second decision to punch Sofia Jean firmly in the solar plexus, while the other children looked on in horror. This time Sofia Jean was the one doing all the crying, and Elspeth decided right then and there that she much preferred this result to the previous day's outcome.

From that moment on she vowed that anyone who dared make fun of her would be very sorry to have done so. Or, in her own words, "If you thay that again, you'll be thorry." And though her ominous threats and fierce reprisals garnered her no friends, they did earn her a reputation as one not to be messed with. And no one did mess with her. Or play with her. Or talk to her. She became a loner, losing herself in books and wild imaginings, though none quite so fantastic as the reality in which she now resided. And, as she would soon discover, things were about to get a great deal stranger yet.

When hard work and anger had finally spurred her to the top of the cliff, she found herself once more out of the desert, standing on a grassy plain beneath the shade of a large tree. Looking out across the plain, her heart sank at the sight of the castle, a tiny dot on the horizon, still perhaps two miles off. On the verge of tears for the second time in one day, she managed to fight them off.

"No," she said, with a long sniff. "This is nothing to cry about. You're tired, that's all. You just need to lay down for a moment, and you'll be as good as new."

"That's *lie* down," came a familiar voice from above.

Elspeth looked up to see Fergus perched upon a low-hanging branch of the tree and looking perfectly smug. "*Lay* is a transitive verb," he added for clarification. "You can lay an egg, but you can't lay down."

"That's where you're wrong," said Elspeth. "I can't lay an egg. Not all of us are birds, you know. And I can lay down. Just watch me."

Fergus gave his wings a quick couple of flaps and glided down to a large rock next to Elspeth, who by then was neither laying nor lying but sitting in the tall grass. "I was speaking figuratively," Fergus said.

"The question is, why are you speaking to me at all?"

There may have been anger in Elspeth's voice, but secretly she was happy to see a familiar face, even one belonging to someone as annoying as Fergus. "Did you follow me all the way here just so you could correct my grammar?"

"No. I followed you here to make sure you made it back to the forest alive."

"For someone so concerned with what other people say, you sure don't listen very well, do you?" answered Elspeth. "In case I haven't made myself clear, I have no intention of going back to the forest. Once I find the way out of here, you and your whiny little friends will never hear from me again."

"There's so much you don't know," said Fergus, gazing off in the direction of the castle. "He's a monster. Believe me. You have no idea what he's capable of."

"Aha," said Elspeth, jabbing a stubby index finger in the direction of the confused owl. The interjection caught Fergus completely off guard. "You just ended a sentence with a preposition," Elspeth explained. Reenergized, she jumped back to her feet and performed a victory dance as if she had just scored a go-ahead touchdown in the Super Bowl. Fergus seemed flustered and at a complete loss for words, able only to sputter out a few syllables that sounded like the beginnings of words.

"You don't like it very much, do you?" Elspeth gloated. "Having someone pounce on you the moment you make a mistake."

"No," said Fergus, finally able to utter an actual word. "I suppose I don't. But please understand, I get no enjoyment out of correcting people, I really don't. It's just that I can't help myself. It used to drive Vera batty."

"Vera? Who's Vera?" asked Elspeth.

The owl's round, yellowy eyes narrowed. "She was my wife," he said. "You would probably know her better as the Pussycat."

"*The Owl and the Pussycat went to sea*," said Elspeth. "Of course. I didn't realize you two were married."

"For many years," Fergus confirmed.

"Seems like an odd match," said Elspeth. "Don't cats usually eat birds?"

"I suppose they do," admitted Fergus. "But not my Vera. She wasn't like that. She was the kindest, gentlest soul one could ever hope to meet. You would have liked her. Everyone did."

"I don't know," said Elspeth. "We have a cat. Mr. Comfy. I'm not terribly fond of him. He throws up in my shoes. Does your wife ever throw up in your shoes?"

"Not much use for shoes," said Fergus, looking down at his talons. "Besides, I'm a widower. My wife is no longer with us, as they say."

"Oh," said Elspeth. "I'm sorry to hear that."

"No, you're not," said Fergus. "The fact is you couldn't care less."

"That's not true," said Elspeth.

"It's quite all right," said Fergus. "I don't judge you for it. Because that cold, cold heart of yours is the very thing that's going to help me avenge the death of my beautiful Vera."

The Owl and the Pussycat went to sea,
In a beautiful pea-green boat.
They took some honey and plenty of money,
Wrapped up in a five-pound note.

Then Krool sailed by on his luxury yacht,
Escorted by two submarines.
Wearing only a Speedo, he cried, "Fire the torpedoes,"
All because he detested pea green.

Chapter 10

Fergus was wrong, or at least partly so, for even Elspeth could not help but feel sorry for the owl upon hearing the full story of his wife's untimely demise. After all, in addition to having lost his beloved Vera, Fergus bore the extra burden of not having been able to save her, as well as the added guilt of being the sole survivor of the attack on the pea-green boat.

"The sad fact is," he said, "that owls can fly for much longer than cats can float. Believe me, I tried my best. I took her by the nape of the neck with my talons, and with all my strength I struggled to lift her from the water. But there's a reason that cats eat birds, as you pointed out, and not the other way around. With her fur soaking wet, she was just too heavy. In time, she slipped from my grasp and vanished beneath the waves, never to be seen again. Eventually, I was rescued by three men in a tub who happened to be passing by."

"Probably should've been wearing life jackets," said Elspeth. "You have heard of the *Titanic*, haven't you?"

Fergus, who had not heard of the *Titanic*, chose to ignore the callous remark. He looked off toward the castle again with those round yellow eyes.

"You see that?" said Fergus, gesturing with his wing. "The part with all the scaffolding?" Elspeth's eyesight was excellent but no match for an owl's, and she squinted off into the distance without success.

"Word is he's putting in a new bowling alley," Fergus continued. "If you can believe such a thing."

"I sure can," said Elspeth. "I love bowling. Knocking those pins for a loop like they were ten Sofia Jean Fleeners all lined up in neat little rows. Bam! Take that!"

"It's not a matter of whether one enjoys bowling," Fergus snipped. "The point is that he's building it while there are people going hungry. I'm confident that once you meet the scoundrel you'll feel just as strongly as the rest of us do about him. Speaking of which, you'd better get going if you want to be back by nightfall."

"You mean you're not coming with me?" asked Elspeth, her nonchalant attitude an attempt to hide her disappointment.

"Don't worry," said Fergus. "I'll be watching."

"Whatever," said Elspeth. "I'm glad you're not coming along. You're just an old stick in the mud, anyway."

"I am not a stick in the mud," Fergus protested.

"You're right. At least with a stick in the mud, you can flick mud at people. You're no fun at all."

"I am very fun," said Fergus in a tone that, to Elspeth, didn't sound the least bit fun. "Ask any of my friends. And I have plenty of them, which is something I doubt you could say for yourself."

Before Elspeth could respond, Fergus took to the air, first flapping in the direction of the castle before banking sharply to the left and disappearing within a grove of trees.

And so Elspeth did the only thing she could. She began walking. Trudging would be a more accurate description, her heavy feet scraping along the ground. For the next half hour she encountered not a single soul, and she eventually felt as though perhaps she'd been too hasty in having thrown Gene, the indignant stick, into the brush.

As it often did when she had no one to talk to, her mind started to wander. She began to find amusement in the look of her shadow, which by now was that of a lanky giant with thick feet and a long, tapered head. She stretched her arms out ahead of her, locked her kneecaps, and began walking like Frankenstein's monster. She even added the accompanying guttural groans for her own amusement. She continued this until she was overcome by the feeling of being watched.

Elspeth stopped in her tracks, lowered her arms, and raised her head to see several sets of eyes gazing back at her. Eight of the eyes belonged to four exhausted-looking horses, while four more pairs occupied the heads of the pudgy men sitting upon the backs of those horses.

The men were all dressed identically, with poufy red hats and dark-blue tunics over bright-white shirts. Each of their faces bore some type of decorative facial hair: a Van Dyke beard on one, a goatee on another, one man with a waxy handlebar mustache, and the fourth with a full beard and thick, shrubby sideburns. In their hands were long spears, the business ends pointing skyward while the butts rested in leather holsters attached to their horses' saddles.

"Elspeth Pule?" asked the largest of the men, the one with the Van Dyke. By the way the others deferred to him, he seemed to be the highest-ranking member of the group.

"You too?" said Elspeth. "How do you know my name?"

"We have been dispatched to escort you to an audience with His Majesty, King Krool, Ruler of All the Land, Lord of the Seas and the Moon, Duke of Banbury Cross, Baron of Gotham, Royal Knight Companion of the Most Noble Order of Silver Bells and Cockle Shells, Earl of St. Ives, Great Steward of the Pumpkin Eaters, Knight Grand Cross of the Most Honorable Order of Knick-Knack Paddywhack, and Royal Grand Champion of the Order of Pickled Peppers."

"Wow," said Elspeth as the man drew in a much-needed breath of air. "That's quite a mouthful. How do you remember all that?"

"Practice, ma'am," the man answered. "Now, if you please, his lordship is very anxious to meet you."

Anxious to meet her? By now Elspeth's irritation was turning to intrigue. Though she had no idea where she was or how she got there, King Krool, a man reportedly capable of unlimited evil, was anxious to meet her. What did that mean, anxious? Anxious as in excited? Anxious the way a person is before a big exam?

The man with the Van Dyke climbed down from the large black steed, an action that seemed to bring the horse much relief. "Madam," said the man. He held the reins in one hand while gesturing toward the horse with the other.

"You want me to get on that horse?" asked Elspeth.

The horse leaned toward Elspeth and whispered, "Please. If you don't get on me, then he will."

"Quiet!" the man sharply addressed the horse. "No talking in rank."

The four-legged beast snapped to attention and dutifully obeyed the order for silence. By now, Elspeth's legs felt as heavy as bags of wet sand, and she would have been agreeable to riding a porcupine. And so, with assistance from the soldier, she climbed aboard the weary horse.

This was Elspeth's first time on horseback, and as the man led the animal on foot toward the castle, she had to admit that she was very much enjoying the experience. Asking for an alpaca now seemed like a ridiculous request when she could have a horse instead. If only Dolly Dew Eyes (or Fashion Farrah, or whatever her name was) could see her now. Wouldn't she be sorry that she had cast her old friend aside so abruptly?

As they drew nearer to the castle, Elspeth was surprised at its appearance. Of the two kinds of castles, she had imagined it would be more fortress and less fairy princess, more dark, roughly hewn stone than symmetrical blocks of bright white, perfectly stacked in slender towers and topped with conical, red-tile roofs. In short, it certainly did not seem like the home of an evil overlord.

Just outside those gleaming walls was a smattering of cottages comprising the village of Banbury Cross. The residents pointed at Elspeth as if she were some sort of celebrity. In fact, with all the attention, she was beginning to feel how she imagined a celebrity might: important and powerful, yet vulnerable and uneasy.

Her level of anxiety increased with each step forward. She had never met royalty before. Unless she were to count William the Umpteenth, but Elspeth saw very little regality in a man the size of a small table lamp who lived in a cave and was prone to bouts of lunacy. This, on the other hand, was the real thing: horses, an enormous castle, and . . . that smell. What was that delectable mingling of odors that greeted Elspeth's twitching nostrils? Eager for more, she took the opportunity to draw in several large breaths. "What is that?" she asked. "It smells unbelievably good."

"The feast, ma'am," said the man with the sideburns that resembled two dead squirrels. "Celebrating your arrival."

And there it was—yet another indication that perhaps the stories Dumpty and the others had told were, if not outright false, then perhaps exaggerated to some degree. After all, how horrible could Krool be if he were thoughtful enough to prepare a feast in her honor? On her very own birthday the best her own parents could ever muster was a store-bought cake and a lousy scoop of ice cream.

As Elspeth and her entourage crossed into the castle's long shadow, the drawbridge was lowered while the portcullis behind it rose up slowly with the grinding of heavy chain. The tired horses clomped across the bridge and into a large courtyard. All around them were small shops that catered to the soldiers and the king's personal staff. With clapboard roofs, the shops sat side by side and offered up everything from candlesticks to fresh meats to scrumptious tarts, some still cooling on the window ledge.

The man leading Elspeth's horse stopped the beast in the middle of the courtyard and offered his hand, which she took as a sign that she was to dismount. "The king's valet will be by presently to tend to your needs," he said. "Until that time, please make yourself at home."

Ride a black horse to Banbury Cross,
To meet a fine man who's made himself boss.
Rings on his fingers, don't step on his toes,
For he will bring torment to all who oppose.

Chapter 11

As the soldiers rode off toward the stables, Elspeth stood in the courtyard beneath a clear blue sky, looking around in awe at the enormous structure that literally surrounded her. Before today, the nearest she'd ever been to a castle was Maryanne Schnecter's seventh birthday party, which was held at a miniature golf course. But this castle was the real deal, and Elspeth loved everything about it.

What she found most appealing were the wonderful smells, and she could not help but wander over to get a better look at the sausages hanging in the window of the butcher shop. She leaned toward them, closed her eyes, and breathed in their rich aroma. Her heart nearly stopped when she heard, "No loitering!"

Until then she hadn't noticed the sign printed with those exact words. Elspeth found herself both startled and annoyed.

"All right, all right," she said. "No need to yell. I was just . . ."

"Do you have any money?" the sign demanded.

"Uh . . . no," said Elspeth.

"Then you're loitering!" said the sign. "Now knock it off."

Elspeth shook her head in disgust and moved on to the bakery. Recently there had been some trouble involving the Knave of Hearts stealing some tarts. As a result, a sign had been posted out front that read, SHOPLIFTERS WILL BE PROSECUTED TO THE FULLEST EXTENT OF THE LAW.

When she was within a few feet of the shop, the sign barked out, "Watch it now! Shoplifters will be prosecuted to the fullest extent of the law!"

"I can read," she snapped back. "Good grief. That's not very good public relations, you know. Threatening potential customers like that."

"No offense, ma'am," the sign replied. "Just doing my job."

"You'll be out of a job when this place goes bankrupt due to lack of sales. Treating people like common criminals. How insulting."

"I'm sorry. I feel horrible now," said the sign, wilting slightly. "I really do. You know what?" Then, despite its complete absence of eyes, the sign appeared to look first left and then right before turning back to Elspeth and whispering, "Why don't you go ahead and help yourself to one of the tarts? On the house."

"Seriously?"

"Consider it a free sample. How's that for customer service?"

"That's very nice of you," said Elspeth as she eyed the tarts, trying to hone in on the most delicious of the lot. "I'll make sure and tell all my friends to shop here."

As Elspeth carefully lifted the chosen tart, she realized her hand was trembling. It had been a very long time she'd last eaten. Greedily she shoved the tart toward her mouth and took a bite. Before the flavor could even make its way from her taste buds to her brain, the sign shouted out, "Thief! She's stolen a tart! Burglary! Robbery! Thievery! Arrest her!"

Elspeth spat out the half-chewed bite and threw the remainder of the tart to the ground.

"What?" she screeched. "You told me to take it."

"If I told you to jump off a bridge, would you do that?" the sign shouted back.

"You should be ashamed of yourself. Of all the sneaky, dirty tricks."

"I'm sorry," said the sign with a sigh. "It's just that I have a quota to meet. Five shoplifters a week or they'll fire me. You understand. Tell you what. Let me make it up to you. See that butcher shop over there? The owner is a personal friend of mine. I'm sure he wouldn't mind if you helped yourself to a sausage or two."

"You think I'm falling for that again?"

"That's quite enough," echoed a voice from across the plaza. The source of the voice, a tall, thin man with longish blond hair and a brownish-yellow mustache hurried over. "I'm quite sorry about that, Ms. Pule," he said as he reached Elspeth and took a moment to catch his breath. "Rest assured this incident shall not go unreported. Pardon me. My name is Georgie, His Majesty's personal valet."

"Georgie? As in Georgie Porgie?" Elspeth replied.

"*Georgie Porgie puddin' and pie*," Georgie replied as if reciting a corporate slogan.

"Speaking of which, when do we eat?" said Elspeth, as she felt hungrier than ever before after having gotten a quick taste of that tart.

"Right," said Georgie. "The feast. You must be very excited to meet His Majesty, King Krool, Ruler of All the Land, Lord of the Seas and the Moon, Duke of Banbury Cross, Baron of Gotham, Royal Knight Companion—"

"Yeah, yeah," Elspeth interrupted. "Duke of pickled peppers and peach pie plum, blah, blah, blah. I just want to know when I can have some food."

"I see," said Georgie, who seemed genuinely disappointed in not being allowed to finish reciting the king's full and official title. "It shouldn't be long. Why don't we get you inside and you can change for the party?"

"I didn't bring a change of clothes," said Elspeth. She looked down at her aquamarine T-shirt and faded jeans, dirty from her encounter with the torcano, and for the first time she worried that she might be underdressed for the purpose of meeting with royalty. "I didn't know I'd be coming here."

"Not to worry," said Georgie. "In anticipation of your arrival, the king's personal tailor has put together an ensemble I think you'll find most elegant. He's quite in fashion these days. Anyone who's anyone is wearing Bobby Shafto."

"You mean *Bobby Shafto's gone to sea, silver buckles at his knee*? That guy?" asked Elspeth.

"He designed this little number," said Georgie. He raised his arms and performed a full pirouette. "What do you think? Is it too much with the ascot and the epaulets?"

Elspeth, who had no idea what an ascot or an epaulet was, just looked at Georgie and said, "Looks fine to me."

"Oh good," said Georgie. "The last thing I would ever want to do is show up his lordship. All right then. This way, please."

Georgie turned on his heel and walked quickly across the courtyard, and Elspeth followed.

"He really is a wonderful man, you know," Georgie said. There was a gleam in his eye as he spoke. "A truly great leader who has done so much for his people."

Georgie stopped and pulled open a heavy wooden door. "We'll take a shortcut through the kitchen," he said.

They stepped from the breezy courtyard to the busy kitchen where workers hustled about, stirring this and dicing that. There were bubbling pots and sizzling fry pans. On a long counter running through the center of the room rested the most enormous pie Elspeth had ever seen, its diameter perhaps equal to that of a tractor tire.

"Wow" was all she could manage at first glance. "I'm more of a cake person, but that looks pretty darned good."

"I should hope so," said Georgie. "It's my most important duty, to oversee the making of all pudding and pie. Tonight we're having the king's personal favorites: plum pudding and everyberry pie."

"Everyberry pie? You mean it has . . . ?"

"Every berry," said Georgie, leaning into the pie and taking in a long whiff.

"Every single one?"

"As the name would imply."

"Raspberries?"

"Raspberries."

"Strawberries?"

"Strawberries."

"Blueberries, blackberries, gooseberries, cranberries, and elderberries?"

"But of course."

"Lingonberries, salmonberries, and marionberries?"

"Child," said Georgie. "It's my job to personally see to it that everything is just right, so believe me when I

102

say this pie contains every berry there is. Huckleberries, thimbleberries, mulberries. You name it, it's in there."

"Loganberries?"

Georgie's face went instantly white. His eyes widened and his jaw dropped. "What?"

"Loganberries. You did say it had every berry," said Elspeth. "You mean to say that you forgot the loganberries?"

Georgie snatched Elspeth by the elbow. "Shh," he hissed as he hurried her away. "You mustn't speak a word of this to anyone."

"Relax," said Elspeth. "It's just a dumb old pie. Who cares if you forgot to put . . ."

Georgie responded by clamping his hand over Elspeth's mouth while hustling her toward the exit at the far end of the room. "What are you trying to do here? Get my head chopped off?"

Elspeth tore Georgie's sweaty and foul-tasting palm from her mouth. "Take your hands off me," she demanded.

"My apologies, Ms. Pule," said Georgie. "Please forgive me. It's just that the king is very particular about these things, and if he were to find out, well, there's no telling what he might do."

Georgie quickly opened the exit door that took them into a windowless corridor, the walls lit with torches and alive with quivering shadows.

"You just got done telling me what a great guy he is," said Elspeth as Georgie shut the door behind them. "So what makes you think he's going to chop your head off just because you forgot the . . . ?"

"Shh! Please," Georgie implored the girl, even though there appeared to be no one but those two in the hall-way. "Yes, the king is a merry old soul indeed and a great and wise man. And that is precisely why he deserves the very best. Now, with any luck he won't notice the missing you-know-what and all will be fine. We'll just have to hope for the best."

Halfway down the hallway, Georgie opened another wooden door, revealing a small, circular room in which nothing stood but a mannequin bodice at the center, out-fitted in the most beautiful gown that Elspeth had ever seen. It was made of silk in a dusty rose and trimmed in bone-colored lace with a large bow that tied at the back. Sleeveless and softly pleated from the waist, it seemed to hover weightlessly above the ground.

"Is that for me?" she gasped while walking slowly toward the dress as if any sudden movement might cause it to run off like a frightened deer. Elspeth had never before been much for fancy clothes, but there was something about this particular dress. It was more than clothing; it was a work of art.

"It is indeed especially for you," said Georgie. "I shall summon the dressers. And please. Not a word of all that previous business if you don't mind."

"Sure," said Elspeth, her mind lost in the breathtaking vision of the gown. A pair of slippers made of the same pink silk, like the ones a ballerina might wear, lay on the floor nearby.

By the time the royal dressers, two pretty and very pale young women, arrived at her room, Elspeth was already wearing the slippers and the dress, though she would need their help in doing up the many hooks that fastened the back.

The young women were abundantly pleasant as they took to their task and, in keeping with their training, spoke only when spoken to. This made for a very quiet room as Elspeth was still quite speechless at the sight and feel of Bobby Shafto's latest creation.

"How do I look?" she said finally, for there were no mirrors in the room.

"You look absolutely lovely," said the paler of the two. "It's just that . . ."

The woman stopped short, and she and her cohort exchanged a look of uncertainty.

"What?' said Elspeth.

"With permission," said the second woman tentatively, "we'd like to do something with your hair."

Bobby Shafto's gone to sea,
Silver buckles at his knee,
The latest fashion accessory
From bonny Bobby Shafto.

Now Bobby's working for the Crown,
Paid in sovereigns and in pounds
To make an execution gown
From bonny Bobby Shafto.

Chapter
12

Elspeth's newly formed curls bounced as she walked, and she felt as though she wore a hat covered in springs, a sensation she was not sure she liked. One of the curls fell to the middle of her forehead, and she brushed it into place once more.

As the pale-skinned ladies in waiting (whom Elspeth learned were named Catherine and Jane) escorted her down the long corridor toward the great hall, she made idle chitchat about the weather as a means of covering up the increasingly loud protests from her empty stomach. The dress, being so snug around her midsection, did nothing to help matters. Bobby Shafto may have been the most fashionable designer in the kingdom, but even he could not properly fit a dress without exact measurements.

Her stomach groaned again, and this time the squeak of the door at the end of the hallway covered it up somewhat. Jane pulled the door open, presenting Elspeth with a view of a large rectangular room with ceilings thirty feet high. At the far end was a fireplace in which fat, dry logs crackled in the busy flames. The sound mingled with the murmur of villagers by the dozens filing in from several doors placed around the perimeter of the room.

Narrow wooden tables lined each length of the great hall and were pushed end to end, giving the appearance of two singularly long tables. While the people trickled in and took their seats upon hard wooden benches, Elspeth was escorted along the smooth, marble floor to one of only three chairs in the entire room. While two of the chairs were rather ordinary, the one in the center was high backed and ornate with a dark blue velvet seat. She assumed this must be reserved for the king and realized that, if this were true, she'd be sitting right next to the man himself.

Just as the last guest took his seat, a set of wide double doors opposite the fireplace swung open, and in walked the same four bearded men who had escorted Elspeth to the castle. With those same long spears in hand they took position, standing at attention, two to each side of the door.

Right on their heels, two other men entered, holding polished brass trumpets. They moved to the center of the room, raised the instruments to their lips, and blasted out a short and sudden tune.

The moment they finished, the men lowered the horns as Georgie, in his ascot and epaulets, strode into the room and said in a loud voice, "Ladies and gentlemen, all rise for His Highness, King Krool, Ruler of All the Land, Lord of the Seas and the Moon, Duke of Banbury Cross, Baron of Gotham, Royal Knight Companion of the Most Noble Order of Silver Bells and Cockle Shells, Earl of St. Ives, Great Steward of the Pumpkin Eaters, Knight Grand Cross of the Most Honorable Order of Knick-Knack Paddywhack, and Royal Grand Champion of the Order of Pickled Peppers."

When he swept in through the doors, the first thing Elspeth noticed about the king was the same thing most people noticed about him at first glance. He was tall and slim (especially for someone so fond of pudding and pie), with an unreasonably handsome face. His jaw was sharp and angular, ending in a prominent chin, dimpled at the center. His smile was broad and easy with teeth so straight and white that, from this distance they appeared, like the tables in the room, to be one continuous thing, a solitary piece of pure white enamel. This made Elspeth think about the gap between her own teeth, and she made a mental note that, when smiling in his presence, she must always do so with lips pursed.

The trumpeters reprised their tune as the king walked with a slow and measured grace toward his royal chair, with Georgie and the four guards following at the required minimum distance of six feet. The king's royal subjects stood and gazed upon the man with placid smiles.

Though Elspeth normally held little or no regard for figures of authority, there was something different going on here. And when the king looked at Elspeth, her heart stopped for a moment.

When the king reached his chair, Georgie quickly slid the throne back from the table. Before taking his place upon it, the king faced the table at the opposite side of the room, stretched his arms out to their full span, and said, in a smooth and commanding voice, "Let the feast begin!"

Cheering and applause filled the hall, and the door from the kitchen burst open. In filed servants, one after the other, carrying platter upon platter of all the foods that had contributed to that wonderful smell Elspeth noticed when she first arrived at the castle.

As four women pushed a squeaky-wheeled table carrying the everyberry pie toward the center of the room, the king turned to his guest of honor and said, "Ms. Pule, welcome to my home."

"Thank you," she said, parting her lips just enough to let the words out.

The king offered his hand, and Elspeth reached out to shake it. Instead the king took her hand in his, leaned forward, and touched it gently to his lips, pulpy and perfectly shaped. "Please, sit down." Then he flashed those flawless teeth and Elspeth returned the smile with lips pinched tightly together.

Sitting in the VIP section had its perks, not the least of which was first crack at the food. No sooner had Elspeth sat down than one of the servants placed a plate before her, loaded with enough food to make Thanksgiving dinner look like a bedtime snack. And though the plate did contain several vegetables (braised carrots, brussels sprouts, and mashed potatoes), it also featured things that Elspeth considered far more edible—things like honey-glazed ham and roasted rack of lamb, which made Elspeth think of Bo-Peep, but only for a moment and not in any way that would suggest empathy.

"You must try the ham," said the king, taking a bite.

"It looks delicious," said Elspeth.

"Let's just say it's a good thing this little piggy went to market," said the king. Georgie, sitting to his right, offered a courtesy chuckle while Elspeth went to work on the enormous plate of food.

Even on the best of occasions her table manners were no better than her manners in general. And now, with her stomach clamoring for food, she nearly forgot them entirely, stuffing her face with one forkful after another.

"Yes, you must be hungry after your long journey," said the king as he watched Elspeth with mild shock. Elspeth offered a grunt of affirmation while continuing to gulp down food with minimal chewing. "I'm sorry to have kept you waiting, but my physical therapy session went longer than expected. You see, I wrenched my back on the golf course today while trying to get out of a sand trap. It's not easy being king, but somebody's got to do it."

Georgie gave out another courtesy laugh, which the king once more failed to acknowledge.

"Make sure you save room for the cheese course," the king said to Elspeth. "It's one of my many culinary weaknesses, I must admit. Époisses, Saint Agur, Beemster. I love it all."

"I like grilled cheese sandwiches," Elspeth responded.

"Hmm," said the king, seemingly unimpressed. "If you're not into fine cheeses, you must save room for dessert. It's everyberry pie. My personal favorite. Contains every berry there is."

Elspeth fought back a smirk. "Don't be so sure," she thought of saying until she noticed Georgie leaning back and staring daggers at her. So instead, she said, "My mother doesn't bake pie. It's not her thing."

"Ah yes, your mother," said the king as if he and Mrs. Pule had gone to high school together or something. "I'm sure you're anxious to see her again after all this time."

"It hasn't been that long," said Elspeth. "But yeah, I guess I would like to see her again."

"You needn't worry, because that's going to happen much sooner than you know. I promise you that."

"Thanks," said Elspeth. "I knew you'd help me out."

"So then," said Krool. "Tell me about your journey. How was it?"

112

"Not great," Elspeth admitted. "Met a bunch of kooks. Almost got killed by something called a torcano."

"Yes," said the king. "It's the season. For torcanos, that is. Not kooks, as you call them. You'll find plenty of those year-round, I'm afraid. Not anywhere near here, mind you. One of my very first proclamations as king, I'm proud to say, was to banish all of the pathetic, whiny little losers to the outskirts where they belong."

Elspeth took this as a compliment. At school, with her gapped teeth and pudgy face and arms, she often felt both unattractive and, as a result, banished from the legions of the handsome and the popular. And now here she was, for the first time in her life, invited to be part of the fashionable crowd.

"So tell me," the king said, leaning closer to Elspeth. "What do they say about me? These kooks you met."

"Hmm," said Elspeth, giving careful consideration to her answer. "Well, they say you have your own bowling alley."

"Do you enjoy bowling?" the king asked.

"Oh yes," said Elspeth. "Very much." She hoped an enthusiastic response would lead to an invitation to play.

"I'm sure they say a great deal more about me than that," said the king.

"I guess," said Elspeth.

"Such as?"

"Oh, you know. The usual. About all the great stuff you've done."

"No insults or threats?"

"Oh no," Elspeth lied, for she saw no reason to mention all the horrible stories Dumpty and his friends had told her about the king. "After all, what could they possibly say?"

The king smiled contentedly. "Good. Then all is in order, it seems." He then turned to Georgie and said, "The time has come."

The king stood and raised his own glass to eye level.

"I would like to propose a toast," he began. "To our esteemed guest, Ms. Elspeth Pule." Elspeth was now aware that everyone in the room was staring at her (and at the same time she was completely unaware that her left cheek was smudged with gravy). Quickly, she cast her eyes downward and stopped chewing for a moment. Even though she was feeling, for the first time in her life, quite attractive, dressed in a beautiful silk gown with her hair done up in curls, Elspeth did not like being stared at, and she hoped this toast would not be a long-winded one like the kind her father sometimes made when he'd had more than one glass of wine.

"She is a remarkably resilient young lady," the king continued. "And she has shown great courage, incredible intelligence, and extraordinary wisdom in choosing to make the very long and very dangerous journey from her home to the castle in order to be with us this evening to turn herself in. Hear, hear!"

"Hear, hear!" the crowd repeated while Elspeth nearly choked on her food before spitting the entire mouthful onto her plate. The king took his seat and resumed eating as if he'd just announced the time of day and nothing more.

"Excuse me, Your Highness," Elspeth said while tugging at the king's sleeve. "I'm sorry, but what did you mean by that? That I came here to turn myself in?"

"That is why you're here, isn't it?" the king answered with a warm, almost fatherly smile. "To turn yourself in?"

"To turn myself into what?"

"Not into what. In to whom. In to my authority, to face the consequences for your crimes."

"Crimes? Hey, that sign told me to take the tart without paying for it."

"You stole a tart as well?" said the king. And then, just like that, his once kind and handsome face changed. His eyes narrowed, and his lips and eyebrows turned sharply downward as if gravity had suddenly taken a special interest in them. "I will consider that a full confession, and I will be sure to add it to the list of charges."

"What list? I haven't done anything," Elspeth protested. As much as she despised having to take responsibility for things she'd actually done, being forced to own up to things she hadn't done made her absolutely livid.

"Haven't done anything?" the king repeated, sounding almost insulted by Elspeth's denial. "You and your family have been plotting my demise for years. And now you will finally pay the price."

"My family? Okay, now this is getting weird," said Elspeth, without stopping to think about how ridiculous a statement that was, being that things had been "getting weird" for the better part of a day now. "My family knows nothing about this place. Everyone here has obviously mistaken me for someone else."

"I think not!" sneered the king. The murmur of conversation throughout the room and the scraping of flatware on china ceased. The king pushed his face toward Elspeth, and she scooted back to the far edge of her chair. "It is without a doubt that you are the one about whom it is written."

"Okay, here we go again with all this 'it is written' stuff," said Elspeth. "What? What is written?"

"The foretelling of your treasonous and seditious acts," replied the king.

"All right, I don't know what 'seditious' means," said Elspeth, "but I do know what treason is. It's betraying your country, which I could not possibly do because this is not my country. I've never been here before."

"Haven't you?" said the king with a smile that was no longer warm in any way.

"No, I haven't," Elspeth answered quite emphatically. "I only came to the castle to find the way out of this miserable country of yours."

Elspeth pushed her chair back and stood up. "Now, if you'll excuse me, I'm going home. With or without your help."

"Silly girl," said the king with a laugh and a shake of his head. "I said that I would see to it that you and your mother were soon reunited. I never said I'd help you find your way home. That's because you are home."

"You're crazy," said Elspeth. "You're all crazy. This whole place. Now, I need to speak with Jack and Jill immediately, so if somebody could show me to the dungeon . . ."

"Don't worry," the king responded. "Someone will be more than happy to show you to the dungeon." Then he turned to the four bearded men standing behind him and said, "Take her to the dungeon to await trial on charges of treason, sedition, and grand theft tart."

Almost immediately, Elspeth found herself in the clutches of two of the men, while the other two opened the nearest door.

"Hey!" she screamed. "Take your hands off me!"

Not only did the men not remove their hands from her chubby arms, they began dragging her toward the open door. "You can't do this to me," she said, kicking her legs and stomping her feet. "I'm an American citizen! I know my rights! I demand to speak with a lawyer!"

She managed to crane her neck far enough to find Georgie, who looked a bit traumatized by the whole ordeal.

"You!" she shouted. "You led me to believe this was a feast in my honor."

"I'm sorry," Georgie mumbled. "I had no idea."

"Quiet!" the king shouted. "You're apologizing to a known enemy of the Crown." To the beefy guards, who seemed to be having far too much trouble subduing an eleven-year-old girl, he said, "Now get her out of my sight!"

When the four men hauled her through the door and just before they slammed it shut, Elspeth hollered, "Dumpty was right! You're a horrible person! And another thing: that pie has no loganberries!"

Old King Krool was a nasty old fool,
And a nasty old fool was he.
He called for his pipe,
And he called for his bowl,
And he called for the cancellation of all federal holidays,
Including Christmas, Easter, and St. Crispin's Day,
And the execution of all enemies of the Crown,
Both foreign and domestic, including,
But not limited to, his fiddlers three.

Chapter 13

While stone is an excellent building material, it's downright lousy for acoustics. Elspeth's high-pitched screams ricocheted off the walls of the dark and narrow stairway to the dungeon, causing the guards much discomfort.

"You'll pay for this, all of you!" she wailed. "My father has sold hearing aids to some very important people!"

The guards had no idea what a hearing aid was, but by the time they'd wrestled Elspeth into the tiny cell, slammed the iron door, and bolted the lock, they might have needed one.

"Get back here," she hollered through the bars, rough and rusted. But the guards hurried down the hall just as fast as their pudgy legs could take them.

It was only when the four men had turned the corner and taken their shadows with them that Elspeth finally realized all the yelling was in vain. She took a deep breath and had a quick look around at her new environment. She quickly noted that, though there may be two kinds of castles, the fortress type and the fairy princess type, a dungeon was a dungeon: dark and cold, the air filled with moisture and hopelessness.

Just then she heard a soft whimpering to her left. She turned and peered into the adjoining cell, the single torch on the dungeon wall lighting it just to the point that she could make out the silhouette of a hulking, two-headed creature.

"Stay away from me," she ordered, backing away as far as the iron bars at the other end of her cell would allow. "I'm not afraid of you."

The beast did not respond. And, as her eyes slowly adjusted to the poor lighting, Elspeth soon realized it was not some double-headed monster at all, but rather two people huddled closely together. The woman was sobbing lightly while the man wrapped his arms about her shoulders.

"Look at her," the woman said with a whispery sniff. "She's beautiful. So strong and beautiful." The smile on the woman's lips suggested that the salty drops running down her cheeks were, in fact, tears of joy, though what one could possibly have to be joyous about in a place like this Elspeth could not fathom.

"Yes, she is," agreed the man. "She is indeed."

Elspeth just stared at the two. The woman was small but sturdy, with a Prince Valiant haircut that framed her gaunt face in sharp right angles. The man was mostly unremarkable, with the traditional trappings of middle age: an expanding midsection and a hairline in retreat.

"Let me guess," said Elspeth. "Jack and Jill."

"Yes," said the man, with a smile that revealed a small gap between his two front teeth.

The woman left her husband's comforting embrace and moved toward Elspeth until the bars stopped her progress. She pushed her face through the space between as far as it would go. "I can't believe it," she said, still sniffling. "I can't believe you're here."

"Yeah, I'm not sure what to believe myself anymore," said Elspeth, studying the floors, the walls, and the ceiling for any quick and easy way out that she might have missed at first glance. "All I wanted to do was to find that stupid well and go home, and instead I'm stuck in this terrible dungeon. This has been the worst day of my entire life."

"Don't worry," said Jill. "Everything will be all right." The woman's very demeanor was soft and soothing, but Elspeth had been fooled by such things before.

"It'll be all right?" Elspeth replied. "I'm sorry, lady, but you don't know what you're talking about. Krool's putting me on trial for treason. Maybe you aren't up to date on crime and punishment, but most people convicted of treason don't end up with community service, raking leaves, or painting over graffiti. They end up in front of a firing squad or whatever they do around here to execute people. By the way, how do they execute people around here?"

"Beheading," said the man. Jill spun around and shot him a very stern look.

"Jack," she scolded. "There's no need to tell her that. What's wrong with you, anyway?"

"Just being honest," replied Jack. "She did ask."

"Seriously," said Jill. "When are you going to learn to keep your mouth shut?"

"There must be a way out of here," said Elspeth, doing her best to ignore the bickering couple. She gave the door a good shake, but it moved only enough to make a small rattling. "Somehow we've got to escape from here so you can show me the way to the well before Krool decides to chop my head off."

"He won't kill you," said Jack. He joined his wife at the bars, and Elspeth noticed that he walked with a very pronounced limp, greatly favoring his left leg.

"Really? What makes you so sure?" she answered.

"Because he failed once before."

"Jack, no," Jill snapped. "We shouldn't. Not yet."

"Shouldn't what?" asked Elspeth. "What do you mean, he failed once before?"

Jack spoke to Elspeth, but his eyes were locked on Jill's searing glare. "Nothing," he said. "I just meant that . . . nothing."

"No," Elspeth persisted. "It wasn't nothing. What did you mean?"

Jack looked at Elspeth then back to his wife's rigid face. He opened his mouth to speak, but before words could find their way out, the door to the dungeon squeaked open once more and the four guards marched in with Georgie firmly in their grasp.

"This is absurd," pleaded the king's former personal valet. "Everyone knows that loganberries are very hard to find this time of year. It was an oversight, a mistake anyone could've made."

Without a word, the man with the Van Dyke unlocked the empty cell next to Elspeth's and shoved Georgie in hard enough that he didn't stop until he hit the back wall and tumbled to the ground in a heap. "Please," he begged, crawling on his hands and knees to the front of the cell as the guards turned and made for the exit. "If I could just have a word with His Highness, I'm sure I could convince him that this is all just a terrible mistake."

The door to the dungeon slammed shut, and once the echo had faded, the room was silent for a brief moment before Georgie began sobbing. "No," he wailed. "I'm too young to die." He stopped blubbering when he heard the clearing of a throat and looked over to see Elspeth staring down at him.

"*You're* too young to die?" she said. "I'm eleven. If you're too young to die then what am I?"

With the help of the bars, Georgie pulled himself to his feet and moved toward Elspeth's cell. "You are an awful person is what you are," he said. "Why did you have to tell him about the loganberries? Because of you, I've lost my job."

"Yeah?" said Elspeth. "Krool's going to chop my head off for treason and whatever the penalty is for stealing a tart."

"It generally results in having one's hand chopped off," said Jack.

"Jack! For crying out loud," said Jill.

"What? She wanted to know."

"If he's in an especially good mood," offered Georgie, "perhaps he'll chop off your head first."

"Oh yay, goodie for me," said Elspeth.

"I'm just saying, it would certainly save you some discomfort."

Elspeth growled and grabbed two handfuls of her curled hair and fought the urge to tear it out by the roots.

"I'll put in a good word for you," Georgie added.

"Quiet!" shouted Elspeth. "Enough! I can't take this anymore. Everyone just stop talking to me for a minute. I need to think."

She shuffled to the darkened back of her cell, leaned against the rock wall, and, with a sigh, slid to the ground. She drew her knees up and rested her muddled head upon them, the silky gown smooth against her cheek. Her prison mates honored her request for silence, and Georgie sat down himself while Jack and Jill just stood and looked upon Elspeth for a good ten minutes before Jill said, "Elspeth, dear."

Elspeth did not answer, and when she failed to respond a second time, it was quite apparent that the girl had fallen fast asleep. And when Jill was absolutely certain of this, she whispered, "Sleep, sweet Jacqueline. Sleep."

Georgie Porgie puddin' and pie
Found loganberries in short supply.
When Krool ate the pie he said,
"Off with Georgie's puddin' head."

Chapter 14

Morning arrived, and Elspeth woke, as she frequently did, with the feeling of having been watched. She took a few moments just lying in the fetal position while trying to piece together the events of the previous day.

Slowly she sat up, gave her stiff neck a good stretch, and jumped at the sight of Jill, peering at her through the bars of her cell with a wistful smile.

"What are you doing? Have you been . . . watching me sleep?" Elspeth said. She quickly wiped the grit from her eyes and ran the back of her sleeve across her mouth for any remaining drool.

"I'm sorry," said Jill. "I couldn't help myself." She spoke in a whisper so as not to waken Jack and Georgie, who were still curled up, fast asleep on their own patches of dirt.

"It is kind of weird," said Elspeth.

"I suppose it seems that way to you," said Jill. "It's just that . . . we had a daughter once. We . . . lost her."

"Yes, I know," said Elspeth, feeling it appropriate to stand up. Out of respect, perhaps? She wasn't sure. Though she may have been entirely unmoved by Bo-Peep's tale of having lost her precious sheep, there was something about a mother speaking of her child in the past tense that could touch even the least accessible of hearts. "Dumpty told me all about it. I can't believe Krool threw her down a well. Of all the horrible things. It must have been awful for you."

"He came in the night," said Jill. By her faraway look, Elspeth could tell that the scene now played vividly in Jill's mind. "Krool and his men. They snatched her away, and we could not stop them no matter how hard we fought, kicked, and clawed. In the end we failed. We failed to protect our own daughter. It was shameful."

"But you did everything possible, right?" said Elspeth, suddenly hit with a very strange and new emotion, an overwhelming desire to relieve the woman of her horrible pain. "You fought them as best you could. There's no shame in that. And you did try to get her back. You did go looking for her."

"For any sign of her," said Jill. "For years we searched every inch of the kingdom. When we heard that she had been cast down a well, we set our sights on exploring each and every one, hundreds of them, until finally, one night . . ."

Jill stopped short and looked away quickly. The shaking of her head launched several large tears onto the dirt floor at Elspeth's feet. Elspeth moved closer to Jill, carefully stepping over the tears, as though they were delicate, living things. "What?" she whispered. "One night, what?"

Jill reached through the bars and took Elspeth's hand while her eyes filled and overflowed. "One night . . . we found her."

Without knowing why, Elspeth pulled her hand away, and, with mild reluctance, Jill released it. "You found her?" Elspeth gasped. "You found your daughter's remains?"

"Not her remains," said Jill, that tender smile returning once more. "We found her. Alive and well."

This new detail nearly knocked Elspeth off her feet. "She's still alive? But Dumpty never told me . . ."

"That's because Dumpty doesn't know," said Jill. "Nor does anyone else. We mentioned only that we had found a passage out. The rest we kept secret. To protect you."

Elspeth's confusion could not have been more complete. "I don't understand. What does any of this have to do with me?"

"The little girl who was thrown down the well," said Jill, "was you."

"What?" said Elspeth. She laughed at this, not because she found it funny but because she felt she ought to, considering the pure lunacy of it. "I think if someone had thrown me down a well I would've remembered."

"You were not even a year old. Let's just say we're all quite fortunate that you've always been very good at holding your breath, or Krool might have succeeded in his plan. What he thought would be the end of you turned out to be a new beginning."

Elspeth looked beyond Jill to the sleeping heap on the ground—the one with the thinning hair, the ballooning belly, and the small space between his front teeth. Without realizing it, she began probing the gap in her own teeth with the point of her tongue. As ridiculous as it sounded, there was something both familiar and familial about these people. Looking at Jill's face, she noticed many of her own features gazing right back.

"But that would make me your daughter," said Elspeth. "And you, my mother."

"Yes," said Jill. And, while she continued to smile warmly, Elspeth slowly backed away.

"No," she said. "You're confused, I'm afraid. Or crazy. Or both."

"Page thirty-five," said Jill.

"What?"

"Of the Book. If you need further proof, it's a very good likeness of you. In fact, it's how we were sure that we'd finally found you."

"I don't want to look at that stupid book," sneered Elspeth. "It proves nothing. Besides, I have parents. Back home."

"The Pules," said Jill with a nod that looked like approval. "They've taken very good care of you, and for that we will always be grateful to them."

Elspeth was flooded with a desire to do something she hadn't in years. She wanted nothing more at that moment than to run to her mother and hug her tightly and without reservation. And then something that Jill had said moments earlier echoed in her mind. The bit about how she'd always been very good at holding her breath.

The last thing Elspeth had done before waking up in the middle of a strange forest was hold her breath until her living room had gone completely dark. It stood to reason then, that by repeating the act she might be transported back home or, at the very least, to some other place far less dreadful.

With nothing to lose as Elspeth saw it, she folded her arms across her chest, took in a very shallow breath (for the goal this time was not to prolong the process but to pass out as quickly as possible) and stopped breathing.

As before, sound was the first to go as her inner ear swelled and pounded. She didn't hear a word that Jill was saying, even though the woman must have been speaking quite loudly because Jack woke abruptly. He sat up, staggered to his feet, and limped over to his wife. The two seemed to be pleading with her, talking over each other and motioning with their hands.

Their voices would eventually wake Georgie, though Elspeth took no notice of that. By then the already poorly lit room was becoming darker still, and in a moment everything—Jack and Jill, the dirt floor and the iron bars, the dank air and the desperate gloom—disappeared, and once more Elspeth found herself in the warmth and brightness of her own home.

Ding dong dell, baby's in the well.
Who threw her down?
He who wears the crown.
Did she survive?
Please see page thirty-five.

Chapter 15

Never before had Elspeth's mother looked upon her with such kindness. With a loving gaze, she brushed the curls from Elspeth's forehead and kissed her softly on the cheek. Her father took his turn, hugging her tightly before walking briskly to the front door. Smiling widely, he opened the door and led in a real live alpaca, white with reddish-brown markings.

Mr. Pule had been selling hearing aids in Peru, he explained, and, wanting nothing more than to make his daughter happy, he had picked out the most beautiful alpaca he could find to bring home. Clenched between the animal's blocky white teeth was a pink silk ribbon tied in a bow around a small gold box.

Taking the box from the alpaca, Mr. Pule described how his flight home had connected in Brussels, affording him the opportunity to pick up a sampling of the finest Belgian chocolate.

Elspeth took the box and gently pulled at the pink bow until it fell away and floated gently to the floor. Removing the lid, she brought the box to her nose and breathed in deeply. There were only four chocolates in the box, but each was a work of art, with clean lines and a subtle but uniform sheen. Carefully, she plucked out a square, flat one with the initials of the maker embossed upon its surface.

Wanting to savor each and every morsel, she snipped off but a small corner with her gapped front teeth and, instantly, her mouth was filled with the rich flavor of . . . blood. What? Wait a minute. Yes, it was the unmistakable metallic taste of blood. Confused, she looked to her father, who only smiled, apparently unaware that he had been duped by Belgians into buying something that tasted so incredibly unlike chocolate.

Before Elspeth could complain about the awfulness of it, the alpaca, for no apparent reason, reared up on its hind legs, then turned and sprinted for the open door. "No!" Elspeth shouted. And when neither her father nor her mother made a move to stop the animal, Elspeth raced after it. In her haste, she tripped over her father's case of brochures and hearing-aid samples and fell face first to the floor.

Slowly, she moved her fingertips to her mouth and brought away a fair amount of blood—far more than could possibly be contained in that tiny bite of so-called chocolate. When her pupils came into focus again, she noticed a small pool of blood on the dirt floor, which caused her to consider the dirt floor itself. This was not her living room at all. It was a prison cell, and her parents were nowhere to be found. When she looked up and saw Jack and Jill peering through the bars of the adjacent cage, she knew it had all been nothing more than hallucination.

"Are you okay?" asked Jack. "You've been unconscious for quite some time. We've been worried to death."

"It didn't work," was all Elspeth could say. "I'm still here." She sat and stared at the wall and ran her tongue over the dried blood on her split lower lip. In addition, there was a golf-ball-size welt on her forehead that throbbed with every beat of her heart.

"I'm sorry," said Jill. "I wish you would have asked me first. There's only one way out as far as I know."

"The well?"

"The well," Jack confirmed. "Unfortunately, now that Krool knows about it he's placed it under heavy guard."

"Listen," said Jill. "I know all of this is confusing and upsetting. But try to look at it as an opportunity, a chance to do something great."

Elspeth shook her fists in frustration. "I just want to go home," she said through teeth clenched tightly. "And don't tell me I'm already home. I want to go to my real home. To my house and my things and all the people I know. I don't want to do something great."

Jill knelt down, hoping to draw Elspeth's eyes to hers. "Don't you see?" she said. "They're the same thing. You can't do one without the other."

"Why not?" asked Elspeth.

"Because of the prophecy," Jill responded. "As long as Krool is allowed to remain on the throne, the passageway home will be forever inaccessible to you. Someone needs to lead the people in rising up to take back what is rightfully theirs. And that person is you."

"And just how am I supposed to lead the people when they're all a bunch of cowards, always running away? The Dish ran away with the Spoon. Little Miss Muffet ran away from a spider. And *when the boys came out to play, Georgie Porgie ran away*."

"That is a lie," Georgie protested loudly while poking his finger through the bars in Elspeth's direction. "And besides, I will not be a party to this in any way. In fact, I will not listen to another word of this treasonous plot." He covered his ears and moved to the far end of his cell and began humming a random series of notes that failed to amount to music.

"Even if I had any interest in any of this, what's the point?" asked Elspeth. "How am I supposed to overthrow a government from inside a jail cell or with my head chopped off?"

"Fate has brought you this far," said Jack, as if that should somehow bolster Elspeth's confidence.

"But why me?" she asked. "This prophecy stuff. I don't get it. I'm an eleven-year-old kid. There's nothing special about me."

"Don't be foolish," Jill whispered. "There's plenty that's special about you. Things that you don't even know about."

"I have no friends," said Elspeth. With those words came tears, but Elspeth, with years of practice, managed to gulp them back down. "How special could someone with no friends be?"

"That tells me only that you're misunderstood," said Jill. "Don't you think it's possible? That you could be so misunderstood because you've been living for so long in a world that's not your own?"

"I don't know. I suppose," said Elspeth. She dug a morsel of dirt from the floor and rolled it between her thumb and forefinger.

"Whether you believe it or not, you were meant to do great things," whispered Jill.

"I'm sorry, but I don't believe it," said Elspeth. "I'm sure you're very nice people and everything, but it all sounds like a bunch of nonsense to me. Still, if it's the only way for me to get home, then I guess I have no choice."

"So are you saying you'll do it?" asked Jack hopefully.

Elspeth sighed and looked first at the ground and then back to Jack's and Jill's expectant faces. "Okay," she said in a resigned sort of way. "I'll do it. That is if we can get out of here somehow before we lose our heads."

The smiles that covered Jack's and Jill's faces were of both happiness and pride. "I knew she'd come through." Jack beamed. "I knew she would save us. A born hero, didn't I tell you?"

Jack's boasting might have gone on indefinitely if not for the sudden sound of heavy footsteps approaching. The prison door pushed open, and in walked the four guards from the day before. Immediately Georgie descended upon them.

"Thank goodness you're here," he said, rushing to the door of his cell. "I'm sure once His Majesty hears my side of the story, he'll see it was all just a simple . . ."

But when the guards unlocked Elspeth's cell instead, Georgie quickly realized this was not about him. "Please." He beckoned to the man with the large sideburns, who stood stoically nearby. "Perhaps I could testify against the girl in exchange for leniency. I'd be more than happy to do so. I've heard some things that might be quite useful." His pleas went ignored, and the man with the Van Dyke led Elspeth from her cell.

"Elspeth Pule," he announced loudly. "You are hereby summoned to appear in the royal court of His Highness, King Krool, Ruler of All the Land, Lord of the Seas and the Moon, Duke of Banbury Cross, Baron of Gotham, Royal Knight Companion of the Most Noble Order of Silver Bells and Cockle Shells, Earl of St. Ives,

Great Steward of the Pumpkin Eaters, Knight Grand Cross of the Most Honorable Order of Knick-Knack Paddywhack, and Royal Grand Champion of the Order of Pickled Peppers."

When he had finally finished his pronouncement, Elspeth looked at the man and said, "Okay, seriously. Are you as tired of saying all that as I am of hearing it?"

"Probably," said the man.

By the time the guards led Elspeth out of the dungeon, across the breezy plaza, down a series of narrow hallways, and into the courtroom, it was abuzz with spectators, all anxious for a look at the young traitor. The same eyes that had looked upon her with what she thought had been envy only the night before, now seemed full of scorn.

She tried her best to avert the piercing stares and found plenty upon which to focus. An entire wall of the room was draped in several enormous, floor-to-ceiling tapestries featuring very flattering likenesses of the king. An oversize table and chair, placed upon an elevated platform, presumably for the judge, sat vacant for now, and Elspeth was led to a wooden bench that seemed to have been reserved for her alone.

Sitting on another bench to her right was a man dressed in a dark-blue suit, his thick hair combed back, straight and tight. A longer look caused Elspeth to consider the fact that the man bore a strong resemblance to Krool.

With a bang, a side door flew open, and in hurried a man looking very much like George Washington after having just been mugged. His white wig, complete with braided ponytail, sat slightly askew on his head, and he struggled to button up a black gown while loose paper fell from a leather satchel wedged beneath his left arm. He stumbled over an untied shoelace and practically fell onto the bench next to Elspeth.

"Hey, watch it," she said.

"Pardon me, Ms. Pule," replied the man. "Sorry I'm late. Very busy morning. Okay then, let's take a look at your file." The man began digging through the satchel, pulling papers to his lap and flipping through them.

"What are you, my lawyer or something?" asked Elspeth, hoping for an answer in the negative.

"Jack B. Nimble," said the man, briefly looking up from the lapful of paper. "Of Nimble, Nimble, Tucker, and Levine."

"So you are my lawyer," Elspeth responded. "And you're just now going over my case?"

"I only got the files late last night. I'm a bit overloaded as it is, being the only one willing to take on these kinds of cases."

"What kinds of cases?"

"The kind where the defendant is obviously guilty," said Mr. Nimble. He found the page he'd been looking for and began reading silently, except for the slight clicking of his lips as he mouthed the words.

"Wait a minute," said Elspeth. "What do you mean, I'm obviously guilty? Aren't you supposed to be defending me?"

Nimble exhaled abruptly and looked up from his paperwork. "I can't very well defend you if I'm unfamiliar with your case, now can I?"

"But how can you be unfamiliar with my case and still think I'm guilty?"

"Because you're accused of a crime against the Crown," answered Nimble as if explaining why two plus two equals four. "So either you're guilty or the king is wrong, and that couldn't possibly be the case."

"Okay, I get it," said Elspeth. "Everyone thinks I'm this girl who's supposed to lead this big revolt against the king, like some kind of modern-day Joan of Arc or something. But even if that were true, it hasn't happened yet. So how can I possibly be charged with a crime?"

"It's a crime to even consider the act of treason. Now, I suggest we enter a plea of insanity," said Nimble. He found a pencil in the bottom of the satchel and began scribbling on the paper. "Have you ever heard voices in your head?"

"I'm hearing one now," said Elspeth.

"Great," said Nimble.

"It's telling me to knock that stupid wig off your head," Elspeth continued.

"Prone toward acts of violence." Nimble wrote some more then scratched it out. "On second thought, maybe we don't mention that."

Double doors behind the judge's chair swung into the courtroom, and in walked the bailiff, an elderly man with stark-white hair that covered his head, most of his face, and sprouted from his ears. He inhaled with a wheeze, and Elspeth was surprised to hear, "All rise for His Honor and Royal Highness, King Krool, Ruler of All the Land, Lord of the Seas and the Moon . . ."

It took the old man four or five separate breaths to get through the entire introduction, which gave Elspeth time to lean over and whisper to her lawyer, "The king is also the judge?"

"Yes, that's bad news," said Nimble. "I was hoping for Judge Contrary. She's tough but fair."

The king entered the room and waited for the old man to dust off his chair with a handkerchief before taking a seat. "Court is now in session," the bailiff managed with a single breath. "In the matter of Case Number 418,611: *The Crown versus Elspeth Pule*, to the charges of sedition, treason, and grand theft tart, how do you plead?"

When Elspeth answered with a forceful "Not guilty," a buzz rippled through the courtroom because, just as Nimble had said, for one to profess innocence to a crime against the Crown, with no further explanation, was to suggest His Highness had erred.

Nimble hastily straightened his wig and said, "My apologies, Your Honor. What my client meant to say is that she wishes to plead not guilty by reason of insanity."

"I'm not insane!" yelled Elspeth. Though, given everything she had experienced in the last twenty-four hours, she wasn't quite so sure. "And furthermore, I would like to object."

"That's my job," said Nimble.

"Then why aren't you objecting to the fact that the person accusing me of this crime is acting as judge, jury, and executioner?"

The king let out a hearty laugh. "Judge and jury, yes," he confirmed. "But executioner? Yuck. No, thank you." The king shuddered as if thinking about having to eat worms or something. Several members of the gallery snickered at this, which caused Krool to slam his gavel several times upon the table. "Quiet in the courtroom! And be seated. I'm prepared to hear opening statements at this time."

All in the courtroom took their seats except for the man with the slicked-back hair. "Good morning, Your Honor and Royal Highness," he said with a perfect-toothed smile.

"Good morning, Dave," Krool replied.

"Dave?" Elspeth whispered. "That's not the king's nephew, Dave? The guy who burned down the kittens' house?"

"That's him, all right," Nimble confirmed. "Spoiled little brat."

Chief prosecutor and nephew to the king, Dave, cleared his throat and began his opening statement. "Your Honor, Crown's Counsel will demonstrate, beyond a shadow of a doubt, that the defendant in this case, Elspeth Pule, a.k.a. Jacqueline Jillson, is not only guilty but ridiculously guilty."

"Jacqueline Jillson?" whispered Elspeth.

"Your name at birth, apparently," Nimble whispered back.

"Yikes," said Elspeth, suddenly aware of how Dolly Dew Eyes must have felt.

"We are confident that, when all the facts of the case are presented, His Honor and Highness will have no choice but to convict on all charges. Thank you."

The king's nephew took his seat, and Krool turned to Elspeth's lawyer with a look of extreme disinterest. "Mr. Nimble," he said. "The court will now hear your opening statement."

As Nimble stood, Elspeth sighed and muttered, "This oughta be good."

"Your Honor and Majesty," Nimble began. "Of course my client is guilty but should not be held accountable because she is completely and totally insane. In fact, she's so insane that, despite all of the evidence pointing to her insanity, she actually believes that she is not. I mean really, how crazy and deluded is that? Anyway, it is our intention to prove this beyond all doubt. Thank you."

146

Nimble retook his seat, and Elspeth leaned in and hissed, "I told you, I am not insane."

"Yes, brilliant," said Nimble. "Keep denying it. As I said, it makes you look even crazier."

"Quiet please," Krool ordered. "The prosecution may call its first witness. And let's make this quick. I intend to be out on the golf course by noon."

"Yes, Uncle Krool . . . excuse me, Your Honor," said the prosecutor. "At this time, the Crown wishes to call to the stand Elspeth Pule."

While refusing to testify might have been the prudent thing to do, Elspeth was anxious to tell her side of the story, and she quickly rose and walked to the witness stand, a small wooden chair resting meekly in the shadow of the judge's table.

Before she could take her seat, the bailiff stood before her and raised his right hand. Elspeth had seen enough courtroom dramas on TV to know what was expected of her. She rolled her eyes, then raised her right hand as well.

"Do you swear to tell the truth, the whole truth, and nothing but the truth, so help you Krool?" asked the bailiff.

"So help me Krool?" Elspeth answered with a sneer. "Seriously?"

"Quite serious, ma'am," the bailiff replied.

"Sure," said Elspeth, just wanting to sit down and get it over with. "So help me Krool."

She plopped onto the seat as the king's nephew swaggered closer. "Good morning, Ms. Pule," he said with a greasy smile.

"Yeah, whatever," said Elspeth, her eyes still angled toward the ceiling.

"Please state for the court your current occupation."

"What?" said Elspeth. "I'm eleven. I'm a student."

"Oh, an intellectual," said Dave with eyebrows raised in a way that suggested mockery. "Isn't it true, Ms. Pule, that you have been planning the overthrow of my uncle's government since you were a small child?"

"There's nothing true about it," Elspeth insisted. "I've had far more important things to do, like going to school, playing chess, and stuff like that."

Dave sauntered back to the bench to retrieve a large leather-bound book, then held it aloft as he walked back toward the witness stand. "The Crown would like to mark this as Exhibit A." He handed the book to Elspeth, and she immediately recognized it as a copy of the same book Bo-Peep had presented to her. "Please turn to page thirty-five."

Elspeth's heart began to race. She sat and stared at the book resting in her lap. "No," said Elspeth softly.

Aggressively, Dave leaned over and snatched the book away. "Fine," he said. "Allow me." He flipped through the pages, fanned the book open, and handed it back to Elspeth. "Now," he said. "Tell me what you see."

Elspeth just stared into Dave's soulless eyes. As much as she despised the look of him, it was far better, she sensed, than what loomed below on page thirty-five.

"What's the matter, Ms. Pule?" said Dave, addressing her while facing the gallery. "Are you afraid of what you might find?"

"I'm not afraid of anything," Elspeth asserted.

"Really?" said Dave. "Then why don't you prove it? Go on. Take a look."

Of course Elspeth was very much afraid. But there's a very good reason that curiosity, and not fear, killed the cat. Slowly, she lowered her eyes until they focused on the open book. Nearly inaudibly, and almost involuntarily, she whispered, "It's me."

"Pardon me?" said Dave loudly.

Like the other pictures in the book Elspeth had seen, this one was a black-and-white woodblock etching. The image was of a girl dressed in some type of military uniform and thrusting a pointed stick high into the air. The girl's hair was done up in curls, one dangling in the middle of her forehead. She wore a triumphant smile, which revealed a small gap between her front teeth. Though the girl in the picture was decidedly slimmer than Elspeth, the likeness was otherwise astonishing.

"But it's not," Elspeth said, shaking her head. "It can't be."

"Let the record show," said Dave, "that when the witness first saw the picture, she said the words, 'It's me.'

Now, Ms. Pule, if you would be so kind as to read the passage below."

Elspeth raised the book closer to her eyes and read silently until Dave bellowed, "Aloud, please!"

As much as she hated reading aloud in front of large groups, Elspeth did so without further prompting, only because she wanted to see if the words uttered out loud would somehow sound even more ridiculous. But when she heard them in her own voice, quite the opposite happened, and by the time she'd finished, she was as convinced as she was afraid that perhaps, just perhaps, they were indeed true.

Elspeth Pule, kicked out of school.
She would not learn the golden rule.
Held her breath until near death,
Then turned her wrath on Old King Krool.

Chapter 16

It wasn't until Dave tried to retrieve the book from her that Elspeth realized she was holding it in a vise grip. "That'll be enough," he said when he finally wrested the book from her hands. "No more questions."

Dave glided smoothly back to his seat on what Elspeth thought must surely be a layer of slime. On the way, he glanced at Nimble and said, "Your witness."

Nimble stood and approached Elspeth slowly. In fact he moved so slowly that Elspeth got the idea that he was stalling, still trying to think of what he might ask her.

"Elspeth, dear," he said finally. "Please state for the court your biological age."

"I'll be twelve next month," said Elspeth.

"Not even twelve years old," said Nimble, facing those in the audience. "And already plotting the overthrow of the government. To think that you, an eleven-year-old girl, could defeat and dethrone the great, the powerful, the infallible King Krool would be nothing short of insanity, would it not?"

"I told you before," Elspeth spoke just below a shout. "I'm not insane."

"No more questions, Your Honor."

Elspeth sat stunned as Nimble walked back to the bench. "Wait, that's it?" she asked.

"You may return to your seat, Ms. Pule," the bailiff instructed.

No sooner had Elspeth retaken her seat than Krool stood and the bailiff shouted, "All rise," causing her to immediately spring to her feet again.

"I'll be back with my decision shortly," Krool announced before turning and abruptly walking out of the room.

Elspeth glared at Nimble, who was frantically rifling through the papers in his satchel. "What are you doing?" she asked.

"Getting ready for my next case," he replied without making eye contact. "Tom Tom the Piper's son has stolen another pig. It's his third offense, so it's not good, I'm afraid."

"What about my case?" asked Elspeth. "You mean to tell me that was the whole trial? That was your entire defense?"

"I think we made our point quite well," said Nimble. "And the good news is the judge really seemed to like you."

"*Like* me? They say he tried to drown me. When I was just a baby."

"Well, he must have had a good reason," said Nimble. "You must have done something."

"I was a baby."

"I've met some very disagreeable babies in my time," said Nimble. "A couple of them were real jerks, in fact."

A second later, the doors to the courtroom opened again, and in walked the bailiff, ordering everyone to rise. Krool entered and instructed all but the accused to be seated. Elspeth, he said, was to remain standing for sentencing. He had come to a verdict after a mere thirty seconds of deliberation.

The four guards appeared at her side, ready to escort her back to her prison home as the judge pronounced her guilty of all charges. Now the only thing left to be determined would be whether the judge would find it in the goodness of his heart to have Elspeth beheaded before chopping off her hand.

Back in her cell, that was all she could think about as she sat on the dirt floor, sobbing loudly into her palms while Jack and Jill looked on with worry and Georgie paced as furiously as one can in the confines of a tiny cell.

"Are you sure?" he asked for a second time. "Are you sure he didn't mention me?"

Elspeth did not dignify Georgie's query with a response. As she saw it, she had already answered enough stupid questions during that horrible excuse for a trial. And now, here she sat, acting every bit like the type of person she had always found so annoying: a sniveling, blubbering, self-pitying mess.

"Three days," she sputtered. "Three days from now he's going to chop off my head. And my hand." She examined her right hand, then brought it to her throat and imagined her head rolling into some cheap wicker basket while crowds of people watched and cheered her premature death.

Jack and Jill exchanged a look, each hoping the other would have some bit of wisdom to impart, something that might give Elspeth a small measure of hope.

"I'll never see my parents again." Elspeth wept. "And they'll never know what became of me. How did this happen? How did my life turn into such a disaster?"

"It's not as bad as you think," said Jill.

Elspeth glared at the woman and said, "Not as bad as I think? You named me Jacqueline Jillson."

"It was a compromise," Jill admitted.

"I think it's quite a beautiful name," said Jack, the undeclared winner of that compromise.

Elspeth resumed sobbing and, for once, made no effort to stop it. In fact, the blubbering went on for the better part of the morning and afternoon. If she had only three days to live she felt it was entirely within her rights to spend them however she wished, and feeling sorry for herself was just as good a way as any.

As nightfall approached, she alternated between crying, dozing on the hard ground, and pacing nervously about her cell. When the man with the handlebar mustache delivered her dinner (for Krool wanted to ensure that Elspeth would be healthy and well nourished for the execution), Elspeth drank some of the water from the metal cup, but left the bowl of boiled cabbage untouched, except to slide it away with her foot so as to better avoid the acrid smell.

Just when she felt her anguish could not possibly be any greater, she felt a sharp, shooting pain in her backside, which caused her to spring from the dirt floor. "Ahhh," she cried, rubbing the affected area while scanning the ground for a scorpion or something else capable of causing such a sting.

"What is it?" Jill asked. "What's wrong?"

Elspeth noticed a small hole in the ground, surrounded by a tiny pile of dirt. From the hole rose something shiny and metallic. It was a teaspoon, and in that teaspoon was a bit of moist soil, which was quickly tossed aside and added to the pile.

With a mild clang, the spoon shot out of the hole and landed on the dirt floor. The head of a small gray mouse popped through the hole. With quick, jerky movements, the mouse climbed out and assessed its surroundings. Elspeth noticed that the mouse, which otherwise had all the parts mice normally have, was missing its tail.

"Excuse me," the mouse shouted as well as a mouse can shout. "Would there be anyone here by the name of Elspeth Pile?"

"Pule," said Elspeth, who had never been very fond of rodents to begin with.

"Close enough," said the gray mouse. "Name is Earl. Earl Grey." He then leaned over and shouted back into the hole, "Come on up, mates. We found her!"

One after the other, two more mice emerged from the hole—the first brown and lean, the second white and plump, and each with its tail every bit as missing as the gray one's. Quite immediately, the chubby white mouse walked right into the brown mouse as if the latter didn't exist.

"Hey," the brown mouse protested. "Watch where you're going. What are you, blind?"

"Not funny," the white mouse replied.

"Enough," commanded Earl Grey. "We don't have time for such nonsense. Now, let's get on with the rescue, shall we?"

"Rescue! Did you hear that?" said Jack with a pump of his fist. "I told you fate would intervene."

"This is fate intervening?" said Elspeth. "A rescue attempt by the three blind mice?"

"Excuse me, madam," said Earl Grey, with hands on his hips. "We're a bit visually impaired perhaps, but not blind, I assure you."

Meanwhile, the white mouse sniffed eagerly at the air. "Is that cabbage I smell?"

"I don't know what it is, to be honest," said Elspeth, "but you're welcome to it."

"Later," said Earl Grey. "Right now we've got heroics to perform."

"You won't get away with this," said Georgie. "Attempted escape is punishable by death."

"Only attempts that fail," said Earl Grey. "And we never fail. Now, allow me to introduce my co-heroes in this daring mission. This is James," he said, indicating the brown mouse. Then, pointing toward the white one, he said, "And this is Barry."

"James and Barry?" said Elspeth. "You're Earl Grey and these two are James Brown and Barry White?"

"You've heard of us," said Earl Grey, his furry little chest puffing out ever so slightly. "Stands to reason, I suppose. After all, this is not our first heroic rescue."

"And how, exactly, do you plan on carrying out this heroic rescue?" asked Elspeth. "Wait, let me guess. We're all going to take a magic shrinking potion and escape through that tunnel." Elspeth gestured toward the mouse-size hole in the floor.

"No," responded Earl Grey, quite impatiently. "We're going to go out the way you came in—right through the door."

"Once more," countered Elspeth, "unless you have some sort of shrinking potion that will allow me to fit

158

between the bars, that won't be possible. The door is locked shut."

"Locks are made to be picked," said Earl Grey with a quick flex of his eyebrows. Then, turning to his fellow rescuers, he said, "Gentlemen?"

James Brown and Barry White popped back into the hole and, a brief moment later, reemerged carrying a long, sharp stick. In fact, it was a long, sharp, familiar-looking stick.

"Well, well, well," said Gene. "We meet again. Look who's in dire need of Gene the Stick now."

"You brought him?" Elspeth asked, not even trying to hide her disapproval. "You do realize he never shuts up."

"Oh yeah," Earl Grey admitted. "On the way here I learned the entire history of sticks and all of their contributions to society."

"I tell you, it's about time people gave us some respect," Gene spouted. "All we get are insults. People will say that someone lives *out in the sticks*, as if it's a bad thing. And if you think for a minute that a wolf could blow down a house made of us, then you'll believe anything you read. Pure fiction."

When Gene finally finished, Elspeth sighed and said, "And you brought him because . . . ?"

"Because he's the only one we could find that was pointy at the end and long enough to reach the lock," replied Earl Grey.

"That's right," said Gene proudly. "Do you know how many sticks are out there? I do. And out of all of them, I was the only one up to the task."

"How lucky for us," said Elspeth. "And don't forget, I'm the one who sharpened you in the first place."

"If you hadn't, I'm sure someone else would have," said Gene. Then the grudge-holding stick began to perform what appeared to be some type of dance, wiggling about while the two mice struggled to keep hold of him.

"What the devil are you doing?" asked James Brown.

"Sorry, it's the water," said Gene. Looking around, the only water in any proximity to him was the amount that remained in Elspeth's metal cup. "My great-great-grand-father was a divining rod. Found most of the wells in this kingdom. It's in my blood, you might say."

"He might have found the well that led us to you," said Jack. "Imagine that."

"Yes," said Gene, still twitching. "Anyway, if you don't mind."

Elspeth took this to mean that she should dispose of the water and did so the most efficient way possible: by drinking it down in one gulp.

"Thank you," said Gene, instantly returning to a more relaxed state.

"All right then, let's get to picking that lock," said Earl Grey, and he and the other mice began carrying Gene toward the back of Elspeth's cell.

"Excuse me," she said. "The door is this way."

The mice quickly performed an about-face and headed for the locked door. "The lighting is terrible in here," Earl Grey offered as an excuse.

He and his fellow mice scurried between the bars and into the corridor.

"Okay, fellas," said Earl Grey. "You know what to do."

Elspeth watched as the three visually impaired mice climbed, one on top of the other, forming a wobbly tower of rodents a whopping ten inches tall, which would be all the additional height they would need to reach the keyhole with the help of Gene, the indignant, pacifist, blabbermouth, grudge-holding stick.

With Gene grasped tightly between his tiny mouse fingers, Earl Grey angled the stick toward the lock, missing on one occasion after another until finally the mice upon which he was standing began to protest, first with grunts and moans and eventually with words.

"Hurry it up, would you?" griped James Brown. "My back is killing me."

"You?" protested Barry White. "I'm the one on the bottom. I'm always the one on the bottom."

"Maybe we'd let you move up a notch if you'd just lay off the cheese and crackers once in a while," Earl Grey snarled.

"It's not my fault," Barry White responded. "I've told you before, I have a glandular issue."

Elspeth could only watch the infighting and ineptitude for so long before finally losing patience and, despite her general dislike of rodents, she said, "If you want, I could just lift you up to the lock."

The three mice froze, their faces cast in the position of those who have just been made aware that they are doing something incredibly stupid.

"Hmm," said Earl Grey, "I suppose that would work just as well. No harm in trying. Right, fellas?"

The others agreed, and Elspeth slipped her palm through the bars, allowing the three mice to climb aboard.

"Brilliant idea." Jack beamed as he and Jill watched. "That's our daughter, you know. A chip off the old block."

Elspeth brought the mice slowly upward, and their presence upon her palm caused an involuntary shiver that almost sent them tumbling back to the ground.

"Easy now," instructed Earl Grey as he inserted Gene into the keyhole and began probing the lock. "I must have a steady surface from which to work."

"I'm sorry," said Elspeth. "No offense, but rodents give me the willies."

Earl Grey seemed amused by this. "Ironic, isn't it?" he said with a chuckle. "Considering it was Willie who gave you the rodents."

"What do you mean?" asked Elspeth.

"King William," Earl Grey replied. "He hired us."

"King William lives?" gasped Jack.

"Oh, he's alive all right," Elspeth confirmed. "And completely out of his mind. Still, I guess it was pretty nice of him to try to rescue me."

"That's King William for you," said Jack. "Nice to a fault."

"Nice has little to do with it, I would imagine," said Jill. "He knows that without our Elspeth, he'll never be king again."

"It's dark in here," said Gene with an echo.

"Quiet," said Earl Grey in a loud, stern whisper. "I require absolute silence." He continued to work the lock while listening intently until, at last, there it was: a distinct and unmistakable click. The door to Elspeth's cell popped open, and for a brief moment, no one said a thing.

"Yes!" Jack cheered at last. He and his wife hugged each other tightly.

"You did it," marveled Jill.

"Of course I did," said Earl Grey.

"You?" said Gene. "Hello? See what I mean? Never any credit."

"Fine," Earl Grey conceded. "It was a team effort. Excellence all around. Now, let's get going while we still can."

"No," said Elspeth. "We're not going anywhere without Jack and Jill."

Earl Grey squared up with Elspeth and spoke as though there were no size difference between them.

"Now listen here, missy. We were paid our going rate for rescuing one person. Now you're suggesting we take two more for the same price?"

"Three more," said Georgie.

"What?" said Elspeth, whipping her head around to make sure Georgie got a good look at her scowl. "What makes you think we'd take you with us?"

"Because if you don't, he'll kill me," said Georgie with a whimper. "And I know you don't want that on your conscience. Please."

"He can't kill you over some stupid berries," said Elspeth.

"Can and will," said Georgie. "After all, he threw you down a well for something he was afraid you might do."

"I don't know," said Elspeth. "Just this morning you were offering to testify against me."

"Yes," Georgie admitted. "And I hope you'll be able to accept my sincere apology. Anyway, I could be quite helpful to you. You may be free of that cell, but we've still got to sneak out of the castle. And no one knows this place better than I do."

Elspeth considered the facts of the matter and decided that it actually made good sense to add a backstabbing, self-serving weasel to a group that already included three bumbling, partially blind mice, two strangers claiming to be her parents, and an annoying, blathering stick. "All right," she said with a sigh of finality. "We'll take you along."

"Thank you," said Georgie, practically melting with relief. "You won't be sorry."

But the matter was not so easily settled. "I don't know," said Earl Grey. "Four people for the price of one? Nope. Afraid that won't do."

"I thought you said you were heroes," snapped Jill, her voice heavy with the kind of disappointment only a mother can convey.

"We *are* heroes," said Earl Grey.

"Heroes don't rescue people because they're being paid. They do it because it's the right thing," said Jill.

"Doing the right thing doesn't put crumbs and garbage on the table," Earl Grey retorted.

"If I can't appeal to your sense of common decency," said Jill, "then perhaps I can convince you to do it for the sake of avenging your missing tails."

"I thought the farmer's wife cut off their tails," said Elspeth.

"Ha! Typical," Earl Grey snorted. "Always blaming things on the middle class. Anyway, they'll grow back. Eventually. Right?" James Brown and Barry White quickly checked their backsides to see if anything might be sprouting up. "Besides, tails are overrated."

When it became apparent that there was nothing Jill could say to convince Earl Grey, Elspeth spoke up. "If you don't take everyone with you," she said, "then I'm not going. And if I don't go, then there's been no rescue and you won't get a thing."

Earl Grey seethed. He was not used to dealing with prisoners and hostages who were anything but grateful for having been rescued. "All right," he finally relented. "We'll take the lot of you. But once we're out of here, I'm bringing the matter up with Winkie right away."

With equal efficiency, Earl Grey and Gene the Stick picked the locks on the other two cells, freeing Georgie, then Jack and Jill, who could not resist the overwhelming desire to hug their daughter for the first time in almost a dozen years.

Under normal circumstances, Elspeth might have objected to such familiarity, but there was something about it that seemed quite natural. Besides, the encounter was brief, as Georgie reminded them that they still had a very long way to go before tasting true freedom.

Three visually impaired mice,
Three visually impaired mice.
See how they run,
See how they run.
They all went after Krool's Monterey jack,
He cut off their tails with a battle-ax.
Now you know the horrible facts
Of three visually impaired mice.

Chapter 17

Creeping down the long, dark passageway and arriving at the door to the dungeon, they soon realized that it, too, was locked and would require the talents of Earl and Gene.

The mouse and the stick quickly went to work on the last lock, which was not the final obstacle that stood between the captives and the outside world. Once they'd gotten beyond the confines of the dungeon there were still guards posted throughout the castle, for a man with as many enemies as Krool can never have too much security.

As it turned out, Gene soon proved quite useful for something other than picking locks. His slightly curved shape made him the perfect tool for peering around corners.

"Well?" asked Elspeth as she pulled him back in.

"It's clear," said Gene.

The group, based on Georgie's knowledge of the castle layout, made a left turn and crept quietly along the corridor until they came to the entryway of a large room. Again, Elspeth carefully extended Gene so he might have a look, both left and right. When she retrieved him once more, Gene whispered so quietly that Elspeth had to bring him very close to her ear.

"Two guards," he said. "One on either side."

"What now?" Elspeth whispered to Georgie.

"It's Thursday," he replied. "That means Weldon and Morgenstern are on duty at this post."

"And how does that bit of knowledge help us now?" asked Elspeth.

"Not sure," Georgie whispered. "But I do know that the two can't stand each other. They've been feuding since grade school."

Elspeth, who knew a fair bit about grade school feuds, thought a moment about how such a thing might be exploited to their benefit. An idea popped into her head surprisingly quickly, and she whispered it to Gene, who considered it briefly.

"I suppose it'd be all right," he whispered back. "As long as I'm only the cause of the violence and not involved in it directly."

Earl and his crew also figured into Elspeth's plan, and she knelt down and whispered instructions like an NFL quarterback calling a play. "I like it," Earl replied with a devilish nod.

Elspeth rose up and inched her face forward until she could see the two guards, both staring straight ahead, their backs to the wall. Their rigidness and silence may have been due to protocol or to a shared hatred, strong enough that they would neither talk to nor even look at one another.

Elspeth slowly moved Gene toward the guard at the left of the doorway, the one known as Morgenstern. With the stick she smacked him sharply on the ear.

"Hey," he cried, as Elspeth ducked quickly back into the hallway. The guard turned to the fellow known as Weldon. "What do you think you're doing?"

"What are you on about?" said Weldon.

"Don't play dumb," snapped Morgenstern. "You flicked my ear and you know it."

"I did no such thing," Weldon argued.

"Do it again and it'll be the last time," threatened Morgenstern.

The argument ended, not abruptly, but slowly, tapering off and dissolving into mumbles. Once the guards had gone back to their silence and straight-ahead staring, Elspeth peeped around to the right and this time smacked Weldon in the ear.

"All right," said Weldon. "That's it." He dropped his spear, wound up, and threw the punch he'd been wanting to throw at Morgenstern's smug face for twenty years. Morgenstern, however, ruined it all by moving that smug face quickly out of the way, which caused Weldon's fist to have an unpleasant meeting with the rock wall immediately behind it. As Weldon screamed in agony Morgenstern seized upon the opportunity and rushed Weldon, tackling him to the ground.

As they wrestled, rolled, and grunted on the floor, Earl Grey and his team of verminous heroes skittered out and surreptitiously took to the task of tying the men's shoelaces together—a dangerous job, considering those big, heavy shoes were in constant motion.

The shoelace tying turned out not to have been necessary as Elspeth, Jack and Jill, Georgie, Gene, and Earl Grey and his friends were able to glide through the room unnoticed due to the fact that the fight between the guards had escalated to the point of eye gouging.

Down another long, torch-lit hall the escapees crept, but they froze when they heard footsteps and voices growing louder by the second.

"Quick," whispered Georgie. "In here."

He pulled open a door, and Elspeth immediately recognized the kitchen, now quiet and dark, though the wonderful smells of the previous night's feast still lingered. Jack and Jill, who had been subsisting on prison scraps for several days now, breathed in the smells so deeply their ribs hurt.

"Is that everyberry pie I smell?" whispered Jack.

"Not exactly," said Elspeth. This garnered a sharp look from Georgie, and Elspeth replied with an innocent-looking shrug.

Following Georgie, the others slipped inside and closed the door. Georgie grasped the knob tightly as the voices and footsteps neared. Then the footsteps stopped, though the voices continued. Elspeth recognized them as belonging to Catherine and Jane.

"I know," said Catherine. "She may be a horrible little beast, but do they have to chop off her head?"

"Such a shame," said Jane. "It'll ruin that dress."

"As for Georgie, I say good riddance," said Catherine.

"No kidding," Jane agreed. "Did you know he tried to kiss me once?"

"Eww, disgusting," said Catherine. As she spoke, Georgie's face reddened and his teeth clenched as tightly as his grip on the doorknob.

Catherine reached for the knob and found it immovable. "Hmm," she said. "Must be locked. We'll have to go around."

When the women continued down the hall, Georgie felt it necessary to whisper. "It's not true." He then turned and led the group through the kitchen.

"Put that down," Earl Grey scolded Barry White, knocking a sizeable breadcrumb from the mouse's mouth.

"But it's pumpernickel," said Barry. He took one last sniff of the morsel then hurried to catch up with the others.

The door at the other end of the kitchen led them back out into the courtyard where the shops had long ago closed down for the night. On the catwalk above stood several more guards, but they were more concerned with attackers or assassins breaking in than with prisoners getting out, and their backs were to the escapees.

Elspeth and the others crouched down into the shadows and away from the glaring light of a half moon as they crept across the plaza, stopping at another closed door. "This is the billiards room," Georgie whispered. "It's under renovation, and the other day I noticed an opening in the outer wall."

"So let's go then," said Jack.

"It's under guard," said Georgie. "The only thing is, I can't remember whether it's Rutherford or Derbyshire on Thursdays."

"What does it matter?" asked Elspeth.

"Why, it matters a great deal," said Georgie. "If it's Derbyshire, we're in good shape. He has a tendency to fall asleep on the job."

"And if it's not?" asked Jill.

"Then it's Rutherford, five-time winner of the Sentry of the Year Award," said Georgie. "To be honest, I'm not sure what to do at this point. This is really the only way out of the castle other than over the wall or through the drawbridge."

Elspeth knelt down in front of the door and tried to slide Gene beneath so he could have a look around, but the space between the door and the ground proved to be too tight, even for a pointy, scrawny fellow like Gene.

"It's no use," she said. "He won't fit. We'll just have to chance it and hope that it's Derbyshire."

"What if it's the other guy?" asked Jack.

"Then we'll all be added to Krool's collection of severed heads, I would imagine," said Elspeth.

"That would never happen," said Jack with a gap-toothed smile. "He'll never get the best of my daughter."

Georgie placed his hand upon the doorknob. "Are you sure about this?"

"Do it," ordered Elspeth with a quick nod.

Georgie inhaled deeply and began turning the knob so slowly that its movement was barely perceptible to the naked eye. When he'd turned it as far as it would go, he looked at Elspeth once more. She nodded, and he pushed the door inward. Immediately, Elspeth gasped at what she saw. Across the room sat a man with round, red cheeks and a double chin, and he was staring right back at them. The man, as it turned out, was Derbyshire, who apparently had a habit of sleeping with his eyes half-open. In fact, it would have been difficult to discern that he was sleeping at all if not for the subtle but consistent snoring. He was sitting on a stack of boards, leaning back against the wall, a mere couple of feet from the opening.

For a moment, Elspeth was concerned that the sound of her heart pounding against her sternum might be sufficient to wake the man, and she took several slow, deep breaths to try to calm herself.

The room was cluttered with a number of obstacles, present as a result of the renovation project. There were tools, piles of boards, and loose stones. The escapees started across, the mice leading the way. Jack's bad foot momentarily failed him, and he stumbled over a mortar-board.

Instantly, everyone froze, and all eyes shot toward Derbyshire. The jowly guard mumbled and stirred, but his own eyes remained at half-mast and he settled back into a deep sleep. Jill glared intensely at her husband, and Jack shrugged apologetically.

They continued toward the escape route without further incident, and when they slipped through the hole in the wall, they found themselves standing beneath scaffolding being used as part of the renovation project. It served as the perfect cover from the eyes of the guards on the catwalk above.

Just being outside the castle walls, Elspeth had a new and overwhelming appreciation for freedom. Breathing in deeply, she wanted nothing more than to run across the field and away from the castle. But Georgie put his fingers to his lips then pointed upward, reminding her and the others of the posted sentries.

From the beginning, this had been an impromptu rescue plan and, as a result, had not been carefully thought out. After all, who could have imagined that escaping from the dungeon and sneaking out of the castle would be the easy part? How were they to get across the open field to the cover of the trees some two hundred yards away without being spotted?

"Okay," whispered Elspeth to Georgie. "What do you recommend?"

"I'm sorry," Georgie replied. "I honestly don't know."

"We could dig a tunnel from here to the forest," offered James Brown.

"Yes," said Elspeth. "And in the three weeks it would take you to dig that tunnel, we will all have lost enough weight to fit through it."

As it turned out, with all eight minds hard at work, none of them had a better idea. There seemed to be no viable solution.

Then out of the blackness came the kind of shriek that curls toes and stiffens hair on the backs of necks. With a second shriek and a whoosh, a shadow shot across the moon.

Elspeth was certain she knew the cause of it. "It's Fergus," she said, searching the darkened sky.

There came another shriek, and a fourth, but these were of human origin as the guards on the catwalk above fought off the dive-bombing owl, ducking for cover and stabbing their spears blindly into the night.

"Now," said Georgie, and with the others close behind he left the cover of the scaffolding and sprinted for the trees.

Elspeth was not a terribly athletic child. Of all the subjects in school, she disliked gym most of all. As a result, she was in very poor shape, and only halfway across the open field she developed a searing cramp in the side of her gut.

She struggled on for as long as she could, but soon the pain became too much and she stopped and doubled over, feeling that she might vomit. Behind her the guards were still locked in battle with Fergus, who continued his daring assault, clawing and shrieking while deftly avoiding the deadly spear tips thrust in his direction. It was a brave and noble effort, but Elspeth wondered just how long he could keep it up.

She stumbled onward until she found herself being scooped off the ground. Jack threw the girl over his shoulder, and with Jill at his side he limped and lumbered the remaining distance to the grove of trees.

Out of the moonlight and into the dreamy shadows they stumbled, falling into a heap upon the soft grass. For the first few moments, they just lay there, catching their breath. Before any of them could say a word, another shriek shot out across the night. This was not a war cry, but a squeal of intense agony, followed by a thick and sudden silence.

"Fergus," whispered Elspeth.

A wise old owl lived in an oak.
Kept to himself unless you spoke
With syntax off or grammar wrong.
Say what you will, 'cause now he's gone.

Chapter
18

Hurried voices carried through the cool, thin air but none that Elspeth recognized. There were no more toe-curling shrieks or corrections of improper grammar. It meant only one thing, she feared. Fergus was dead.

"He was a good friend," said Jack.

"First his wife and now this," said Jill, her head lowered. "Terrible."

"We should keep moving," said Gene anxiously.

Elspeth peered through the trees, back toward the castle. Risking her life to save others was not something she could ever imagine having the courage to do. "Wait," she said.

An all-too-brief moment of silence was the only thing Elspeth could offer as a means of thanking Fergus. "Okay," she said at last and slowly brought herself to her feet. "Let's go." But pulling her gaze from the castle and her shoes from this hallowed patch of ground was easier said than done. Doubtfully, she scanned the sky one more time for any sign of a passing shadow.

"We'd better hurry," said Georgie. "It won't be long before they realize we're gone."

About this, Georgie couldn't have been more correct. Back in the castle, the hatred shared by Weldon and Morgenstern eventually gave way to fatigue, and now the sworn enemies lay beaten, breathless, and exhausted on the cold stone floor. And when they'd had time to consider it, they realized that no matter how devious the other might have been, neither was clever enough to have tied both sets of shoelaces together.

With the tip of his spear, Morgenstern sliced through the laces and the guards raced immediately to the dungeon, where they found the door open and the three cells vacant.

Right away there was an argument over who should be responsible for waking the king and sharing with him the fact that several high-profile prisoners had escaped while on their watch? Luckily for Elspeth and her friends, for the first time in twenty years the fierce rivals agreed upon something: that neither would be the one to report this horrible bit of news. Instead, they would work together and would themselves escape the castle, for they believed their chances of survival would be greater in the wild than in close proximity to an angry King Krool.

It wasn't until nearly an hour later, at the changing of the guard, that Krool finally learned of the prison break, and he predictably spun into a violent rage.

"How?" he demanded of his four most trusted guards as he paced around his palatial sleeping chambers. Krool punctuated his question by thrashing a washbasin with the nine iron he kept beneath his pillow for self-defense. The ceramic bowl exploded off its stand, shattering and skittering out across the marble floor. "How did this happen?"

"Weldon and Morgenstern," replied the terrified men. "They're missing as well, I'm afraid."

"Double-crossing backstabbers!" Krool swung the club again, this time knocking over an entire suit of armor that had been standing next to the door. "I want them found," he fumed. "I want my prisoners and those two traitors hunted down like dogs!"

The four men just stood, looking somewhat confused and hesitant.

"What?" Krool demanded.

The guards exchanged looks, as a means of determining which of them would be the one to convey what they were all thinking. "Yes, Your Highness," volunteered the man with the sideburns. "We're not sure how we should . . . what I'm trying to say is . . . it's just that we've never hunted dogs before. I mean, it's generally not an accepted practice. I've hunted foxes with the use

181

of dogs, but hunting dogs just isn't done, so we're a bit at a loss as to how we would . . ."

"Fine!" yelled the king. "Then hunt them down like foxes! Or rabbits, or badgers! I don't care. Just find them and bring them to me. Alive. After all, we wouldn't want me to miss out on any of the fun, now would we?" Krool sneered and kicked the helmet belonging to the suit of armor across the floor, out the door, and down four flights of marble stairs.

By the time the resulting clang stopped bouncing off the castle walls, Elspeth and the others had reached the cliff and had begun zigzagging down the hillside, in search of Winkie's cave. Earl Grey, with his keen sense of smell, led the way.

"I don't know why we have to stop here," griped Elspeth. "The sooner we get back to the forest, the sooner we can get started with this whole stupid . . . rebellion thingy."

"I know you're anxious to go home," said Jill, "but crossing Torcano Alley at night is much too dangerous."

"But you've done it before, haven't you?" Elspeth replied. "When you were looking for me . . . for your daughter, I mean. You said you went out at night and searched the entire kingdom."

"Yes," Jill agreed. "But not without incident. We had many close calls, and poor Jack nearly lost his foot to a sinkhole full of lava."

Up ahead Jack's hobbled gait was even more pronounced on the steep downward slope.

"So that's why he limps," said Elspeth.

"That's why he limps," said Jill.

Elspeth decided that one night in Winkie's castle away from home would be preferable to falling into a sinkhole, and so she argued no further for attempting a night crossing. The others followed as Earl Grey scampered up the hillside and into the cave.

"Who's there? Who is it?" echoed Winkie's voice from the darkness.

"It's us," said Earl Grey. "The conquering heroes have returned."

When Winkie spied Elspeth crawling into the cave, he emerged from the shadows, smiling broadly. "You've done it, Earl," he exclaimed. "You pulled off the rescue."

"Yes," said Earl Grey angrily. "And at four for the price of one, I might add."

"Four?" Winkie replied. He then watched as Jack and Jill and finally Georgie crawled into the cave, which may have been suitable lodging for a man of Winkie's stature, but add four mice, three regular-size adults, and an eleven-year-old girl, and things were more than a little cramped.

Despite the issue of overcrowding, Winkie seemed delighted to have them, with one notable exception. "Well, look who's here," he said, glaring at Georgie. "If it isn't little Georgie Porgie puddin' and pie."

"Hello, Winkie," said Georgie.

"That's King William to you," said Winkie with a snarl. "You've got a lot of nerve showing your smug little face around here."

"Okay, you're obviously upset with me," said Georgie. "But what was I to do? I had to stay behind. Krool offered me a big promotion with a sizeable increase in salary. I would have been a fool not to take it."

"Then what are you doing here now?" Winkie demanded.

"Uh . . ." Georgie's eyes shot around the cave as if looking for an answer etched upon the walls. "I would like to be able to say that I've seen the error of my ways and have come to my senses," he muttered. "But the truth is, I'm . . . I'm here not so much by choice as by necessity. You see, Krool has declared me an enemy of the Crown and was planning to have my head chopped off."

"And what makes you think I won't do the same?"

"Because," said Georgie softly, "you're not like him. He's a monster."

"That's right," said Winkie. "A monster that you helped create and unleash upon the world."

Georgie seemed genuinely puzzled. "I don't know what you're talking about," he said.

"Don't you?" said Winkie. "Strange then how Krool and his men were able to gain access to the castle on the very night you were on duty. And a mere coincidence, I suppose, that the day he replaced me upon the throne you just happened to be made his personal assistant."

"I admit it looks bad," said Georgie, "but I have no idea how he and his men got in and that's the truth."

"You wouldn't know the truth if it slapped you in the face," said Winkie, fighting a strong impulse to do just that.

"I never did like him, just for the record," said Gene.

"Okay," said Georgie. "It seems as though you all have your minds made up about me. But regardless of what may have happened in the past, I'm here to offer my help. To do anything I can to get rid of that tyrant."

"I'm not interested in your kind of help," said Winkie, folding his arms and turning his back on Georgie.

"Hear that?" said Gene. "He's not interested."

Georgie sighed and nodded his head slowly. "All right then," he said. "Good luck to you all. And thank you for saving my life. At least temporarily."

As Georgie backed his way toward the cave entrance, Elspeth half expected Jack or Jill to stop him or for Winkie to change his mind. When neither happened, she said, "Hold on."

"Yes?" Georgie asked.

But Elspeth turned her attention not to Georgie but to Winkie. "He did help us escape the castle," she said.

"He helped himself," said Winkie. "You heard him. He did it to save his own head."

"He does know a lot about Krool," said Elspeth. "And about the castle. The inner workings, schedules, things like that."

185

"He can't be trusted." Winkie finally spun around for the purpose of giving Georgie one final dirty look.

"Maybe not," Elspeth agreed. "But we have no choice. Defeating Krool without his help might be impossible. And if I'm the one supposedly leading this uprising, then I say he stays."

Winkie dropped his arms and shook his head. To Jack and Jill, he said, "Your daughter is very stubborn."

Jill smiled. "I prefer the word 'spirited,'" she said.

"Excuse me," said Georgie, not wanting to interrupt but also not wanting to remain half-inside the cave and half-out. "It's just that I'm not sure whether I'm supposed to go or . . ."

"You're staying," said Elspeth. "You are now an official member of my military advisory committee."

"Fine," Winkie responded. "But if he double-crosses us, I'm holding you personally responsible."

"He won't double-cross us," said Elspeth. "Will you, Georgie?"

"Of course not," said Georgie. He spoke with a smile that looked cunning and smarmy, just because that was the only way Georgie knew how to smile. "If I were going to double-cross you, would I have helped you escape? If not for me, you'd probably still be there."

"If not for everyone involved," said Earl Grey.

"Yes," said Elspeth, thinking of another who had been part of the rescue but not of the celebration. "I'm afraid I have some bad news as well."

"Bad news?" said Winkie.

"Fergus," said Elspeth. "He attacked the guards so we could get away. I'm afraid he wasn't so lucky. He made what we call in chess a positional sacrifice."

"Oh dear," said Winkie. "That is most dreadful news. So now you understand how important it is to rid the world of that awful Krool."

Before Elspeth could answer, Earl Grey shouted, "Quiet!" He was pressing his left ear firmly to the ground, with his eyes closed tightly.

"What is it?" asked Jack, ignoring the plea for silence. "What's the matter?"

"Horses," said Earl Grey. "Perhaps a hundred or more. And they're coming this way. Fast."

Star light, star bright,
First star I see tonight;
I wish it weren't, with all my might,
A large torcano, burning bright.

Chapter 19

Though crossing Torcano Alley in darkness may have been a foolhardy venture, to just sit around and wait for Krool's soldiers to show up and arrest them would be stupidity in its purest form.

The half moon, hanging in a clear night sky, provided some light but also created long, dark shadows that could be mistaken for the seemingly bottomless cracks in the earth.

The other travelers followed Jack and Jill, crisscrossing and sidestepping, while placing all their trust in the unpredictable ground beneath their feet. Again Gene demonstrated firsthand the usefulness of sticks when Jill used him to tap at the ground in front of her as she walked, testing it for stability.

The silk slippers provided Elspeth's feet with little comfort on the rocky ground as she followed behind Jill and directly in front of Jack, while Winkie and the trio of tailless mice rode upon Jack's broad shoulders. Georgie, at the end of the group, stopped to make frequent checks of the cliffs behind them.

It was hard to tell in that faint, blue moonlight, but after an hour without incident it looked as if they'd made it nearly halfway across. That was when Georgie turned, stood silent for a moment, and said, "Uh-oh."

There they were, one hundred strong, lined up along the edge of the cliff—dark, spear-holding silhouettes that, from this distance and in this light, strongly resembled a wrought-iron fence.

"It's okay," said Jack in a less than convincing voice. "They'll never come after us while it's still dark."

No sooner had Jack uttered those words than Krool's men began guiding their horses down the zigzag trail and into Torcano Alley, where they would have a distinct advantage over their prey.

"I don't believe it," said Jill. "What do we do? They're sure to catch us on horseback."

"There's only one thing we can do," said Earl Grey. "We've got to pick up the pace."

Without discussing it further, Jill continued, this time faster and less certain than before. "Watch it here," she cautioned, while using Gene to point out a large crevasse hidden in the shadow of a petrified oak tree. By the time they'd gotten around it safely, they could hear the sounds of horses' hooves, some four hundred strong, clip-clopping across the desert floor.

"We're not going to make it," said Georgie, glancing over his shoulder.

"Don't be ridiculous," said Elspeth. "Of course we'll make it."

"Only if we run," said Jill.

"Then let's run," said Elspeth, confused as to why any discussion of it was necessary.

"But if we run," said Jack, "we could fall to our deaths."

"Seriously," said Elspeth. "You people are absurd." Elspeth pushed her way to the front, hiked up her gown, and broke into a jog. Not surprisingly, she was in no better shape now than she had been several hours earlier when running from the castle to the forest. As before, a searing pain developed quickly across her abdomen as she sucked in more oxygen than her atrophied lungs could process. Just when she thought she could continue no farther, the ground beneath her feet crumbled and she began to fall.

She barely had time to scream when her arm was nearly dislocated at the elbow as she found herself dangling above a large sinkhole, rocks and pebbles plopping into a bright-orange bed of magma some fifty feet down. The only thing that had stopped her from plunging into it herself was Jack, who held firmly to Elspeth's wrist, while Winkie clung tightly to her hair. When Jack had seen the girl falling, the lunge he'd taken to save her had caused Winkie to tumble off his shoulder, roll down his arm, and land squarely on Elspeth's head.

"Sorry," said Winkie, though he did not loosen his grip on Elspeth until Jack had hoisted her up and placed the shaken girl on more solid ground.

"Thought we'd lost you there," said Jack. "Again."

"I hate this place." Elspeth panted, breathless from both the near-death experience and the running that had preceded it. Then, remembering that her life had just been saved, she added, "Thank you, Jack."

"No problem. You know, you can call me Dad, if you want," Jack said hopefully. His face exposed the disappointment he felt when Elspeth replied only with "I know."

The sinkhole, in addition to having nearly been the end of young Elspeth Pule, also allowed Krool's men to close the gap even farther. The healthy head start that Elspeth and her friends once enjoyed had withered and wasted away to a mere five-minute lead, while the forest was still a good hour away.

"I'm afraid it's over," said Georgie.

They stood and watched the horsemen moving nearer and nearer, and while Georgie and the others hung their heads in defeat, Elspeth did what she did best. She got mad. "No!" she growled with fists in the air. "It's not going to end this way! We're not going to take this! Do you hear me? We are not going to take it!"

The longer she yelled, the louder she got. Strangely, however, the louder she got, the more difficult she was to hear. A competing noise was rising up across the desert. From this distance it could have been a large, twinkling star hanging just above the horizon. But of course it wasn't.

"Torcano," said Jill as it grew closer, larger, and hotter.

"It's a big one," said Jack, now yelling because, in addition to the whirring of rocks and lava, there was the sound of a hundred panic-stricken horses, rearing up, snorting, whinnying, and throwing riders to the ground.

"We should run," said Georgie.

"No," said Jill. "We don't know what path it will take. We're better off to stay where we are and hope it spares us. Trust me. Jack and I have been through a few of these in our time."

"Easy for you to say," said Gene. "You're not made of wood."

"Maybe it'll hit Krool's men," said Barry White.

"If there's any justice in this world," Jack added while taking his wife's hand and squeezing tightly. He felt someone gripping his other hand and looked down to see that it was Elspeth, her eyes lost in the fiery funnel racing toward them.

Those few who have seen and survived it will tell you there's nothing quite so beautiful and mesmerizing as a torcano at night. Like a towering bonfire of gas and stone spinning across a darkened sky, it would seem certain that this is what the birth of the universe or the beginning of our galaxy must have looked like.

For the record, Jack had been right. This was a big one, the narrow end of its funnel nearly as wide as the gap separating Elspeth and her friends from Krool's men and their terrorized horses. But neither the horses nor the soldiers had need to worry because the torcano had chosen its path. When it became all too apparent which direction it would favor, Jack yelled, "Run!"

But running was of no consequence to a monster of this size and speed. Those of Krool's men who had not been thrown to the ground sat atop their horses and watched as the torcano quickly chased down the escaped prisoners and mercifully (if nature can show mercy) swept across them in an instant.

The soldiers took no joy in what they had seen as the torcano continued on its path. Once the terrible noise had faded and the horses were again relatively calm, the large man with the Van Dyke beard led his horse to the site where Elspeth and the others had last been seen.

He climbed down from his mount, and when the dust had settled sufficiently he spotted on the ground a single slipper, its once-pink silk now charred black and still smoldering.

As a rooster crowed somewhere far off in the distance, the man knelt and plucked the shoe from the ground. "That's it then," he said in a quiet voice. "That's the end of her."

Cock-a-doodle-doo!
My dame has lost her shoe.
Or if you prefer, her shoe lost her
When away she flew.

Chapter 20

"Are you certain?" Krool demanded while clutching the blackened slipper. He brought it to his nose and breathed in the sour, smoky smell.

"That's all that's left of her," said the man with the Van Dyke, the other three of Krool's most trusted guards by his side. "That's all that's left of any of them."

Krool walked across his sleeping chambers and peered out through the East Tower window. When he turned away from the window, the look on his face made the guards fear that they had failed him somehow. They would have expected a smile or some look of satisfaction. "I would have preferred her head," he said, looking at the slipper resting upon his open palm. "But I suppose this will have to do as souvenirs go."

He returned his gaze to the sunrise and said nothing for such a long time that the guards quietly slinked out of the room without further words among them.

Elspeth was the first to regain consciousness. Lying on her back, it took her several minutes to realize exactly what she was looking at. It was pure blackness, punctuated by a thin stripe of orange and pink running down the middle. The stripe, she eventually determined, was the sky, while the darkness was provided by the steep walls of the crevasse in which she lay.

She felt a dull ache, not in any specific place but all over. Slowly, she sat up and the sound of her movement and the pained groans she emitted began to stir the others lying nearby.

Jack and Jill, Georgie, Gene, Winkie, and the mice—they were all there, and each remarkably intact for having suffered such a fall. There were bumps, bruises, and partly singed clothing, not to mention a missing slipper, but no broken bones or fractured skulls. Looking up, Jack estimated the drop at no less than a hundred feet. "The upward pull of the torcano must have slowed us down," he said. "We're very lucky to be alive."

"Yes, but for how long?" said Winkie, giving voice to what they all were thinking. Even for the most accomplished of mountaineers, outfitted with the best equipment money could buy, climbing out would be impossible. "Better that we had died from the fall than from starvation."

"Starvation?" said Barry White, worried that his plumpness might qualify him as a food source should it come down to that.

"There must be a way out," said Elspeth, looking this way and that along the dark, stone alleyway.

"Perhaps tunneling downward, we might come out on the other side of the earth," said James Brown.

"That's absurd," said Georgie. "We're doomed."

The situation did seem quite hopeless and did not become any less so until Elspeth noticed a strange noise at her feet. Squinting into the darkness, she soon realized the scratching sound was the result of Gene, lying on the ground, wiggling uncontrollably.

"Gene?" she asked, kneeling next to him. "What is it?"

"Water," said Gene. "Somewhere nearby. Please, take me away from it."

But Elspeth did just the opposite. Quickly, she picked up the quivering stick and pointed him first in one direction and then the next. "This way," she said.

Jack and Jill looked at each other and shrugged. Then Jack placed Winkie and the mice aboard his shoulders, and they all followed Elspeth through the narrow passageway, groping the walls for guidance in the dim light of early dawn.

"I fail to see how this is helpful in any way," said Georgie. "We can't survive on water alone."

"If there is water," said Elspeth, "it had to get down here somehow."

With each step, Gene grew more and more animated until finally there came the unmistakable sound of someone stepping in a puddle. That someone was Elspeth, and the puddle actually proved to be a small stream, running across their path from another crevasse that intersected their own at a right angle.

"Yes," said Elspeth. "Good job, Gene."

"What can I say?" Gene replied. "I do what I do."

"But which way now?" asked Jack, turning in a full circle to consider all four directions.

"Water runs downhill," said Elspeth. "This way."

She took a sharp right, leading them upstream. As they walked, the small trickling of water slowly became faster, deeper, and wider. In ten minutes' time the underground creek covered Elspeth's ankles, and in ten more it reached nearly to her knees. She bunched up the soaking-wet gown and trudged onward, badly missing her old tennis shoes and her favorite pair of jeans. The rushing water directed them to another right turn and then a left. By now it was waist deep, and moving through it was slow and difficult work, especially for Jack with his injured foot and the combined weight of four hitchhikers upon his shoulders.

"Come on, Jack," his wife urged. "Keep moving."

"I'm doing my best," the man grunted.

But as the water became swifter and deeper it also became brighter. In fact, it began to sparkle like a starlit sky. Elspeth stopped and looked up to see a brilliant amber sun reflecting off a bubbling waterfall, which cascaded into the crevasse from the surface just twenty feet above.

"We made it! You did it, Elspeth," said Winkie. The praise caused Gene to clear his throat. "Yes, you too, Gene. You both did it."

Though climbing up a twenty-foot waterfall may have been easier than trying to scale the walls of a crevasse five times that height, it was still no simple task. The rocks were smooth and slimy in places, and a firmly planted foot could easily slide off or be forced away by the rushing water.

Elspeth had a particularly tough go of it, being that her left hand was full of bunched-up execution gown while her right hand was full of Gene. One foot was bare and the other was covered by a nearly useless silk slipper. Still, determination and anger spurred her on once more until finally her eyes were hit with a flood of sunshine, spreading out above the tops of the trees that stood less than a hundred feet away.

"The forest!" she cried.

Before she could climb any farther, Winkie called out, "Hold on! Krool's army. They could be waiting for us."

In her excitement to be out of that crevasse, Elspeth had not considered this. She turned slowly like a groundhog looking for its shadow and was happy to report that she could see no sign of Krool's army or of any other living thing—unless you count rocks, sticks, and bushes, of course. "They're gone," she announced.

"Maybe the torcano reversed course and got them," said Winkie.

Elspeth pulled herself out of the hole, and one by one the others joined her, each of them overjoyed to once again be on the surface of the earth. For some time they all just stood in the bright sunshine, allowing their wet clothes and cold bodies to draw in its warmth, while at the same time considering the horror that some of the king's horses and some of the king's men might have endured.

"Well," said Jack. "If the torcano did get them, that's one hundred fewer we'll have to fight."

"Come on," said Jill. "The suburbs are this way." They followed her into the shadows of the trees, and just before entering the forest Elspeth took one look back for friend or foe and came away both disappointed and relieved.

As Elspeth trudged on, it became increasingly difficult to stay focused and awake. She pined for her lavender room back home and her soft, spongy bed with its smooth sheets and pillow that sometimes smelled of West Coast rain. She even missed the mildewed, water-stained carpet.

The longer they walked, the more familiar the path became, until finally Elspeth recognized a particular willow just ahead.

"Hello, Manuel," said Jill to the guardian tree.

"Señora!" he exclaimed. "I was afraid I would never see you again."

In Elspeth's world, people sometimes used the term "tree hugger" to describe one who advocates for the environment. This was the first time she had ever seen a tree doing the hugging. Manuel wrapped his wispy branches around Jill and gave her a hearty squeeze. "Little Robin Redbreast said you'd been sentenced to life in prison."

"We were," said Jill. "And we'd still be there if King William hadn't arranged for our rescue."

"King William the Umpteenth?" Manuel replied.

As Jack stepped forward, Manuel immediately noticed the small man perched upon his shoulder. "His Majesty returns," he said with a gasp. "Long live the king."

"Thank you," said Winkie, pleased to have been addressed by that title for the first time in many years. "But I won't officially be king again until this young lady rids us of that evil Krool."

"Wait a minute," said Manuel. "Are you saying she's . . . ?"

"Our daughter," Jack said proudly.

"Your daughter?" said Manuel. "But I thought that Krool . . ."

"He did," said Jill. "But she survived. And here she is."

"This is little Jacqueline?" said Manuel.

"My name is Elspeth, not Jacqueline," said Elspeth. "And I've only agreed to any of this because apparently it's the only way for me to get home. Speaking of which, before we get started I'm going to need some sleep."

Winkie nodded to Manuel. The tree pulled back his branches, and there was the encampment just as Elspeth had last seen it only two days prior. Loitering about was the same group as before with one noticeable addition. Winkie was the first to lay eyes upon the newcomer.

"Who, pray tell, is that?" he asked, wide eyed and loose jawed.

When Elspeth caught sight of Dolly Dew Eyes, sitting on a tree stump and playing chess with Bo-Peep, she was initially angry. That anger was soon mixed with admiration as she watched the doll now known as Farrah step onto the board and lug her queen knight to c6, which immediately prompted Bo-Peep to capture it with her king rook.

"Yes," Elspeth muttered. "Now queen bishop a3." And when Farrah did just that, Elspeth said, "Boden's mate. Absolutely brilliant."

"Yes," Winkie agreed. "She's a vision of loveliness."

"What?" said Elspeth. "Who? Her? She's a doll."

"You can say that again," said Winkie.

"No, she actually is a doll," said Elspeth.

"It's just an expression," said Winkie. "You didn't really have to say it again."

"You don't understand," said Elspeth. "She used to be my best friend."

"You know her?" said Winkie, barely able to maintain his composure. "Perhaps you would do me the honor of an introduction."

"Sure." Elspeth sighed. "But just to warn you, she's a real heartbreaker."

"I'll bet," said Winkie, his eyes blinking for the first time since landing on Farrah, the only woman he had ever encountered who was anywhere close to his own height. In addition, her near complete lack of hair made him feel far less self-conscious about his own baldness.

So engaged in pleasant conversation were Farrah and Bo-Peep that neither noticed they had been approached until Elspeth cleared her throat.

"Oh. Hello," said Farrah, sounding both guilty and defensive.

"I see you've found a new chess partner," said Elspeth, not even trying to hide her annoyance.

"Not a very good one, I'm afraid," chuckled Bo-Peep. "She's beaten me nine times straight."

"What can I say?" said Farrah. "After all, I learned from the best."

"Yeah, save it for someone who cares," said Elspeth. "Anyway, I just came over to introduce you to Winkie. I mean, William."

From the ground below, Winkie offered a shy smile and a half wave. "King William!" Bo-Peep gasped and jumped to her feet. "Forgive me. I didn't see you there."

"Not to worry," said Winkie. "I'm used to it. Besides, I know you weren't expecting me."

"Did you say *King* William?" asked Farrah.

"Yes," said Winkie. "William the Umpteenth."

"I've heard wonderful things about you," the doll replied with a smile so sweet that it activated Elspeth's gag reflex. "A real man of the people, I'm told. I'm Farrah."

"It is indeed a pleasure to meet you," said Winkie.

"Oh, but the pleasure is all mine," cooed Farrah.

Elspeth's tolerance for this type of talk was quite low to begin with. Being that it involved her former best friend fawning over someone who was not her made it downright unbearable. "I'll leave you two to get acquainted," she snipped.

But Winkie would have to wait to further acquaint himself with Farrah because word of his return had spread throughout the encampment. The tiny former king was soon surrounded by his loyal subjects, many of whom had supposed he must be dead.

And while William the Umpteenth basked in adulation, he was not the only one to be lavished with attention. Looking out across the compound, Elspeth spied Jack and Jill, who were busy receiving warm greetings from many people and one nonperson, namely a very self-involved wheel of cheese.

"Don't ever do that again. You had the Cheese worried sick," said the Cheese.

It was obvious that Jack and Jill were among the more well-liked residents of the suburbs, or "Loserville," as Elspeth decided it should be called. She wondered what it must be like to be so popular, to have so many people light up just at the sight of you.

"What have we here?" boomed a voice she immediately recognized. She turned to see Dumpty, smiling as broadly as the hardened scars on his face would allow. "I had a feeling you'd be back. And I see you've managed to bring your parents with you."

"What?" said Elspeth. "You mean you've known about that all along?"

"Not all along," said Dumpty. "But once I went back and checked the Book, it was quite obvious. You should take a look at page thirty-five when you get a chance. Lack of chubbiness aside, it's quite a remarkable likeness."

"Yes, I've seen it," said Elspeth. "At the trial."

"Trial?"

"I was accused of treason . . . or for thinking about treason, I don't know. Anyway, Krool was planning to execute me in three days when luckily the mice showed up to rescue us."

"Must have been terribly traumatic for you," said Dumpty. "The important thing is that you all got out in one piece."

"Actually," said Elspeth, scanning the treetops one last time, "not all of us, I'm afraid."

The news of Fergus's death turned out to be much harder on Dumpty than Elspeth had imagined it would. While Dumpty may have found the owl annoying and at times unbearably so, the two, as it turns out, were very old friends. They'd grown up together, and Dumpty had even served as best man at Fergus and Vera's wedding.

"I'm sorry," said Elspeth. She placed a hand on Dumpty's arm. "If it weren't for me . . . if I had listened to you about going to the castle . . ."

"No," said Dumpty, turning away momentarily. "You did what you had to do." There came a couple of long, wet sniffs before he was finally able to continue. "It's not your fault. War is a nasty business. These things are just some of the many unsavory aspects." When he turned back to Elspeth, his eyes were noticeably red and he appeared anxious to change the subject. "So then. We lost one of ours, but I see you've recruited one of theirs."

Georgie sat on the ground, alone as one can be amid a large group. Each of the residents seemed to be making a considerable effort to ignore him.

"According to Winkie, Georgie's the one who sold him out," said Elspeth. "He's the one who opened the castle gate to let Krool in."

"That is the rumor," said Dumpty.

"He denies it, of course," said Elspeth. "And he promised to help us. To tell us everything he knows about Krool."

"That would certainly be most useful," said Dumpty. "Still, I think it best to keep a very close eye on him."

Jeepers creepers, people eaters,
Awful beasts and evil creatures.
Hide us in a pumpkin shell,
So they can't find us very well.

Chapter 21

When Dumpty assembled the crowd to announce that the young girl they'd met previously was indeed the famous Jacqueline Jillson, the reactions ranged from disbelief to absolute euphoria. Could it really be her? No, too chubby. And obnoxious. But Jack and Jill would certainly know their own daughter, wouldn't they? And wise King William seemed to think she was the real deal. Then it must be her. Oh glorious day! Unless it wasn't her. Then what?

Whether ecstatic or skeptical, the response was nearly universal to the news that Elspeth's presence would make it necessary to pull up camp and move deeper into the woods, where Krool's soldiers would likely never set foot, being that strange and horrifying beasts were rumored to live there.

"But what about the Nine-Horned Skewerodontus?" asked Jack Sprat.

"Or the Great Spiny Gleekin?" begged his portly wife.

"Or the rabbits?" whined Simple Simon.

"There's no such thing," said Dumpty. "All those things are legends, nothing more. Except for the rabbits."

"Not true," shouted Goosey Goosey Gander, a very high-strung goose with patches of missing feathers and a nervous twitch. "Just last week my nephew spoke to a very good friend who was nearly devoured by a Devourasaur."

"Fine," said Dumpty, throwing up his hands. "If you want to believe in fairy tales, that's your business. But there is another threat that is very real, and that's Krool's army. You can bet he'll be sending more soldiers after Elspeth, and if we stay here we'll be nothing but sitting ducks."

"I'm a goose."

"It's just an expression," said Dumpty. "The point is, if we don't get out of here soon, our goose will be cooked."

"That's offensive," said the goose.

"Dumpty's right, for a change," shouted the Crooked Man. "Instead of being afraid of a bunch of made-up nonsense, we should be worried about a real monster dwelling right within our midst." He straightened his crooked arm as well as he could and shot a crooked finger at Georgie. "This man. He's sold us out once before, and it's only a matter of time before he does it again."

Soon a grumbling, mumbling crowd began to close in around Georgie. When verbal threats escalated to shoves, Elspeth shouted, "Stop! Leave him alone. Anyone who lays a finger on him will have to answer to me. Is that clear?"

The crowd murmured in reluctant agreement, and Georgie was relieved when finally they wandered away to begin folding their tents and packing up their meager possessions in preparation for the move.

Jack and Jill stepped up beside Elspeth, one on either side, and Jack placed a hand upon her shoulder. "They listen to you," he said. "They respect you. That's important."

"I hope you realize what a great thing it is you're doing for everyone," said Jill.

"I'm not doing this for them," said Elspeth. "I'm doing it for me."

"Still," said Jill, "you've given hope to us all."

Elspeth looked at the gloomy group around her. "They don't look very hopeful," she said.

"Yes," Jack was forced to agree. "They're not the peppiest bunch, I must admit."

"That's where you come in," said Jill. "If anyone can fire them up, it's you."

"I don't know," Elspeth said doubtfully. "It'll be a bit like firing up a wet match. Maybe a change of scenery will help."

There was no question that the suburbs had been an awful place to live, but it had also been a place to call home, and with that always comes certain attachments. Some of the residents had lived there long enough to put down roots, quite literally speaking. In fact, no one was more upset by the decision to move than Manuel.

"If I could come with you, I would," he said now that it was official and Dumpty had ordered the group to form a single file for the long march ahead. "You will come visit me once in a while, *si*?"

"Of course we will," Winkie promised. "And if you and your fellow trees and shrubs could relay any useful information our way, it would be greatly appreciated."

"You can count on us, Your Highness," said Manuel. "If Krool sends his army into the forest, I'll make sure you get plenty of warning."

Then, as they trudged by, Manuel hugged each member of the group—with only two exceptions. The first was Georgie, to whom he gave the cold shoulder (or in this case, the cold limb). The second was Elspeth. Savior of the people or not, he still considered her an outsider and remained cautious of her. When she passed by he offered a branch, and she shook it firmly. "Good luck, señorita," Manuel said. "I hope you know what you're doing."

"You can hope all you want," said Elspeth. "But the truth is, I have no idea what I'm doing."

The search for a suitable place to set up camp was one long, somber parade with talking kept to a minimum so frightened ears could remain alert for a sudden attack by a poisonous Tiger Snake or the giant Germese Stranglerat.

"I think we've gone far enough," said Carol Sprat. She spoke from both fear and exhaustion, though the perspiration that streamed down her face was mostly from the latter.

"Just a little farther," said Dumpty. Dealing with such a disgruntled group was a stressful business, and his vertigo was getting the better of him. He stopped and leaned against a tree for support. "It's important to make sure we have at least a half day's head start on them once they enter the forest."

With a few deep breaths Dumpty's equilibrium soon returned, and they continued on, the group growing increasingly fearful and paranoid with each turn along the path. Elspeth wondered just how she was going to fire up these wet matches.

"What was that?" shrieked Jack Horner, spinning quickly around. "I saw something out of the corner of my eye. It was black and moving along the ground."

"That was your shadow," said Elspeth. "See?"

"Oh," said Jack Horner, giving his shadow a wave. "That's a relief, isn't it? Next time we might not be so lucky."

"Ahh! What was that?" shouted Little Miss Muffet only moments later. She spun in circles while desperately slapping at the nape of her neck. "I felt something touch my back."

"That was your wig," said Elspeth.

"It's not a wig," sobbed Miss Muffet, highly insulted. "It's a weave."

"I don't care if it's wicker basket," said the Cheese. "Can we just keep rolling? It's hot out here. If we don't get there soon the Cheese is gonna turn into a giant puddle of fondue." Instantly, the Cheese had second thoughts as to the wisdom of his chosen words.

"Hey, Carol Sprat, don't you be looking at the Cheese that way. And I don't want you three anywhere near me," said the Cheese to Earl Gray, James Brown, and Barry White, who had been following as closely behind him as possible just to bask in his wonderful aroma.

"And you, Jack Horner. If you don't get your tongue back in your mouth I'm liable to give you a knuckle sandwich."

Jack Horner just stood and stared, salivating at the notion of a knuckle sandwich with cheese.

Still, the journey continued without imaginary monsters eating any of the travelers and without any of the travelers eating the Cheese. The spot that Dumpty eventually settled upon looked similar to the old camp, if not a bit more overgrown and noticeably darker with the closely knit trees allowing less sunlight to reach the forest floor.

"Okay, this looks good," Dumpty said to the grousing crowd as they stumbled into the site of what they hoped would be a very temporary home.

"New Loserville," Elspeth dubbed the place with a whisper to herself. "If that was the suburbs, this is definitely the slums."

"Yes, it's not much," agreed Winkie. "Let's just say I'll be happy once we're back in the castle where we all belong."

"You mean where you all belong," Elspeth reminded him.

"Yes. Pardon me," said Winkie.

Looking about the camp, Elspeth noticed something she considered strange. When the journey had first begun, Winkie was riding on Jack's right shoulder and Farrah on his left. Now the two sat side by side on Jack's left. And were they holding hands? Yes, they were holding hands. Disgusting, thought Elspeth.

When the complaining had tapered off to a manageable level, Dumpty directed attention to himself and advised everyone to set up their tents right away and settle in for a good night's rest. Their new commander in chief was anxious to begin training first thing the following morning.

There was none among them in greater need of sleep than Elspeth herself, and as darkness fell upon the forest, she was happy to be shown to a large tent reserved for her alone. Though it would not qualify as a mattress by anyone's standards, there was a folded-up blanket on which to lie and a small cloth sack of dried beans that would serve as a pillow.

When Elspeth first placed her head upon it, the resulting crunch made her think she would never get to sleep with such noise. In nearly twelve years of living, she had never been more wrong, for the crunching only happened when she moved, and for the next nine hours she didn't. Not even the slightest bit. No flailing, no horrible nightmares, no grinding of teeth.

It was essentially her first time camping in the savage outdoors, and by sunrise she had inhaled more savagely fresh air than she ever had before. She awoke energetic, invigorated, and intrigued by the parcel resting on the ground next to her.

About the size of a throw pillow, it was wrapped in brown paper and held in place with twine tied in a bow. Gently and ever so slowly, she tugged at the bow, and when the twine fell away, the package unfolded, presenting a uniform. There were pants, a shirt, and a coat made of wool in crimson and gray with brass buttons down the middle of the coat and partway up each sleeve. It was identical in every way to the one worn by the girl on page thirty-five.

Little Boy Blue,
Come blow your horn,
Asleep in the slums
And nigh is the morn.
Where are the ones who will rid us of Krool?
They're snoring and snorting and covered in drool.
Will you wake them?
Oh no, not I,
For knowing them, they'll surely cry.

Chapter 22

With lack of practice, his lip had gone weak, and it took Little Boy Blue several attempts to get something that sounded like reveille to come out of the bell of his horn. After that, he was forced to play it four more times when the initial response to it was less than unanimous.

When the troops had finally assembled, General Pule stood before them in her crisp new uniform, the work of Old Mother Hubbard, she'd been told. With her team of advisors (Winkie, Dumpty, and Georgie) at her side, she surveyed the ranks, for the first time getting a good look at what she had, or did not have, to work with.

Even without the Cheese, who maintained his isolationist policy, insisting on continuing to stand alone, they were nearly two hundred strong—though "strong" may not have been the appropriate word, considering that that number included a highly neurotic goose, an incoherently mumbling dish, a spoon who spoke only Portuguese, an old woman who, until recently, had lived in a shoe, a painfully crooked old man, three visually impaired mice, and a plum-pie-loving boy with two broken thumbs.

Elspeth stepped away from her troops in order that she might confer with her advisors. "I don't know," she said with an exasperated sigh. Firmly clasped in her right hand was Gene, whose heroic actions at the castle and in the crevasse had earned him the position of Elspeth's right-hand man. "They don't look like much of an army. Maybe that'll change once we start issuing weapons."

"Weapons?" said Dumpty.

Elspeth spun around so quickly she nearly threw her neck out of joint. "What? You do have weapons," she said.

Dumpty and Winkie looked equally embarrassed at failing to have given consideration to what most would list as an essential ingredient in a political uprising. "Uh, not as such," said Dumpty.

"That's it!" Elspeth exploded. "You expect me to defeat a well-trained army with an unarmed bunch of misfits, losers, and scaredy-cats?" Elspeth realized her voice had risen to the point that it was audible to all. She turned to face her troops. "No offense."

Not surprisingly, her recruits all looked far too complacent to be insulted.

"Okay, this is war, and we're going to need weapons, plain and simple," she said, while repeatedly pounding her fist into the palm of her hand. "I need every bit of metal we've got gathered up right away."

"I'll get the word out," said Dumpty.

"Of course all the metal in the world does us absolutely no good unless we have a blacksmith."

"We do," Dumpty said excitedly. "Simple Simon is a blacksmith."

Elspeth's eyes narrowed. "Would that be the same Simple Simon who's afraid of rabbits?"

"That . . . sounds like him," said Dumpty. "But he's a very good smith."

"Even so," said Elspeth, "we're still going to need some kind of edge."

"An edge?" Georgie echoed.

"I've played in quite a few chess tournaments in my life," Elspeth explained. "I've lost to people I should have beaten, and I've beaten people who were ranked much higher than me. Each time I won one of those matches, I did so by finding some tiny little weakness and taking advantage of it. I read their biographies and articles written about them, looking for anything about their personalities that might help me predict their actions. And that's what we need here."

"Yes," said Winkie. "But what would give us that edge?"

"Not sure," said Elspeth. "If only we had some way of getting into the castle. Didn't you say that's how Krool was able to take you by surprise?"

"Yes," Winkie confirmed, "thanks to your friend Georgie here."

"I told you once and I'll say it again: I had nothing to do with that," said Georgie. "And I resent the implication."

"It's not an implication; it's a statement of fact," said Winkie.

"Enough!" shouted Elspeth. "We've got plenty of problems as it is without having to fight each other."

The verbal spat quickly turned into a glaring contest with each man refusing to turn away from the other.

"Now listen, Georgie," Elspeth said. "As his former personal assistant, no one knows Krool better than you. I want you to make a list of everything you know about him. His likes, his dislikes, his daily habits. Everything."

Georgie brought his hand to his forehead in a sharp salute. "You can count on me, ma'am. I'll get on it right away."

Georgie sneered at Winkie one more time then marched off to carry out the order. Dumpty looked back at the troops milling around and sprawled about on the ground. "So you really think that's it then? You think finding a weakness is the key to victory?"

Elspeth surveyed her sorry excuse for an army and said, "I think to win this fight we're going to need more keys than a janitor."

While Simple Simon went to work on turning forks, spoons, and other bits of metal into instruments of warfare, Elspeth tried to her best to whip the troops into top physical shape. But they seemed far more interested in grumbling about living conditions and strange noises coming from beyond the trees.

"Quiet, please!" Elspeth shouted. "For the last time, there's nothing behind those bushes but more bushes."

"How do you know that?" asked Goosey Goosey Gander. "Have you looked behind all of them?"

"No, I haven't," said Elspeth. "I'm a little busy trying to prepare for battle right now, in case you haven't noticed."

"Permission to speak freely," said Gene.

"When do you ever not speak freely?" said Winkie.

"I wasn't speaking to you," said Gene. "I was just thinking that maybe if we did some team-building exercises it might result in less complaints."

"That's *fewer* complaints," said a familiar voice.

Elspeth turned quickly to her advisors. "What did you say?"

"I didn't say anything," said Winkie.

Just before Dumpty could make the same denial, something across the way caught Elspeth's eye.

"Fergus!" Elspeth shouted. Without thinking, she threw Gene to the ground and ran across the compound. She wrapped her arms around the owl, and he immediately pulled away.

"Ow, ow. Easy there," said Fergus. "My wing."

"Sorry," said Elspeth, stepping back to have a look at the injured bird. "How did you . . . it's just that . . . I thought you were . . ."

"Dead?" said Fergus. "I very nearly was." Before he could continue, Dumpty caught up to them.

"Fergus, old boy," he said. "I can't tell you how good it is to see you."

"Oh, give it a try," said the owl.

Dumpty smiled. Same old Fergus. "All right then. It is unbelievably and overwhelmingly good to see you."

"Thank you," said Fergus. "I assure you the feeling is quite mutual."

"So what happened?" asked Elspeth. "Where have you been?"

"I've been lying in a ditch is where I've been," replied Fergus. "When I finally found the strength to pull myself out, I realized that my left wing was nothing but a useless flap, thanks to one very sharp spear."

"Then how did you get here?" asked Dumpty.

"Walked," said Fergus. "Something we owls are not designed to do, I might add. My talons are killing me."

Dumpty laughed again and shook his pointed head. "The important thing is that you're back with us," he said. "I'm going to spread the good news."

Once Dumpty had run off to tell the others, Fergus turned to Elspeth and said, "You know, I thought you were dead too."

"Why would you think that?" asked Elspeth.

"While I was lying in that ditch below the castle wall, I overheard some very interesting things. For example, Krool thinks you and the others were killed by a torcano."

"Really?" said Elspeth. "We almost were. I guess the fact that he thinks so is good news for us. If he really believes we're dead, it certainly gives us more time to prepare. Not to mention the element of surprise."

"Yes," said Fergus. The owl looked uneasy. "I feel obligated to tell you that there's quite a bit more to it than that."

"What do you mean?"

"Apparently," said Fergus, "Krool is so convinced of your death that he has ordered the guards to be taken off the well."

"Wait a minute," said Elspeth. "The well? You mean the way home? The way out of here? That well?"

"Yes," said Fergus. "That well."

For a brief few seconds, Elspeth looked as if she were working out a complicated math problem in her head. "If that's true," she said, "then all of this is completely unnecessary. All this armed rebellion nonsense is just a total waste of time."

"I wouldn't agree that it's a waste of time," Fergus argued. "Not to your soldiers it's not. To them it's everything. Still, the decision to continue on with this or to be on your way is ultimately yours."

"Yes," said Elspeth. "I suppose it is."

"I imagine it won't be an easy one to make," said Fergus.

Elspeth looked at Fergus and his badly disfigured wing. She took time to consider the risk he had taken and the sacrifice he had made so she might live. "Actually," she said, "it'll be incredibly easy."

"You're what?" shouted Winkie as he paced about his royal tent. "You're leaving?"

"Shh," said Elspeth. "There's no need for everyone to know about this."

"No need? Look at these people." Winkie threw open the tent flap, and there they were, some eating peas porridge, others just moping around, and each of them oblivious to the drama unfolding on the other side of a wall made of canvas. "They've placed every ounce of faith they have in you."

"Then they shouldn't have," said Elspeth. "They should try putting faith in themselves for a change. Though I don't know what good that would do either. They're hopeless."

Coming as close to slamming a door as one who lives in a tent can, Winkie threw the flap with a huff. This was followed by a prolonged silence. It was clear there was much he wanted to say, but he seemed to be carefully weighing the implications of doing so.

"I don't know why you're so upset," said Elspeth, no longer able to endure the silence. "I didn't ask for any of this, you know."

"A hero never asks for his lot in life," said Winkie. "It is handed down from sources unknown. And when it is, he accepts his fate and all the burden and glory that comes with it."

"That's big talk for such a little man," said Elspeth, refusing to be bullied.

"Fine," said Winkie. "If you feel it's the right thing to do, if that's a decision you can live with, then I won't try to stop you. But if you're going to leave, you should probably do it as soon as possible."

As Winkie made for the door, Elspeth said, "Wait a minute."

"Yes?" Winkie said hopefully.

"About the uniform . . ."

"You can keep it," said Winkie. "After all, it was made especially for you."

Elspeth twisted a brass button between her finger and thumb. "I never got a chance to thank Old Mother Hubbard," she said. "If you could tell her . . ."

"I would if I could," said Winkie. "But for that I would need a time machine or a necromancer. Old Mother Hubbard died several years ago. Her daughter, Young Mother Hubbard, does all of our sewing and tailoring now."

Again Winkie tried to leave, and again Elspeth stopped him. "Hold on. That makes no sense," she said. "You just told me she made the uniform especially for me."

"If you don't understand it by now, you never will," said Winkie, and this time he walked out, leaving Elspeth alone in the tent.

For a long while she stood in place, rehearsing just what she would say to Jack and Jill, Dumpty, Fergus, and the others. When she finally got up the nerve to face them she found the reactions to her decision mixed, from disappointment to anger to sadness.

"We'll miss you greatly," said Jill, wiping away a tear and then another until there were too many to brush away.

"Are you sure about this?" asked Jack. "It's just that everyone's counting on you."

"And what about the prophecy?" said Georgie. "You can't deny the prophecy."

"Leave the girl alone," said Dumpty, moving his oval body between Elspeth and the others. "She has no obligation to any of us, prophecy or no prophecy. If she wants to return to the Deadlands, that's her prerogative and we should leave it at that."

"Thanks," whispered Elspeth, her eyes lowered. She was anxious to be on the road before the guilt reached unbearable levels. She was therefore disappointed when Jack insisted it would be much safer to wait until after dark to make the trip.

"Crossing Torcano Alley at night is risky, as you know," he said. "But potential for disaster is far greater traveling in the light of day. Krool thinks you're dead. Let's be sure to keep it that way."

"I'm sorry," Elspeth said to all of them while making eye contact with none. And then, no longer able to bear the stares and the whispers of those hovering about, for word had obviously gotten out, Elspeth announced that she would wait for nightfall in the privacy of her tent. In just a matter of hours, the arriving darkness would provide cover from both the eyes of the enemy and the eyes of all those whom she had disappointed.

The privacy she sought was quickly ended when she heard a voice she recognized outside her tent. "Hello?" said Farrah, not sure how to knock on the door of a house made of cloth. "May I come in?"

"What do you want?" said Elspeth.

Not waiting for an invitation, Farrah walked in. "I hear that you're leaving," she said.

"Who told you? Your boyfriend?" said Elspeth.

"Fiancé," said Farrah.

"Well, that was quick," Elspeth said bitterly.

"Yes," Farrah agreed. "William is a very passionate man."

"I suppose congratulations are in order," said Elspeth but then offered none. "Sorry I won't be here for the big day."

"You're not the only one who's sorry. There are a lot of people counting on you."

"I don't see how this is any business of yours," said Elspeth.

"The problem seems to be," said Farrah, "that you don't seem to see how it's any business of yours."

"Why should it be any of my concern?" said Elspeth.

"Because these are your people."

"What? They're not my people. In fact, most of them aren't even people at all. There's a stick, a spoon, a goose, a slab of cheese, and one guy who's half-egg on his mother's side."

"Is that how you determine whether someone is worthy of your help?" asked Farrah. "By their shape? By what they look like?"

"You know what I'm saying," said Elspeth, who was very close to picking up the doll and hurling her out of the tent.

"Yes, I do know what you're saying," said Farrah. "Do *you*?"

"Of course I know what I'm saying," said Elspeth. "You're trying to confuse me, but it's not going to work. Besides, this isn't about them, is it? It's about you wanting Winkie back on the throne so you can be queen."

"Yes," Farrah agreed. "You're right. I do want to be queen. His queen. And whether he ends up as a butcher, a baker, or a candlestick maker, I will be his queen, regardless. Other than that, you're wrong. This has nothing to do with me."

"I don't believe you," said Elspeth. "And if you're through trying to make me feel guilty for wanting to go home, I'd like you to leave."

"Okay," said Farrah. "But first I have a proposal."

"I don't want to hear any proposals you might have," said Elspeth. "I've made up my mind and that's that."

"One game," said Farrah.

"What?"

"One game of chess. You against me. If I win, you stay until Krool is defeated. You win, you go on your not-so-merry little way and never look back."

"Why would I agree to that?" asked Elspeth. "There's nothing in it for me."

"Perhaps not," said Farrah. "But if you don't play me, you'll always wonder whether you could have beaten me."

"Of course I can beat you. Any day."

"Then you have nothing to worry about, do you? So? What do you say? One game."

Elspeth stared at Farrah with fists balled up in fiery resentment. "Fine," she said at last. "One game. But we'd better get started. Because once the sun goes down, I'm out of here."

Sing a song of eight pawns, for king and queen they warred,
Two and thirty black squares upon the checkered board.
When the game was over, the crowd began to sing,
"We'll make a dish that's best served cold to set before the king."

Chapter 23

Past tournaments in which Elspeth had competed usually drew no more than a handful of spectators—mostly parents, teachers, and certain oddly fanatic chess enthusiasts. In addition, the stakes were no higher than personal pride and, on occasion, a trophy, a certificate, or a small cash prize.

Now, as a crowd of two hundred gathered around that mossy log, most of them secretly rooting against her (and some not so secretly), she could hear her heart accelerating, could feel her palms growing moist.

It helped to remind herself that she was competing against a doll, though there was certainly something to be said for being the underdog.

As a show of confidence, Elspeth chose black. Farrah would enjoy the nearly insignificant advantage of moving first.

As the match began, each player opened conservatively and predictably with an eye on controlling the center. At first, the opponents mirrored each other's moves, as can happen when student and teacher compete head to head.

As play entered the middle game, there would be a few minor exchanges, with each giving up a knight for a bishop and bishop for a knight. But as the sun inched toward the horizon and the spectators crept closer to the players, Elspeth began to develop a slight positional advantage.

Farrah had learned much from her mentor, but she was outmatched, though it wouldn't become apparent until the endgame when she made a move and immediately realized her blunder. She sighed and ran her hands across her bristly sprockets of hair. Because of her mistake, all Elspeth would have to do would be to move king rook b2 and Farrah would be forced to sacrifice her queen to remain out of check. After that, it would be just two more moves before Farrah would find herself in checkmate.

Farrah could only stand and watch as Elspeth placed her fingers upon the rook. For the first time in the match, Elspeth looked up from the board at her opponent, something she only ever did when she knew the game was in hand, for to do so at any other time, she believed, showed doubt and weakness.

Farrah nodded as if to say, "Go ahead. Get it over with."

Elspeth gazed out upon the audience members, who were impatiently leaning forward. Most of them had no understanding of the game and thus no idea that Elspeth was about to wrap it up. She picked Fergus out of the crowd, and the bird gave her not a sneer or a scowl, but instead a very surprising wink. When she looked at Jack and Jill, they offered her a reassuring smile. And when she found Dumpty, he gave her an affirmative nod and a thumbs-up. Despite the fact that a victory here would forever doom them all to a life of misery, they were rooting for her. But why? And then it occurred to Elspeth. They wanted victory for her because they knew how badly, how desperately she wanted to go home. Despite the devastating effect it would have on their own lives, they wanted what was best for her.

Elspeth shifted her attention back to the board. She paused for the longest minute since the dawn of time. She gnawed on her lower lip until the taste of blood told her to stop. Then, quite inexplicably, she removed her hand from the rook and instead took hold of her queen bishop and captured white's queen rook. Not only had she failed to take advantage of Farrah's mistake, Elspeth had completely turned the tide of the game—and not in her own favor. Three quick moves later, Farrah moved her spared queen c4, creating a situation in which either player would lose were it her turn. And it was Elspeth's turn. In chess terms it is known as a trebuchet, named for a medieval device used in siege warfare and similar to a catapult.

"Yes," Elspeth whispered. "Of course. That's it." Without hesitation, she made her move.

Farrah countered and, with not a trace of pride or triumph, flatly declared, "Checkmate."

As Dumpty raised Farrah's right hand, hats were tossed into the air and the crowd erupted in wild cheering, singing, and applause.

"That's it then," said Elspeth, offering her hand to her opponent. "Well played."

"Well played indeed," said Farrah. "You did that on purpose."

"I don't know what you're talking about," said Elspeth.

"You're far too good a player to have made a mistake like that. You threw the game."

Elspeth made no further attempt to deny the accusation. She just looked at Farrah and smiled. "I'm sorry I didn't congratulate you," she said.

"I deserve no congratulations for that," said Farrah.

"I was referring to the wedding. I want you to know that I'm very happy for you both."

"Oh. Thank you," said Farrah. This seemed to have caught her off guard, to the point that she stammered for a bit before saying, "Your blessing means a lot to me. You know, I'll be needing a maid of honor."

Elspeth felt her throat tighten. "And you would ask me?"

"I know I've said some pretty horrible things to you," said Farrah.

"It's okay," said Elspeth. "They were all true."

"They may have been at the time. Anyway, I would be honored if you'd stand with me. It won't be anything fancy. No gown, no ring, no cake. Only the things that matter."

"I would be happy to," said Elspeth. Then she squinted and moved closer. Could it be? It certainly seemed that way. "Your hair. It's . . . gotten longer."

Unconvinced, Farrah brought her fingers to the bristly sprockets and felt them for length. "You're right. It's growing. My hair is growing back."

"Now I feel slightly less guilty for chopping it off," said Elspeth just as Winkie showed up and wrapped his fiancé in a victory hug.

"Excellent game," said Winkie, who knew not the first thing about chess. "I'm quite proud of you."

"Don't be," said Farrah, while staring directly at Elspeth. "I had nothing to do with it."

"You're just being modest, my dear," said Winkie. "The important thing is that we still have our commander in chief, which means we still have a chance of defeating Krool."

"A trebuchet," said Elspeth.

"A what?" said Winkie.

"I've always been quite good at throwing things," said Elspeth. "It's one of my greatest talents, and I've always found it to be very effective. A trebuchet is like a catapult. Can we build one?"

Winkie folded his arms and scrunched up his forehead. "May I ask what you plan to do with it?"

"Why, attack the castle, of course," said Elspeth.

"You mean my castle? You . . . want to throw rocks at my castle?"

"Unless you'd rather wait until it falls apart on its own."

"All right then," said Winkie. "A trebuchet you shall have. But building it is one thing. We'd still have to figure out a way to get it across Torcano Alley and up the cliffs."

"Yes, but let's worry about that when the time comes," said Elspeth, whose list of things to worry about was getting longer by the day.

Eeny, meeny, miny, moe,
Catch an ogre by the toe,
When he hollers, make him pay
For his awful, wicked ways.

Chapter 24

The next morning, Elspeth woke at dawn to the sound of whippoorwills calling an end to a long night. Again she'd slept well, and the resulting energy surged through her core. She donned the crimson-and-gray uniform and buckled up the shoes that somehow fit perfectly despite the fact that they, like the uniform, had been made years before. As a military leader, she felt it her duty to get herself into the same kind of shape she would expect of her troops. The girl on page thirty-five of the Book was lean and muscular, and Elspeth was determined to mold herself to that ideal.

Stepping out of her tent, she saw no sign of life. She was the first one up, it appeared. "Stretching," she thought. "Yes, I must do some stretching first."

She bent forward with the aim of touching her toes and settled on reaching halfway down her shins. "Okay," she thought. "Enough stretching."

She set off down the main path, beginning with a brisk walk and soon breaking into a jog. A familiar, sharp ache soon attacked her midsection, but this time she refused to let it stop her. She pushed on until the pain in her legs took her mind completely off her gut. Only when a large blister began to form on the ball of her right foot while on the way back to the camp did she finally give in. She pulled up, leaning forward, her hands upon her knees, her face red and pounding.

As her heavy panting slowly eased back into normal breathing, she heard a strange whirring and slapping noise coming from up ahead. Could it be the mating call of the Great Spiny Gleekin or some type of warning issued by the Germese Stranglerat?

Slowly, Elspeth inched forward toward the source, breathing slowly through her mouth. A twig crackled beneath her feet. She stopped abruptly, but the sound up ahead continued. She crept closer toward a small tree. She reached out and took hold of a branch. With one last deep breath, she pulled it aside and saw, standing in a clearing, Bo-Peep. Though to say she was standing would not be entirely accurate. She was standing, twirling, and lunging, all while thrusting, spinning, and swinging her shepherd's pole. Her actions looked to be part ballet, part warfare.

The beauty, grace, and violence of the movements kept Elspeth entranced for a solid ten minutes until finally Bo-Peep finished the routine and paused to rest.

"Wow," said Elspeth.

Bo-Peep quickly resumed an aggressive stance and pointed the staff in Elspeth's direction. "Oh," she said and lowered the weapon. "Sorry. You startled me."

"What is that?" asked Elspeth. "What you were doing?"

"It's Shaolin stick fighting," Bo-Peep said shyly. She gave a quick, casual twirl of the staff. "I took it up after my sheep were stolen. It's very good for mind, body, and spirit."

"Do you think you could teach the others?"

"Teach them?"

"Stick fighting," said Elspeth. "I think it may be just the thing we need."

"I don't know," said Bo-Peep. "If they'd be willing to learn, I'd be willing to try."

In the days to follow, Simple Simon was relieved of his weapon-making duties, and everyone worked together to turn two hundred tree branches into two hundred smooth, polished tools of battle that could both bludgeon the enemy and, at the same time, yell at him. As the talkative sticks were being issued to all those with opposable thumbs, Gene could not help himself. "Well, look at this," he gloated. "Once again, it's sticks to the rescue. Makes you want to treat us with a little more respect, now doesn't it?"

Elspeth made her best effort not to hurl Gene into the woods while handing the troops over to Bo-Peep. "Okay, listen up," barked Elspeth. "Today we begin learning the ancient art of Shaolin stick fighting. During this time you are to give Bo-Peep your undivided attention. Is that understood?"

She was met with a "yes, ma'am," spoken in concert and with a surprising level of enthusiasm for a group that had always been so down in the mouth. Perhaps these wet matches were finally beginning to spark. "They're all yours," Elspeth said to Bo-Peep. "And don't be too nice to them."

"Sure," said Bo-Peep. As she took the troops through the very basics of a highly complicated discipline, Elspeth ordered that the chessboard be delivered to her tent, where she would spend the next several hours playing against herself. By doing so she hoped to formulate a strategy by which her underdog forces might have a chance against an army that Georgie had described as well trained and armed to the teeth.

So intense was Elspeth's concentration on the board that it took Dumpty several tries to get her attention. "Excuse me," he repeated for the third time. "May I come in?"

"Huh? Oh. Yes," said Elspeth. "Sorry."

"No worries," said Dumpty as he pushed his way past the tent flap. In his right hand was a plate and on it a hot cross bun that had long ago gone cold, and a dollop of what looked like mashed potatoes. "I thought you'd like some lunch."

"Oh. Thanks," said Elspeth. "I'm starving." She took the plate in hand and immediately went for the bun, using her molars to break through its staleness.

With a middle-aged groan, Dumpty bent his spindly legs and took a seat on the floor next to Elspeth. "So tell me, how are you holding up?"

"I'm okay," said Elspeth. "A little tired, I guess."

"I must say you're doing a remarkable job of dealing with all the pressure," said Dumpty. "It's a lot to be expected of you, I know."

"I just want to get it over with as quickly as possible."

"Speaking of which, how goes the battle? Or should I say the planning of such?"

"I'm glad you asked," said Elspeth. The fatigue left her instantly, and a look of excitement washed across her face as she slid the chessboard aside and picked up a small stick. "I believe I may have figured it out. I'm thinking of a two-pronged attack, which is why I plan to divide the troops into two separate divisions, A Company and B Company. Naturally, I will take charge of A Company. I've decided to place Bo-Peep in charge of B Company."

"Excellent choice," said Dumpty.

Elspeth drew a crude diagram of the castle in the dirt with the stick. Not Gene. As Elspeth's right-hand man, that would be beneath him. It was another stick, whose name is not important.

"Now I noticed there are archers positioned here." She tapped the stick on the east wall of the castle.

"One good shot at the wall with the trebuchet should knock them out of position just long enough to get A Company from the trees to the castle gate." She drew a few cloud-like shapes meant to be treetops and scraped out a line from there to the castle. "Once inside, we will seal off the barracks and the stables. This should keep most of the king's horses and most of the king's men completely out of the game."

She scratched another line from the trees to the rear wall of the castle. "At the same time, Bo-Peep will lead B Company here, using the scaffolding to climb over the west wall, where they will attempt to isolate the king. In chess we call it a double attack, which might lead to a windmill."

"One question," said Dumpty. "Is a windmill a good thing?"

"Unless it's happening to you, a windmill is a very good thing."

Dumpty smiled at Elspeth. "You're enjoying this."

Elspeth thought about that for a moment and had to agree. "I like a good fight," she said.

"That you do," said Dumpty. "Just one more question."

"Yes?"

"Your plan seems like a marvelous one, don't get me wrong. It's just that . . . pardon me, but how do you plan on getting through the castle gate?"

"Not sure yet," Elspeth was forced to admit. "I'm hoping that report from Georgie will give us some ideas. I'm not sure what's taking him so long. You haven't seen him by any chance, have you?"

Dumpty realized that he had not seen Georgie since the previous evening. This became all the more troubling when Farrah rushed into the tent, gasping for breath. "Elspeth," she said, her face stiff with worry. "I'm sorry to interrupt, but there's word from Manuel."

Immediately Elspeth feared the worst—that Krool's army had entered the forest and would be upon them in half a day's time. Thankfully, her assumption would prove incorrect when Farrah said, "No, it's not Krool. It's something else. Apparently Manuel has taken a traitor into custody. Someone on his way to the castle to give away our position."

"No," said Elspeth, reluctant to believe what must certainly be true. "Not Georgie."

"I'll dispatch a security detail to have him brought back right away," said Dumpty. Then he added, "You tried to do a good thing. Don't blame yourself for this."

"Of course I blame myself," said Elspeth. "I'm the one who hired him. I'm the one who ignored all the warnings. This is my doing. Which is why I would like to go along. I want to look into his eyes when he tries to explain himself."

"Yes, ma'am," said Dumpty. "We'll depart presently."

In addition to Elspeth and Dumpty, the security detail consisted of Maury, Cory, and Rory, three lads

245

of imposing stature, and all with a keen dislike of King Krool, the man responsible for their having to live in a shoe for most of their formative years.

Armed with their newly issued Shaolin fighting sticks, the brothers escorted Elspeth and Dumpty along the trail back to the suburbs. Georgie's betrayal was more than just an embarrassment to Elspeth. It also dealt a strategic blow to her rebel army. "I wondered why he was taking so long with that report," she said. "All this time he was supposed to be writing up information on the enemy, he was really compiling information about us."

"The enemy to him," said Dumpty.

"I suppose," said Elspeth. "The problem is, I was counting on that information to give us an edge."

"I had an idea," said Dumpty. "About how we might get that edge."

"Yes?" said Elspeth. "Go on."

"It occurred to me that the mice have tunneled into the castle once before. What's to stop them from doing it again?"

"I'm sorry," said Elspeth, "but I fail to see how three tiny mice could be of much help."

"Let me ask you this," said Dumpty. "What is the one thing that Krool's army has that ours does not?"

"Real weapons?"

"Okay, what is the other thing they have that we don't?"

Elspeth thought for a moment. "Horses?"

"Exactly. If there's one thing I know about horses, besides the fact that they can deliver a rather mean kick to the face, it is that they are curiously frightened of rodents."

"I can relate to that," said Elspeth. "Rodents give me the creeps. But I like your idea."

It had been a long time since someone expressed appreciation for one of Dumpty's ideas. "Thank you," he said.

Before they could see Manuel, they could hear him, loudly chastising his captive for betraying his friends. Speaking back, the prisoner was defiant, indignant, and, as Elspeth and Dumpty would realize when they rounded the final bend, not Georgie.

Hours of pleading for release and struggling to break free had left the Crooked Man both hoarse and near exhaustion, while his equally crooked cat sat upon one of Manuel's broader branches, fast asleep.

"Ah," said Manuel when he saw Elspeth and her entourage approaching. "I'm glad you are here. Any more lip out of this guy and I might have poked him in the eye with a twig. When I overheard him talking to his cat about giving up your position to the enemy, I snatched him up right away."

"Howard?" said Dumpty when he'd gotten a good look at the Crooked Man. "Why would you do this?"

"For the same reason I did before. Because she's right," he said, pointing at Elspeth. "You're all a bunch of pathetic losers."

247

"Before?" said Elspeth. "You mean you're the one who let Krool into the castle?"

"That's right," said the Crooked Man. "And I'd do it again if I had the chance."

Dumpty's jaw grew tight. He stepped forward and appeared very close to punching the Crooked Man in his crooked face. "The blood of everyone he's killed is on your hands," he said in a quavering voice.

"I only helped facilitate what was an eventual certainty," said the Crooked Man.

"But why help Krool?" asked Elspeth. "He ran you over with his carriage and then banished you to the forest."

"Just a story I concocted," said the Crooked Man. "My affliction is actually the result of being in the wrong place at the wrong time as London Bridge was falling down. Krool pulled me from the rubble and saved my life. It was then that I vowed to help in any way possible to see him on the throne and to do my best to keep him there."

"So you've been spying on us for years," said Dumpty.

"I'm a better spy than you'll ever be," said the Crooked Man with a wicked cackle.

"The day before I was attacked," said Dumpty. Again, he ran his hand across the scars on his face. "I told you of my plan to spy on Krool."

"That was your first mistake."

"So it's true then. You sold me out. They could've killed me."

"They should have," said the Crooked Man. "Would've finally put you out of your misery."

Elspeth was both shocked that the traitor had turned out to be the Crooked Man and relieved to find out it was not Georgie. Still, none of this answered the question of what had become of one of her closest advisors.

The mystery would be solved when Elspeth and the others returned to the new camp to find Georgie waiting impatiently. "Aha," he said upon seeing the Crooked Man, with hands tied, being escorted into the clearing. "I thought there was something about your accusations. A little too enthusiastic perhaps."

"You're a fool, Georgie," clipped the Crooked Man. "And you'll be sorry you sided with these washouts."

"We'll see who's sorry," said Georgie as Maury, Rory, and Cory led their crooked prisoner away to a crooked stockade currently being built especially for him, though when construction began earlier that day, it had been intended for someone else.

"It's okay," said Georgie. "I don't blame you for assuming it was me."

"Well," said Elspeth, "you did sort of disappear on us."

"I've been hard at work," he said while giving the handwritten report over to Elspeth. "And I think I may have found a way into the castle. Look at number four under the Likes column."

Elspeth ran her finger down the page and stopped at number four, immediately intrigued by what she saw.

"Yes, I remember that from the feast at the castle," she said. "His love of fine cheeses. Interesting."

"Isn't it?" said Georgie. "And we just happen to have a very large wheel of it."

"But how does this help us?" asked Elspeth. "As I seem to recall, the Cheese stands alone."

"The Cheese stands on the side of justice," said the Cheese, who had rolled up silently behind Elspeth. "Count me in."

"Okay," said Elspeth, both surprised and happy to see the Cheese. "We'd be very grateful for your help. But are you sure about this? It could be very dangerous."

"Danger is my middle name," said the Cheese. When Elspeth chuckled at this, the Cheese felt it necessary to explain. "No, seriously. Danger really is my middle name. First name Rodney."

"Your name is Rodney Danger Cheese?"

"At your service," said the Cheese.

"So what did Georgie say to change your mind?" asked Elspeth.

"It was nothing he said. It was something you did," said the Cheese. "I heard about how you lost that chess match on purpose. You could have gone home and left this whole lousy mess to someone else. But you stayed. When I heard that . . . man. Let me just say, you make me want to be a better cheese," said the Cheese, unaware for the moment that he was being licked by a tiny tongue.

"Couldn't get much better, if you ask me," said Barry White, the owner of that tiny tongue.

"Hey," said Rodney. He spun around quickly and then lurched forward, threatening to flatten the three mice. "Nobody licks the Cheese unless I say so."

"Sorry," offered Earl Grey. "It won't happen again. Will it, Barry?"

"No, sir," said Barry, hanging his head but still smacking his lips.

"You wanted to see us, General?" said Earl Grey.

"Yes," said Elspeth. "I need you to leave first thing tomorrow morning."

"But it was just one little lick," Barry protested.

"On a mission," Elspeth clarified. "To the castle."

"What kind of mission?" said James Brown.

"One that only you three could pull off."

There was a crooked man, and he walked a crooked mile
On his way to betray Elspeth's army, rank and file.
He and his crooked cat met a willow named Manuel;
Now they both live together in a little crooked cell.

Chapter
25

It was no small victory that the Cheese had agreed to exploit Krool's love of aged cheddar by acting as a decoy, luring the king's men into lowering the drawbridge. But the ploy would only be effective if Elspeth's troops could make the sprint from the cover of the trees to the castle entrance before the bridge could be raised again.

In addition to that, getting the Cheese into place unnoticed meant that the plan would have to be carried out under the darkness of a new moon. The next one would occur in nine days, and Elspeth had made it clear that she was unwilling to wait any longer than that. Getting ready in time would mean doubling up on an already grueling regimen of training and conditioning.

By day three of this super-intense boot camp, Elspeth was far from hopeful. Her ragtag army, it seemed, had maxed out.

"Miss Muffet," said Elspeth during one particularly frustrating episode. "What seems to be the problem?"

"I thought I saw a spider," replied the sobbing woman. "Turns out it was just a crunched-up leaf, but for a second there I thought I was a goner."

"May I remind you that you have two feet?" said Elspeth. "And on those feet are shoes. And in your hands is a large stick."

"That's the problem," blubbered Miss Muffet. "When I'm not looking, a spider could easily crawl right up this stick and attack me."

Elspeth threw up her hands. "Okay, let's take five and regroup, shall we?"

While her fellow soldiers sought to comfort the very distraught Miss Muffet, Elspeth expressed her concern privately to Dumpty and Bo-Peep. "I don't know," she whispered. "I'm beginning to think that maybe this is the best they can do. And it's nowhere near good enough."

"If I may," said Bo-Peep.

"Yes?" said Elspeth.

"The first day of stick fighting, when you handed them over to me, you reminded me not to be too nice to them. Pardon me for saying so, but I think that might be part of the problem here."

"That I'm being too nice?" Elspeth chuckled at the thought. "I don't think anyone has ever accused me of being too nice."

"Exactly my point, ma'am," said Bo-Peep. "After all, there's a reason you're the one who was chosen to lead us." She spoke slowly, treading carefully around the subject. "What I'm trying to say is, you have a certain . . . reputation. One that, it seems, would lend itself to holding a position of authority."

"Forgive me," said Dumpty, "but I think what Bo-Peep means is that you can sometimes be very . . . how shall I put this?"

"Spirited?" offered Elspeth.

"Yes," said Bo-Peep with a huge sense of relief. "That's it exactly. And I think that when you first came here, you had a certain edge that seems to have diminished slightly as you've gotten to know everyone a bit better. Many of us now see you as a friend as opposed to a superior officer."

"A friend? Really?" said Elspeth.

"Yes," said Dumpty. "Unfortunately, at this moment in time what most of these people need is not so much another friend but a good kick in the bum."

Elspeth pulled slowly at her chin. "I see," she said, then immediately ordered the troops to fall in and to stand at attention.

"Okay, listen up," she yelled while walking the ranks so close to her troops that she stepped on more than a few toes along the way. "In just six days we will be attacking the castle. That means I've got six days to turn you whiny, sniveling, pathetic, yellow-bellied sacks of goo into a well-oiled fighting machine. From now on there will be no slacking, no griping, and, above all, no crying."

She spoke the last line directly to Miss Muffet, close enough to her face that Elspeth's breath visibly moved the tresses of her weave.

Jack leaned over and whispered to his wife, "She's really fired up now," which caused them both to chuckle.

"Quiet!" Elspeth shouted. "No talking in rank! Now let me make one thing absolutely clear. I am not your friend, and I am not your babysitter. I am your commanding officer. If I say jump, you say, *How high?* If I say run, you say, *How fast?* And if I say drop and give me fifty push-ups, you say, *How delightful, we thought you'd never ask.* Is that understood?"

"Yes, ma'am!" two hundred voices shouted in unison.

"Good. Now drop and give me fifty push-ups!"

"How delightful, we thought you'd never ask!"

Elspeth looked back at Dumpty and Bo-Peep and gave a smile. Halfway through the push-ups, many of the troops had collapsed to the ground, exhausted. Still, it was a start, thought Elspeth.

Just then Winkie showed up, confused as to why half the army was engaged in something vaguely resembling push-ups while the other half lay on the ground, nearly coughing up blood. "What's going on here?"

"Push-ups," answered Elspeth.

"Oh, so that's how they're doing them now," said Winkie. "Anyway, I thought you would like to know that the trebuchet is finished and ready for testing."

"Great," said Elspeth. "Let's go have a look at it."

Its construction was far more primitive than Elspeth had imagined it would be, but Winkie assured her they'd done the best they could with their very limited resources. He then instructed Cory and Rory to load a large rock into the sling.

"Stand back," Winkie ordered, his hand upon the trigger. "This is a powerful weapon. I just hope there's no one standing a hundred feet straight ahead."

Winkie pulled the firing mechanism and the counterweight dropped, sending the arm shooting forward and the rock flying sixty, eighty, one hundred feet . . . not straight ahead but straight up. Then, as the laws of physics would dictate, it fell straight back down.

"Run!" shouted Winkie, sending spectators scattering in all directions. With a strange, low whistle, the rock plummeted downward and landed with a crunch right on top of the trebuchet. Though it may not have been a highly efficient castle-wrecking machine, Winkie's trebuchet did turn out to be a pretty good trebuchet-wrecking machine.

"It would appear," said Winkie, looking upon the useless pile of lumber, "that we need to make a few adjustments."

Farrah, Farrah, no tiara,
How will your wedding go?
No silver bells, no cockle shells,
No pretty maids all in a row.

Chapter 26

Training from sunup to sundown had left Elspeth exhausted. She wanted nothing more than to bed down for the night, but there was one more thing she had to do: pay a visit to the small, humble tent of Young Mother Hubbard.

"Hello?" she said, the parcel wrapped in brown paper tucked beneath her arm. "Anyone home?"

Young Mother Hubbard turned out to be young in the same way that New York is newer than York. That is to say, she looked much older than her name might have suggested, but her weathered face was kind and inviting.

"I'm sorry to bother you," said Elspeth when she noticed the sewing in the woman's hands. "May I come in?"

"Of course," said Young Mother Hubbard as she held back the flap, allowing Elspeth to duck inside. "It's an honor to finally meet you."

"The honor is mine," said Elspeth. Then, of the sewing, she said, "That's very nice work."

"It's a flag," said Young Mother Hubbard. "My mother started it before she died and entrusted me with finishing it. I should have had it done ages ago, but I never thought we'd have much use for it. Until now." Holding it by the corners, the woman let the banner fall to its full length. It was bright gold with a shield in red, and upon that shield were two eyes, one open and one shut. "It's the Winkie family crest," she explained. "One day soon it will fly above the castle as it did for so many years."

"That depends on how things go next week," said Elspeth.

"It would mean a lot to me if one of your soldiers could carry it into battle," said Young Mother Hubbard. "In honor of my mother."

It occurred to Elspeth that, in addition to being an expert seamstress, Young Mother Hubbard was also a very good daughter. In fact, if Elspeth could somehow make it back home, it was the kind of daughter she now aspired to be.

As far as carrying the flag into battle, one especially worthy of the task came to mind right away, and Elspeth promised that if she and her army were so lucky as to gain entrance to the castle, the flag would come with them.

"I wish I'd had a chance to meet your mother," said Elspeth. "But I'm told she died several years ago."

Young Mother Hubbard began refolding the flag with short, angry movements. "Yes," she said. "My mother was one of Krool's most outspoken critics. She sewed large banners outlining his many crimes and hung them from the castle walls. It was only a matter of time before she became the victim of one of those crimes."

"I'm sorry," said Elspeth. "I'm sure she was a wonderful person. And I know she was a wonderful seamstress. The uniform is perfect."

"She was the best in all the land," said Young Mother Hubbard. "And lucky for me, she taught me everything I know."

"That's obvious," said Elspeth. "Listen, I'm sure that work on the flag is probably keeping you quite busy, but I have a favor to ask of you."

"Anything," said Young Mother Hubbard.

Elspeth placed the parcel on the ground, wrapped in the same paper and tied with the same twine as her uniform had been. "I know the royal wedding is only four days away," she said. "But I was wondering if there might be something you could do with this." She opened the package and there was the Bobby Shafto gown, water stained in some places, muddy in others, and in some, just as perfect as the day it was made.

"It's beautiful," said Young Mother Hubbard, running her slim fingers across the pink silk. "But what is it you would like done with it?"

"I'm told the bride has no wedding gown," said Elspeth.

Young Mother Hubbard smiled. "I could make her a dozen gowns with this."

"She'll only need one," Elspeth replied.

"True. And rest assured, it will be the loveliest you've ever seen."

While Young Mother Hubbard went to work on Farrah's dress, Elspeth went to work on her troops, drilling them mercilessly. She berated them when necessary, punished them when warranted, and drove them to exhaustion. Just three days later the change was noticeable. No longer was there any crying, grumbling, or coughing up blood while trying to do push-ups. They were strong, disciplined, and near masters in the art of Shaolin stick fighting. To watch Bo-Peep take them through their full repertoire of moves, all executed in perfect unison, was both beautiful and intimidating.

If Jack and Jill were understandably proud of their daughter, they were also proud of themselves. "Look at this," said Jack, thrusting his chest forward. "I think I've lost weight."

"I think I found it," said Jill, playfully grabbing his belly in two big handfuls.

Jack responded by tickling her mercilessly as she laughed, squealed, and finally fell to the ground, breathless.

Elspeth smiled, amused to see an old married couple having fun together for a change. She wondered what life might have been like growing up here, with them as her parents. Of course Jack and Jill had often wondered the same thing, but only for brief periods, for to dwell too long on what might have been can often lead to regret and bitterness, and they were not those kind of people.

That evening, as Elspeth prepared for another night of well-deserved sleep, she received a visitor to her tent. "Come in," Elspeth said to the last person she expected to see after the tongue-lashing she'd handed out.

"It's okay, ma'am," said Little Miss Muffet. "I don't need to come in. This won't take long. I only wanted to tell you that I saw a spider this morning."

"Oh," said Elspeth. "I'm sorry to hear that."

"I smashed it," said Little Miss Muffet. "With my foot."

"I see," said Elspeth, still uncertain as to where this was leading.

"I'm not afraid anymore," said Miss Muffet. "I'm angry. We're all angry. Thanks to you, our fear has been replaced with outrage. I just wanted you to know that. I just wanted you to know that we're ready."

"Good," said Elspeth with a smile. She agreed that they were ready for battle. She also knew they were ready for a break.

The timing of Farrah and Winkie's marriage ceremony could not have been better. Nothing boosts morale and puts people in a good mood quite like a wedding, which is why it had been scheduled to take place two days before the attack, with that extra day built in to allow the troops time to recover from the festivities as they traveled to the castle. After all, it's not every day that one attends a royal wedding.

The day had begun overcast but by the late afternoon, when Mayor Dumpty took his place beneath an archway made of evergreen boughs and fern leaves decorated with white and purple flowers, the sun was sprinkling through the treetops like tinsel.

The weather was gorgeous and, just as Young Mother Hubbard had promised it would be, so was the gown.

From Shafto to Hubbard, the gown had gone from beautiful, yet predictable and confining, to soft and flowing, almost to the point of being musical. It featured a detachable train nearly ten feet long that Jill and Bo-Peep, Farrah's official bridesmaids, would carry past the two hundred spectators on the way to the altar.

"You look stunning," said Elspeth as Bo-Peep adjusted Farrah's lacy veil and the crowd waited impatiently for her emergence from the tent.

"Not bad for a two-bit garage sale item," quipped Farrah.

"That was a horrible thing for me to say," said Elspeth. "Please forgive me."

"I'm only kidding," said Farrah. "If not for you, none of this would be happening. I can't thank you enough."

"I'd give you a hug, but I don't want to wrinkle your dress," said Elspeth. Farrah quickly settled the matter by initiating a hug of her own. "You'll make a wonderful queen," said Elspeth.

"Speaking of which," said Bo-Peep, "your king is waiting."

As maid of honor, Elspeth took her place next to Dumpty and across from Winkie. If the groom was nervous, he did his best not to show it. As the music began and Farrah stepped out of the tent, he watched her glide toward him as if upon a cloud. When she passed by, each guest fell to one knee, honoring Farrah as if she were already queen. After all, it would be official in but a few minutes.

"Dearly beloved," began Dumpty. "We are gathered here today to join in holy matrimony, King William the Umpteenth and his lovely bride, Farrah."

Handkerchiefs were at the ready as the bride and groom recited their vows to love, honor, and cherish. Looking on, Elspeth wondered if there ever was a time when her own parents were so fond of one another.

When the bride and groom had finished their vows, Dumpty spoke to the crowd, saying, "Ladies and gentlemen, sticks and stones, dishes and spoons, giant wheels of cheese, I present to you your new queen!"

"Long live the queen!" they shouted in return.

"You may kiss the bride," said Dumpty. It was a directive that Winkie was all too happy to carry out, and Elspeth, Bo-Peep, and the others watched and cheered as he kissed the woman he'd been waiting to meet his entire life. William the Umpteenth had been officially wed to Farrah the First.

"I'm sorry that the honeymoon will have to wait," said Winkie, gazing deep into Farrah's eyes, once soulless and plastic. "But do tell me. When the time comes, where would you like to go?"

"The seaside," Farrah said without hesitation. "I miss the smell of it."

"The seaside you shall have," said Winkie. "If we're able to defeat Krool, I promise you will want for nothing."

"What a ridiculous thing to say," said Farrah. "I already want for nothing."

"I hope our children get your charm," said Winkie. "And your hair."

As the sun faded, the party began. Famine or not, there now seemed to be an abundance of food as people broke into their personal hoards in honor of the occasion.

Those who could play instruments did, and those who could not danced around the bonfire until they were no longer able to stand. Little Boy Blue played his horn, Little Miss Muffet kept the rhythm, beating upon her tuffet like a drum, and Carol Sprat belted out vocals with the power one might expect from a woman her size.

Winkie danced with Farrah, Jill with Jack, the Dish with the Spoon, and Dumpty with Bo-Peep, until the mayor's vertigo got the better of him and he fell over, nearly rolling into the fire. Elspeth sat on the outskirts, upon a large speckled rock, looking out at those who somehow seemed to know the secret of enjoying themselves.

Leaving the party behind, she found Gene propped up against an old oak tree and so deep in thought that he failed to notice the triangular bundle she carried. "I guess we'll be shipping out soon," he said.

"Tomorrow at noon," said Elspeth. "We want to be across Torcano Alley before dark. Then we'll wait until nightfall before making our way to the trees."

"I'd be lying if I said I wasn't nervous," Gene admitted.

"We're all nervous," said Elspeth. "And with good reason. None of us has ever gone to battle before. Speaking of which, I have a favor to ask of you."

"Sure," said Gene. "What is it?"

Elspeth unfolded the triangular bolt of cloth, revealing Young Mrs. Hubbard's completed flag. "I need someone to carry it into battle."

"And you're asking me?"

"A flag is nothing without a stick on which to hang it. What do you say? If you carry the flag, I'll carry you—and together we'll raise it high upon the East Tower."

"Providing we make it that far," said Gene.

"We'll make it," said Elspeth. "In case you haven't heard, it is written."

Old Mother Hubbard moved to the suburbs
When Krool took over the throne.
On the front of her shirt
She stitched "Krool's a jerk."
'Twas the last thing she'd ever sewn.

Chapter 27

With a few minor adjustments and a couple of major ones, the trebuchet seemed to be working much better. However, in order to transport it across Torcano Alley, up the cliff and across the field to the cover of the trees, it would have to be taken apart. Whether it would still work when reassembled in darkness remained to be seen.

In regard to the troops there was no question as to their preparedness. They were sufficiently conditioned, expertly trained, and appropriately angry. They were a team, and every team, Elspeth decided, should have a name. And that's how her army, two hundred strong, came to be known as the Quick Stick Brigade. She ordered them into marching formation and then turned to Fergus.

"We'll send for you tomorrow when it's all over."

"I must say, not being a part of the attack is a bitter pill to swallow," said the owl. "But with this useless wing, I'd be nothing but a burden to you."

"Don't worry," said Elspeth. "We'll make sure you get your revenge."

"It's not revenge with which I'm concerned. It's you. Please, be careful."

Fergus was not the only one to remain behind. Queen Farrah would not make the trip nor would her official bodyguards.

"Little Robin Redbreast will deliver word of our victory," said Winkie to his bride. "Only then will it be safe for Rory, Cory, and Maury to escort you to the castle." He then removed a small slip of paper from his pocket and handed it to Farrah.

"What's this?"

"From Jack and Jill," said Winkie. "The location of the well. If we're not victorious, if something bad should happen to me, get away from this place. Promise me."

Farrah studied the paper for a moment then handed it back to her husband. "If something bad should happen to you, I promise you I will dive into a well, but not this one."

"You're as stubborn as you are beautiful," said Winkie with a smile. "I suppose I had better do my best to emerge from this intact." He kissed his bride for what each of them hoped would not be the last time, then he joined the marching ranks sitting astride the nape of Jack's beefy neck.

Their weapons at rest upon their right shoulders, the Quick Stick Brigade followed Elspeth through the forest as she held Gene out at such an angle that the flag could be seen in all its glory. Though talking in ranks was prohibited, the march was by no means a quiet one as trees and bushes they passed along the way gave out shouts of support.

"Go get 'em!"

"Give 'em one for us!"

"Quick Stick Brigade! Hurrah!"

None of them was more enthusiastic than Manuel as Elspeth took the time to thank him once more for apprehending the Crooked Man.

"Glad to do it, señorita," said Manuel. "Anything to help the cause." Then he reached up with one branch, snapped off a small twig, and handed it to Elspeth. "If you would do me the honor of planting this in the castle courtyard, it will make me happy to know that I'm with you all in some little way."

"You have my word," said Elspeth, carefully pocketing the twig.

Manuel snapped to attention and raised a branch in salute, holding it there until the last member of Elspeth's army had passed.

When they reached the edge of the forest, there stood the three posted signs, Keep Out, Do Not Enter, and Don't Even Think About It.

"Where do you think you're going?" Keep Out demanded. "Can't you read?"

271

"Read this," said Elspeth as she smacked the sign with the heel of her hand, the force knocking it to the dirt.

"You won't get away with this!" Keep Out threatened as the other two signs snickered behind his back.

Snaking out across Torcano Alley went the Quick Stick Brigade, and soon Elspeth recognized the crevasse into which she and the others had fallen. She was therefore pleased when Jack informed her that torcano season was nearly at an end by now and the odds of encountering one this time of year were unlikely.

Other than having to make a few unscheduled stops so Dumpty could regain his balance and composure by leaning upon his stick, they crossed without incident or being noticed. They continued past Winkie's former home in the side of the cliff, then lugged the heavy parts of the trebuchet up the switchback until they'd reached the plateau. All in all, it had a been a six-hour march, and the troops were thankful for a chance to sit in the tall grass and rest until dark, when it would be time to move into position for the next day's assault on the castle, barely visible from this distance.

Once the final leg of their trip began, there would be no talking. This was the last opportunity Elspeth would have to address her army before the attack and, depending how it all went, perhaps the last chance to ever speak to them again. "Listen up, everybody," she said. At the mere sound of her voice, her soldiers began scrambling to their feet until she said, "At ease, at ease. You've all done enough standing for the time being."

For the last hour she'd been thinking about the message she wanted to convey but hadn't decided on quite how to say it. "In case I don't have a chance to tell you later," she began, "in case something should happen to me, I wanted to be sure you all knew how proud I am of you. As your commanding officer, I would like to thank you for your hard work and dedication. I would also like to take this opportunity to apologize for something." Her voice raised slightly in pitch as her throat tightened. "You see, I'm afraid that I haven't been completely honest with you all."

This statement sent a soft murmur through the crowd. What could it be? What horrible lie had she told them? Would she abandon them as she had once threatened to do?

"Several weeks ago," Elspeth continued, "I made a speech in which I said I was not your friend. That was as untrue then as it is today. Before I came here, I had no friends. And now I've got more than I can count. More than I ever imagined. And certainly more than I deserve.

"Together we've come a long way. As a very big man once said to me, a hero's fate is handed down from sources unknown. And when it is, he accepts his fate and all of the burden and all of the glory that comes with it. We've endured the burden. Now let's taste some of that glory."

It was the kind of speech that one might expect to result in wild cheering and deafening applause, and it very well may have had that castle not been just a couple of miles away. Instead, it ended in quiet nods of affirmation and handshakes—two hundred of them as Elspeth moved among her troops, thanking them individually for their efforts.

When the sun had set and the white castle now showed only in black silhouette against a purple sky, Elspeth gave the order to advance. In silence the two hundred marched toward the cover of the trees where they would spend their last night as second-class citizens, for by day's end tomorrow, either they would be free or they would be dead.

The cottages outside the castle gate were mostly dark, though a few gave off a glow from candle or fireplace. To speak poorly of Krool was a most serious offense, so one could never know how the people of Banbury Cross truly felt about him. Outwardly, they sang his praises, though it was equally probable that they loathed him just as much as did Elspeth, Jack and Jill, and the others.

Playing to the side of caution, Elspeth led her troops in a wide berth around the houses so as not to be detected by those within.

When they finally arrived at the grove, she was pleased to find Earl Grey waiting for her. He was happy to report that the job of tunneling into the stables had been completed as of the day before. As discussed, he and his fellow mice would remain hidden until hearing the signal that it was time to spring into action. With a tiny salute, he hurried off to a hole near the castle wall and disappeared.

Putting a trebuchet together in near complete darkness and in total silence could not be a more difficult task. It took three attempts before it was assembled to Winkie's satisfaction, with no extra parts still lying on the ground.

Elspeth whispered to her troops that once the job was finished they would be wise to try to get some sleep before the attack. Sage advice perhaps, but also, as they discovered, nearly impossible to follow. In the thin night air, even a whisper could find its way to nearby ears. After all, every word that the guards spoke to each other, every petty complaint and obvious joke, was clearly audible to those hiding amid the trees. So then, with talking prohibited and sleep elusive, there was nothing to do but lie there for hours, imagining all that could go wrong.

The Cheese stands alone.
The Cheese stands alone.
High in cholesterol,
The Cheese stands alone.

Chapter 28

It was an hour till dawn when Dumpty gave the Cheese a double tap with the palm of his hand, indicating that it was time for him to leave the cover of the trees and roll toward the castle gate. This time, it never occurred to Dumpty to lick his hand after touching the Cheese. There were other things on his mind far more important than flavor.

Danger may have been his middle name, but that did nothing to quell the trembling as the Cheese rolled out across the open space, between the cottages, until finally he stood alone before the castle, where he could do nothing but wait for the rising sun to reveal his position to the guards on the catwalk. What if something went wrong, he thought. He could easily end up as an hors d'oeuvre at Krool's victory party.

Then again, if all went according to plan, this could be the stuff of which legends are made. Future generations for centuries to come would speak of him as they do the Trojan horse. "The Trojan Cheese," he thought to himself. It certainly had a nice ring to it.

At first, the guards couldn't decide what it was, exactly. "It's a wagon wheel," one suggested. "It's a grinding stone," said another. It wasn't until the rays of the rising sun began to heat up the Cheese that the resulting aroma finally solved the issue. It was, without a doubt, a wheel of sharp, aged cheddar.

The next thing to be determined was what should be done about it? It was much too early to awaken the king, even concerning a matter of such importance as fine cheese. Then again, did any of them really want to be responsible for letting such a find slip away?

"I don't know," said one of the guards. "We can't just open the gate without permission."

"Yes," said another. "But think what might happen to us if the birds get to it before we do."

"Birds?" thought the Cheese. That was something he hadn't considered, but now that the guards mentioned it, he clearly noticed several crows circling overhead, getting lower and lower with each pass.

He contemplated turning and rolling back to the safety of the trees, but that would jeopardize the entire mission, so he remained motionless as the guards continued to debate the issue. Soon the Cheese was relieved to hear the clunking of the oversize chains as slowly the drawbridge started down.

One hundred feet away, Elspeth turned to her troops and gave a thumbs-up, which signaled them to move into attack position. Like sprinters intently listening for the starting gun for the one-hundred-meter dash, they crouched with fighting sticks in hand.

Elspeth watched the gate closely. The timing must be perfect. There would be a short delay between the rush toward the gate and the realization by the guards that the castle was under attack. Those precious few seconds could prove vital to the mission's success.

Elspeth turned and made eye contact with Winkie to make certain he was ready at the trigger of the trebuchet. He nodded slowly in response, and Elspeth turned her attention back to the drawbridge, now halfway to the ground. As a mechanism, it was painfully slow. The better side of that was that it would be even slower on the way up. If Georgie's calculations on the velocity of the drawbridge were accurate, there should be just enough time for A Company to scramble through.

While the platform inched closer to the ground, all eyes focused on Elspeth's left hand as she raised it high above her head. When it dropped, that would be the signal to fire the trebuchet. The order to charge would follow immediately with Little Boy Blue blasting his trumpet.

When the drawbridge was a mere three feet from the ground, Elspeth's left hand sliced through the air.

Winkie pulled the trigger and . . . nothing happened. He pulled it again with the same result. Panic quickly set in as Dumpty shoved Winkie aside and began tugging furiously on the lever with all his might, but with the same awful result. The drawbridge hit the ground with a thud. The misfire of the trebuchet had already cost them precious seconds. A look of terror crossed Elspeth's face. It was far too late to abandon the mission, but without the trebuchet, the archers would have a clear shot at them.

With no other option, Elspeth yelled, "Charge!"

At the sound of the trumpet, the three visually impaired mice jumped out of a small hole in the dirt of the stable floor and began terrorizing the horses, while B Company raced to the west wall scaffolding and A Company charged toward the main gate.

The two guards sent out to retrieve the giant wheel of cheddar were nothing less than shocked to see one hundred stick-wielding warriors charging toward them, years of anger derived of suppression and exploitation spilling forth from their lungs in a wild, almost inhuman cry of war.

Villagers threw aside sashes and peered out their windows at the commotion while others ran out, still in their nightclothes.

"Go!" yelled the Cheese as Elspeth, Georgie, Jack and Jill, and the others stormed past. "Go!"

"Raise the gate!" the guards commanded, sprinting back the way they'd come. "We're under attack!"

By now B Company was scrambling up the scaffolding while on the catwalk of the east wall a half dozen archers loaded and drew their bows. Each an expert marksman, it was only a question of which of Elspeth's soldiers would go down first. Or would Elspeth herself be a quick and easy casualty? As the archers took aim, a low whistling noise rose up above the sounds of thundering feet and savage howls.

The boulder from the trebuchet slammed into the top of the wall with enough force that those archers who were not thrown off the catwalk found themselves knocked to the ground, their bows sliding across the stone and over the edge to the courtyard below.

No time to celebrate, Winkie ordered the trebuchet reloaded immediately as Elspeth, flag shimmering in the early morning sun, reached the drawbridge, which had already begun inching slowly back off the ground. And as she and her army poured into the castle courtyard, she realized her mistake.

Though a drawbridge is a painfully slow mechanism, a portcullis can be lowered quite quickly and that's exactly what was happening. The thick iron gate came sliding down from above. Once it hit the ground, it would leave half of A Company trapped outside the castle walls, with Elspeth and the other half sealed off inside. Divided, they would be slaughtered. A windmill had been put in motion, but it was not in Elspeth's favor.

She admonished her troops to hurry as the drawbridge crawled upward and the portcullis raced down.

"Run!" she yelled. But all her urging was no force to compare with gravity.

And then, just as it appeared that defeat was a foregone conclusion, her advancing troops heard another voice, this one coming from behind them. "Look out!" yelled the Cheese. "Coming through!" Those who were not fast enough to get out of the way were quickly mowed over by the giant rolling dairy product.

Rodney hit the rising drawbridge at full speed. The gap between the platform and the ground caused him to fly several feet into the air upon impact. When he hit the downward sloping drawbridge, he picked up even more speed and rolled beneath the portcullis. Its iron tines sunk deep into his waxy rind with an awful squishing noise that caused Elspeth, and anyone else watching, to gasp. Like a dull meat cleaver into an overripe tomato the gate crushed the Cheese, pushing his malleable body toward the ground until, just like that, it stopped. Three feet from the ground, a big enough gap for Elspeth's troops to fit beneath, the portcullis stopped. And when Jack and Jill came to Rodney's aid, he groaned, "I'm all right! The Cheese stands alone! Now, go!"

Quite obviously, he was not all right and was in no condition to stand, alone or otherwise, but his friends had no choice other than to leave him.

By the time the last of A Company scurried beneath the gate with the drawbridge continuing to rise, Bo-Peep and B Company had climbed onto the catwalk and were well on their way to isolating the king by cutting off his escape from the East Tower.

Meanwhile, Elspeth led A Company to the barracks to pin the soldiers inside. But the misfiring trebuchet and the near disaster of the portcullis had cost them far too much time. When they finally reached the barracks, soldiers were already streaming out. They charged the rebels with swords drawn and spears leveled.

"First position!" Elspeth ordered. The Quick Stick Brigade, their backs to the wall, formed a wedge and met the attacking soldiers with lunges and parries, taking them out with sharp smacks to the temples and thrusting uppercuts to their jaws. Down the soldiers went, one after another, in piles while others turned and ran.

In stark contrast to Elspeth's well-conditioned troops, years of complacency had left Krool's men in terrible shape, and even running away was a difficult task. Some of them dropped their weapons and surrendered on the spot, begging not to be bludgeoned.

By now, all this commotion had awoken the king. He dressed hurriedly as his four most trusted guards filled him in. "What is it? What's going on?" he demanded.

"The castle is under attack," said the man with the sideburns.

"Under attack by whom?" Krool demanded. Quickly he buckled up his shoes and did up his belt.

"It appears that we were mistaken, sire," said the man with the Van Dyke. "As it turns out, she's alive."

"Who's alive?" asked Krool, though there could really be only one answer to the question.

"Jacqueline Jillson," the man replied. "Also known as . . ."

Krool reached out and grabbed the man by his pointy beard. "I know who she is. You assured me she was dead!"

"Prematurely, it would appear," said the man. "I'm sorry, Your Highness."

"You're sorry? You'll have plenty of time to show everyone how sorry you are when your sorry head is displayed on a pike!"

Krool pushed his way past the men on his way to the door.

"Sir?" said the man with the Van Dyke. "Perhaps you should wait here where it's safe."

"Are you suggesting I should hide? From an eleven-year-old girl?"

"Yes, sir, I am."

In an instant, the tower shook from the base to the turret with a direct hit from the trebuchet. Cracks appeared on the wall, and plaster rained down upon their heads. "On second thought," said the guard, "perhaps we should get moving."

Krool clipped his scabbard to his belt, drew his sword, and followed the others out the door and down the stairs to the catwalk.

With the rebel forces inside the castle walls, Dumpty and Winkie put the trebuchet to rest for fear of hitting their own troops. All they could do now was sit and hope with eyes trained on the East Tower, waiting for the appearance of the Winkie flag.

Stepping out onto the catwalk, Krool saw for the first time just how serious the situation had become. The castle wasn't under attack from an eleven-year-old girl. It was under attack from an eleven-year-old girl and her well-trained and highly disciplined army.

Bo-Peep's B Company was advancing quickly along the catwalk toward Krool and his guards.

"Stop them!" he ordered. The guards rushed toward the attackers but soon proved a poor match. Bo-Peep herself took out three of them singlehandedly. A sharp chop to the legs of the man with the goatee delivered him quickly to the ground. The one with the handlebar mustache tripped over the first guard, and as he stumbled forward he was met with the end of the stick in the forehead.

Stubbornly the man with the sideburns raised his spear with the intention of throwing it through Bo-Peep's heart. He released the spear and might have been successful if not for Bo-Peep's intense concentration and incredible quickness. With her stick, she sideswiped the spear, sending it twirling away toward the courtyard floor.

She followed with a full 360-degree spin, which generated such power that when the stick landed aside the man's head, it sent him crumpling into a useless pile.

All that now stood between Bo-Peep and the person who had murdered her sheep was the man with a Van Dyke beard on his pale, quivering face. He dropped his spear, raised his hands, and fell to his knees. Bo-Peep pushed him roughly aside and rushed toward Krool, her stick lowered, eyes locked on her target.

But Krool's eyes were focused elsewhere, for that spear that Bo-Peep so deftly deflected had claimed an unintended victim, and that victim was Elspeth Pule. Like a helicopter blade, the tip of the twirling lance had sliced through her forehead, causing her to sink to the ground, her face awash in blood. Next to her lay Gene and the Winkie flag, its gold background spattered in red.

Krool crouched down and jumped from the catwalk. He landed on the roof of the butcher shop and slid down across the shingles, absorbing each bump until his feet hit the stone floor of the courtyard just inches from Elspeth's bleeding head.

Her followers watched with shock and utter horror as Krool pulled the girl to her feet and placed the cold blade of his sword across her throat.

"Stop!" he commanded.

With that singular word Elspeth's entire army immediately froze.

"Drop those sticks this instant!" Krool's rich baritone voice volleyed off the stone walls and across the sudden silence, where it eventually made its way to the ears of Winkie and Dumpty.

"What was that?" gasped Dumpty. "It sounded like Krool."

"It sounded like Krool demanding surrender," said Winkie.

And that was exactly what he was demanding: complete and immediate surrender. He demonstrated his resolve by pressing the blade so firmly against Elspeth's throat that it made breathing difficult.

"Well?" he said to the sea of stunned faces before him. "Do you think I won't do it? I once threw her down a well, remember?"

"No," Elspeth gurgled. "Don't do it. He'll kill me anyway."

What Winkie and Dumpty heard next was the sound of two hundred fighting sticks hitting the ground almost at once.

"What do you think is going on?" asked Winkie, still holding out hope.

"I don't know," said Dumpty. "But I'm not going to wait here to find out. To the scaffolding!"

Dumpty scooped up Winkie and sprinted from the trees to the castle, where Krool was busy berating

287

and belittling his soldiers for having lost to a bunch of stick-bearing peasants. He ordered them to pull their battered bodies off the ground and retrieve their weapons. As they complied with the order, Krool gritted his teeth and prepared for the nasty business ahead. He'd been judge and jury for Elspeth and would now add executioner to that list.

As they had years ago, Jack and Jill once more watched helplessly as Krool prepared to end their daughter's life, this time not by frigid water but by cold steel. But before Krool could complete the task, a sudden blow to the back of his head knocked the sword from his hand. His knees wobbled, and he dropped like a sack of potatoes.

"No loitering!" sneered the sign standing directly behind him.

Jack quickly rushed over and placed his good foot on the back of Krool's neck, pinning him to the ground.

"I never did like him," said No Loitering.

Jack retrieved the fallen sword and positioned it directly over the left side of Krool's back where his cold heart was beating rapidly. Eleven years of shame, sorrow, and loss gave way to eleven years of anger as Jack raised the blade and prepared to plunge it in every bit as deep as the pain he'd endured.

"No," said Elspeth. "Please."

Jack looked at his daughter, reluctantly because he knew the moment his eyes met hers, he would have no choice but to comply with her wishes.

"It's much too good an end for him," she said. "Prison. That's where he belongs."

Gently, Elspeth pried the sword from her father's hand, and he seemed grateful to have been relieved of it. She then knelt next to Krool and moved her lips very close to his ear. "Don't worry," she said. "You'll get a fair trial. I have an excellent lawyer for you. Jack B. Nimble. Perhaps you've heard of him."

"This is not over!" yelled Krool into the dirt. "Attack! Let's go, you idiots! Attack them!"

Elspeth's army grabbed their sticks and prepared to do battle, but instead something strange happened. It began slowly then built up momentum as Krool's soldiers began not attacking, but cheering. They dropped their swords and their spears, raised their hands, and, though clearly defeated, somehow managed to let out what sounded like a triumphant cheer.

Once the confusion had passed, Elspeth's soldiers joined in until the sound in that courtyard was absolutely deafening. Still, above the din there was one voice that could clearly be made out. Wiping the blood from her eyes, Elspeth looked up to see Dumpty, skipping and prancing back and forth along the castle wall, screaming at the top of his lungs while showing absolutely no signs of dizziness.

Humpty Dumpty danced on a wall,
Humpty Dumpty having a ball.
All of Krool's horses and all of Krool's men
Never would harm poor Dumpty again.

Chapter 29

The afternoon breeze showed up just in time to give some life to the flag flying from the pole on the East Tower. By way of Little Robin Redbreast, word of the great victory had reached the forest, and in a matter of hours Fergus and Farrah would arrive to take part in the celebration of a military victory that resulted in only a few minor casualties and one major one.

Though he would never be quite the same, Simple Simon and Jack Horner were able to push the Cheese back into a mostly roundish shape by placing him in the oversize dish that had been used to bake that giant everyberry pie and using it as a mold.

"How do you feel?" asked Elspeth as the Cheese rolled around the kitchen like a car with a flat tire.

"Are you kidding? The Trojan Cheese has never felt better," he said. "Now let's get this party started."

Now that Krool was firmly locked within the dungeon, life-size statues of the former ruler were toppled and smashed. Those giant tapestries bearing his likeness that hung from the walls of the courtroom where so many had been sentenced for nonexistent crimes were torn down and burned in the middle of the square, along with his blue velvet chair.

Those who had once sworn allegiance to Krool were all too happy to devote themselves to King William and to his new bride.

"Long live the queen," they shouted when Farrah and Fergus were finally carried into the square, which by now was alive with music and dancing. Winkie rushed to greet his wife, and the cheers only grew louder as they embraced.

"Welcome to your new home," he said.

"It's beautiful," said Farrah, taking in her surroundings. "Though it could do with a woman's touch. I am a fashion doll after all."

"Whatever you think, my dear," said Winkie. "Whatever you think."

As much as she wanted to partake in the victory party, Elspeth was feeling terribly anxious about her parents back home and about what they must be going through by now. "What day is it, anyway?" she asked, having not thought about such things for weeks.

"It's Wednesday," said Georgie.

Elspeth chuckled to herself. "Winkie Wednesday," she said.

"Yes," said Winkie with a gleam in his eye. "What do you know about that?"

Elspeth apologized for having to duck out on the first of what they all hoped would be many Winkie Wednesdays to come.

"Don't worry," said Winkie. "It's quite understandable. You've done enough for us. It's time you did something for yourself."

"Of course you know I'll be back," she promised.

"You'd better come and visit us," said Fergus. "Or I'll hunt you down. And we owls are quite good hunters, broken wings notwithstanding." Fergus issued a salute with his good wing, and Elspeth sent one back.

They formed a line, did the Quick Stick Brigade, that stretched the entire length of the courtyard. One by one Elspeth bid farewell to each of them on her way toward the castle gate, where Jack and Jill were already waiting to escort her to the well.

There was no shortage of gratitude as she moved from one friend to the next. Georgie thanked her for putting her faith in him and for giving him a second chance. Bo-Peep thanked Elspeth for allowing her to take charge of her life. And Gene thanked her for all she'd done in helping to give sticks the recognition they deserve.

Saying good-bye to each of them was difficult. Saying good-bye to some of them was downright painful.

"I'm not sure what I'll do without you," Elspeth said to Queen Farrah. "I'll have no one to talk to. No one to play chess with."

"Oh, I don't know," said Farrah. "I have a feeling you'll end up with plenty of people to talk to. If not, you know where to find me. I'm not planning on going anywhere for a long time."

Elspeth gave her best friend one last hug.

And then there was Dumpty.

"I'll never forget you," she said, having no success in fighting back tears.

"Nor I you," said Dumpty, who was failing just as badly. "I owe you a great deal. For the first time in years, I'm stress free. As a result, my vertigo seems to have completely abandoned me. I feel like a young man again." He performed a quick little dance that made Elspeth laugh right through her tears.

"You are a young man," she said. "And don't worry. I'll be sure to tell everyone the original stories." She ran the sleeve of her uniform across her eyes. "I'll spread the word, just as soon as I get back to the real world."

"The real world?"

"Sorry. The other world. The Deadlands, as you call it."

An embrace followed that would have lasted much longer if not for Elspeth's concern about her parents' well-being. Reluctant as she may have been, that force pulled her toward the castle gate.

The walk to the well was mostly silent with each of them, Jack, Jill, and Elspeth, wondering what they might say and afraid of how they might feel when they got there.

The route took them over Krool's golf course, past the zoo, and around the mulberry bush. When Jack and Jill stopped walking it took Elspeth a moment to realize that they'd arrived at their destination. The well looked quite unlike she'd imagined it would. There was no tiny shingled rooftop and no wooden bucket hanging from a crank. This well was nothing more than a circle of crumbling stone, in places only a foot or two high.

"This is it?" asked Elspeth.

"This is it," said Jack, though it was not clear whether he was referring to the well or to the end. Or, perhaps, to both.

Elspeth leaned over and peered into the dark hole. "You went down there?" she asked. "Voluntarily?"

"There was nothing voluntary about it," said Jill. "Someday, when you have children of your own, you'll know what I mean."

Elspeth nodded but did not remove her gaze from the well.

"I know it looks a little scary," Jack admitted. "But it's quite easy, really. The passageway is at the very bottom on the northern side. When you find it, just pull yourself through and you'll be home."

"Home," said Elspeth, not sure if she completely understood the meaning of the word anymore.

"You will come out a bit wet on the other side, I'm afraid," said Jill.

Only now did Elspeth make the connection. She felt foolish for not having done so before. "The puddle on my carpet," she said. "It was you, wasn't it? You've been watching me sleep."

"Yes," said Jill. "I'm sorry. It's just that . . ."

"No," said Elspeth. "You needn't be sorry. You can come and watch me sleep whenever you wish. Or you could come in the daytime. I could introduce you to my parents . . . my other parents. I'm sure they'd like you."

"We'll see," said Jill. "We only want what's best for you."

She took Elspeth by the shoulders and looked at her from arm's length as if trying to form a mental picture that could last her a very long time. "You've grown up so well," she said. "So strong and so smart."

"Don't forget spirited," said Elspeth.

Jill smiled at this. "Yes. No doubt about that."

"I guess it goes without saying how proud we are of you," said Jack.

"You could say it anyway," said Elspeth. "I won't mind if you do."

"We're unbelievably proud of you," he said. He embraced his daughter, and Jill joined in. It was a family hug, and Elspeth could not remember ever having been part of one before.

"Good-bye, Mom," said Elspeth. "Good-bye, Dad."

She sat down on the stone and swung around until her feet dangled into the blackness. She looked at Jack and Jill one more time for reassurance, then she took in a deep breath and pushed herself over the edge.

Falling into a crevasse one hundred feet deep had done nothing to prepare Elspeth for the experience of purposely jumping into a dark, narrow hole in the ground. In the movies, people always scream when they fall, but as much as she wanted to she couldn't make a single sound.

As she continued to fall, she began to fear that she'd taken her breath too soon. She quickly exhaled, and just as she was about to fill her lungs anew, she hit the water. If there was anything more disconcerting than being at the bottom of a dark, narrow hole, it was being at the bottom of a dark, narrow hole while, at the same time, being underwater.

Already desperate for air, she used her arms and legs to propel herself downward, frantically looking for the bottom while brushing her palms across the sides searching for the passageway on the northern side. But which way was north, she wondered? In fact, the longer she remained without air, the less certain she became of which way was up.

And then she saw it—a dim, wavy light just a few feet away. She continued to push herself downward, but with every foot of progress the light seemed to move away faster than she could swim toward it.

Finally, it was in within her reach. But just as she stretched out her hand to take hold of the passageway and pull herself through, she blacked out.

One, two,
Buckle my shoe;
Three, four,
Prepare for war;
Five, six,
Pick up sticks;
Seven, eight,
Crash the gate;
Nine, ten,
Home again.

Chapter 30

Elspeth greedily filled her lungs with oxygen while sitting up so quickly that if her mother had not been as agile, she would have broken the poor woman's nose.

"Elspeth!" gasped Mrs. Pule. "You're back!"

Elspeth wiped the water from her eyes and looked frantically about the apartment. It was all here, just as she'd left it so long ago: the furniture, the commemorative spoons, her parents. She lunged forward and hugged first her mother, then her father.

"I'm sorry," she blurted out.

"It's okay," her mother comforted her.

"No, it's not. I'm sorry. For everything. I don't want an alpaca, and I don't want a llama. I don't want anything from you. You've given me so much already. And I'm sorry I worried you. I'm sorry I was gone for so long."

Mr. Pule checked his watch, and Elspeth noticed he was holding a washcloth stained with blood. "Yes," he said. "You've been out for nearly ten minutes."

"Ten minutes?" said Elspeth.

"You should lie back and take it easy," said Mrs. Pule. "The paramedics are on their way."

"What?" said Elspeth. "No, call them off. I'm fine, really. There's nothing at all wrong with me."

Delores Pule looked at her husband, and he answered her look with a shrug. Against her better judgment but not wanting to upset her daughter, Delores picked up the phone, dialed 9-1-1 and cancelled the paramedics.

"Are you sure about this?" her father asked. "That's quite a cut on your head."

Elspeth brought her hand to her forehead and felt the gash, the blood now dry and tacky.

"You hit the coffee table pretty hard," her mother said.

"What?" said Elspeth. "No, no. I got this in the battle . . . fighting the evil King Krool and restoring William the Umpteenth to the throne."

"Call them back," said Mr. Pule.

Mrs. Pule picked up the phone once more and began to dial, but Elspeth grabbed her wrist and pulled the phone from her hand. "I know you don't believe me, but it's true. I had to defeat Krool in order to get home. I came back through the well. See? I'm all wet. How do you explain that?"

Mr. Pule presented a drinking glass, half-full of water. "I'm sorry," he said. "I threw water in your face trying to bring you around. I saw it in a movie once."

It was then that Elspeth realized that it was not her uniform that was soaked but her aquamarine T-shirt. She ran her fingers across the denim of her jeans. "My uniform," she said. "What happened to my uniform?"

"Your uniform?" said Mr. Pule. "You won't get your uniform until you're officially accepted at Waldorf. You're going to be quite a sight at the interview with that lump on your head."

"No," said Elspeth. "I'm not going to Waldorf."

"But dear," said Mrs. Pule. "I'm afraid it's our last option."

"I'm going back to my old school. Tomorrow."

"But they said you could only return if you . . ."

"Yes," said Elspeth. "I'm going to apologize. To Mrs. Weed and to the class."

Mr. Pule snatched the phone from Elspeth's hand. "I'm calling them back," he said. While he summoned the paramedics once more, Elspeth did nothing to stop him. She just sat and stared at the wall. The absence of her uniform certainly seemed to suggest that none of it had actually happened. It had all been a horrible, wonderful dream or the result of having cracked her head on the coffee table. And then something occurred to her.

She looked to her left, then right. She spun around and checked behind her. She lifted her bum and made sure she wasn't sitting on anything.

"What is it, dear?" asked Mr. Pule. "What are you looking for?"

"Where's Farrah?" asked Elspeth.

"Farrah?"

"Dolly Dew Eyes," said Elspeth. "My doll. I was holding her when I . . ."

Mr. Pule looked around but saw nothing. "I'm sure she's around here somewhere. Perhaps she slid under the couch." He crawled on his hands and knees toward the couch and peered beneath it. "Nope. Nothing here."

"Don't worry," said Mrs. Pule. "If we can't find her, we'll get you a new one."

"I don't want a new one," said Elspeth.

"Then we'll find the old one," said Mr. Pule.

"I don't want to find the old one," said Elspeth. "That's the last thing I want."

"I'm confused," said Mrs. Pule.

"So am I," said Elspeth, and then, quite abruptly, and without knowing exactly why, she began to sob.

Mrs. Pule placed her arms around Elspeth's shoulders, and, as the sirens grew louder and nearer, she rocked her daughter as she hadn't done since she was a toddler.

*

The next morning, Elspeth sat with her father at the breakfast table and watched as her mother hurried about the kitchen, scrambling eggs and buttering toast. It struck her how little resemblance there was between herself and these two people, and she abruptly blurted out, "Was I adopted?"

Mrs. Pule dropped the buttery knife to the floor, and Mr. Pule burned his tongue when he inhaled a mouthful of hot coffee.

"What did you say?" asked Mrs. Pule.

"Was I adopted?" Elspeth repeated.

Slowly, Mrs. Pule left the stove, pulled out the chair next to Elspeth, and sat down. She took the girl's hand in hers. "We were going to tell you," she said, "when you turned twelve. I suppose we should have done it sooner, but we never wanted you to feel as if you were unwanted by anyone. You must know that we love you every bit as much as if you were born to us."

"I know," said Elspeth. "Where did you find me?"

Mrs. Pule chuckled, imagining a basket on the front doorstep. "Where did we find you? Through the adoption agency, of course."

"Oh," said Elspeth.

"A very lovely woman named Mrs. Hubbard," said Mr. Pule.

Elspeth sat up straight. "Hubbard?"

304

"Yes," said Mrs. Pule. "She's since passed away, I believe."

In her mind, Elspeth added this to the list of strange coincidences, but her thoughts were soon interrupted by a horrible shrill noise. The smoke alarm had detected the smell of burning scrambled eggs. Mrs. Pule rushed to the stove and removed the pan from the burner then went about opening windows and fanning away the smoke with a dishtowel.

"I have to go," said Elspeth over the loud squealing.

"What's that?" yelled her mother.

"I HAVE TO GO!" she shouted just as the alarm abruptly shut off. "I have to go. I don't want to be late."

"Yes," said Mrs. Pule. "We'll talk more when you get home. I mean when we get home." Mrs. Pule explained that she and Mr. Pule would be out until around four due to a very important medical appointment.

"Is everything okay?" asked Elspeth.

"Oh yes," said Mrs. Pule. Despite the paramedics finding nothing wrong with her, Mr. and Mrs. Pule were so concerned with their daughter's strange behavior after hitting her head on the coffee table that they'd called and pleaded for a last-minute emergency meeting with Dr. Fell.

"Everything's fine," said Mr. Pule. He handed Elspeth a key. "You'll have to let yourself in. You're practically twelve, so it should be okay."

Elspeth took the key, and as she shoved it into the

305

pocket of her jeans, her face froze. She felt something, and, pulling that something out, she realized it was a small twig—the twig of a willow tree. "Manuel," she whispered. "I forgot to plant it."

"What's that, dear?" asked Mrs. Pule, still whipping that dishtowel through the air.

"Nothing," said Elspeth. She spun the tiny branch between her thumb and forefinger.

"You'd better get going," her father said. "You don't want to miss the bus."

"Yes," said Elspeth, failing to move toward the door. Then, looking up, she said, "When you get back from your appointment I may not be here."

"Oh?" said Mrs. Pule with surprise.

"Yes. I think I'd like to visit some friends after school."

"Friends?" said Mr. Pule, with even more surprise.

"Are these people we know?" asked Mrs. Pule.

"No," said Elspeth. "But you should."

Her parents conferred briefly and agreed that it would be okay for Elspeth to visit with friends after school providing she was home by dinnertime. Elspeth promised she would be, then thanked them with a hug and hurried off to catch the bus.

On the way, she accidentally kicked a rock, and it said nothing. She picked up a stick and said hello, but it only resulted in silence and strange looks from people walking by. The world around her, the Deadlands as Dumpty had called it, seemed so dull and void of life and, at the same time, busy and loud.

At school, she wasn't the least bit bothered by the stares and the whispers as she walked by with her bandaged head held high. In addition, she found the apology to be much easier than she had thought it would be. Even speaking before the class was a piece of cake. It was the rest of the day that was terribly difficult, and she spent most of it staring at the clock, silently and ineffectively urging it forward.

When the dismissal bell finally came, Elspeth raced to the bus stop and climbed aboard the bus. She'd gotten there so quickly that she had to wait forever for the bus to fill up. Soon, impatience took over. Finding herself completely unable to sit still, she abruptly stood up and began pushing her way upstream, past those boarding the bus. "Excuse me," she said. "Sorry. Pardon me."

She finally reached the front, then bounded down the stairs and took off running for home.

It was four miles at least, but her lungs did not ache and her legs did not tire. When her building came into view she ran even faster, then sprinted up the stairs, the key already in hand. She opened the door and slammed it shut behind her. She tore off her knapsack and her jacket and tossed them onto the couch.

She slid the coffee table to one side and stood in the middle of the living room. Then, with the twig of the willow held tightly between her fingers, she took in a shallow breath and held it.

The adventure continues in Long Live the Queen.

Elspeth Pule's friends from New Winkieland
are in trouble. An evil witch has kidnapped
Queen Farrah, and now Elspeth may be
the only one who can get her back.

Elspeth hated school, and the idea of returning to it in less than a week was unbearable. How could she go back to such a tedious place after a summer of frequent and wonderful trips to New Winkieland, where she had argued with rocks, made friends with a blabbermouth stick, and had witnessed a pillow fight between two pillows named Andy and Kyle? (Not that it matters, but Andy won by technical knockout.)

You see, in New Winkieland, just about everything—from sticks to shrubs to pillows—is alive. And once school started, Elspeth would have to curtail her visits to this magical place to which she traveled by means of holding her breath until she passed out. Each time she awoke to find herself in the land of Humpty Dumpty, Little Bo-Peep, Georgie Porgie, and the Cheese. You know, the one so very fond of standing alone.

In New Winkieland, Elspeth had made the kind of friends she had never been able to in her own world. Dumpty referred to Elspeth's world as the Deadlands, because it was simply that by comparison—dead, as lifeless and devoid of spark as any of her teachers at school. For instance, Elspeth felt convinced that there were B-movie robots with a greater capacity for voice inflection than her Advanced English teacher, Mrs. Weed. And then there was Mr. Evans, the P.E. teacher, who smelled of stale cigars and was so out of shape he used a whistle app on his smartphone, being that he lacked the energy and lung capacity to operate an actual whistle.

Yes, Elspeth hated school. Yet here she was, preparing for the start of another academic year by engaging in one of her least favorite activities: back-to-school shopping at the mall, which seemed to be an annual exercise in determining just how badly her mother could embarrass her by using words that no longer exist.

"Here," Delores Pule said, using her thin, brittle-looking fingers to hold up a pair of jeans from the forty-percent-off rack. "Try on these dungarees. They're on sale."

"Mom," pleaded Elspeth in the kind of harsh whisper that can only be delivered by a mortified twelve-year-old. She nervously scanned the store for anyone she might know. "They're jeans, not dungarees."

"You know what I mean. Now try them on while I go take a look at the sneakers."

Sneakers? Dungarees? How old was her mom? A million?

Actually, Delores, with her rigid posture, poofy, cotton-candy-like hair, and frequent use of outdated phrases, *was* quite a bit older than the mothers of Elspeth's classmates. It was only after Delores had passed her childbearing years that she and her husband, Sheldon, decided to try adoption, a process that proved to be highly discouraging.

Part of the problem was that Mr. and Mrs. Pule were quite adamant that they wanted a girl. Actually, this was a stipulation that was insisted upon by Mrs. Pule, who had always found boys to be too rambunctious.

"But I think it would be every bit as nice to have a boy," Sheldon once suggested.

"Absolutely not," replied Delores. "They're always running around, knocking things over, and making disgusting noises with their armpits and with other parts of their anatomy. We will wait for a girl and that is that."

And so they waited. Soon four years had gone by, and the Pules considered giving up and instead adopting a puppy or a stretch of highway. Then one day, while Mr. Pule was out of town on business, Delores received a call from a lovely woman at the adoption agency named Mrs. Hubbard. The news was just what they had been waiting for but had practically given up on. The agency had taken in a one-year-old girl, and the Pules just happened to be next on the waiting list.

Two days later, they walked into their apartment toting a precious bundle of joy along with a second bundle full of other stuff you need in order to take care of the first bundle: diapers, miniature jars of mashed peas, earplugs . . .

Sheldon and Delores doted on the child to the point of spoiling her silly, and, despite an astonishing lack of physical resemblance between Elspeth and the Pules, the girl grew up believing that Sheldon and Delores were her birth parents. And though they insisted they had fully intended on telling her the truth once she'd turned twelve, Elspeth wasn't so sure that she would have found out if she hadn't encountered her actual birth parents, quite by coincidence, while visiting New Winkieland.

It's one thing to find out you've been adopted by way of accidentally running into your biological mother and father and quite another to discover that they are people you've always thought to be fictional characters. Imagine, for instance, learning that you are the son of Romeo and Juliet or the daughter of Mary Poppins and Zeus. (Not likely as, to my knowledge, the two never dated.)

In Elspeth's case, she initially struggled with the idea before coming to terms with the fact that her real parents were Jack and Jill—two people known to the world mostly for their inability to successfully negotiate a hill while carrying a bucket of water.

As unlikely as the whole thing might have seemed, Elspeth suddenly found herself with two sets of parents: one with whom she lived in the greater Seattle area and another who resided, hidden from the "real world," in the land of nursery rhymes, known once again as New Winkieland now that Elspeth had helped restore Wee Willie Winkie to his rightful place upon the throne while casting out the horrible King Krool.

She was reliving that moment now as she stood in the changing room surrounded by so many angled mirrors that she could actually see the back of her own head, which ached with boredom and an intense longing for the wild exhilaration that could only be had by leading an armed rebellion against an evil tyrant.

Here in the Deadlands, Elspeth was just another middle schooler, destined for a middling life of great inconsequence and staggering mediocrity. But in New Winkieland she was a legend. In fact, during her most recent visit several weeks ago, she was both flattered and slightly embarrassed that King William the Umpteenth had commissioned a statue of her likeness to be erected in the castle courtyard.

"They're a little big around the middle," said Delores, tugging at the waistband of the sale-priced jeans and pulling Elspeth out of the daydream and back to the

Deadlands. "You could wear a belt with them. I think it would look very sharp."

"Sharp?" said Elspeth, staring blankly at the back of her head.

"Yes. You know, snazzy."

Elspeth and her mother left the mall and walked out into a rain-soaked parking lot with two pairs of snazzy dungarees (jeans), two pairs of slacks (pants), a pair of sneakers (tennis shoes), and six new pairs of skivvies (underwear). This rather unimpressive haul had more or less exhausted Elspeth's back-to-school clothing budget. The Pules were not wealthy by any means. In fact, you would be hard pressed to call them middle class. Sheldon Pule was employed as a door-to-door hearing aid salesman while her mother worked from home part-time preparing other people's tax returns.

That home was in a small, four-story apartment building covered in white stucco and dotted with small outcroppings of concrete and iron that were barely big enough to be called balconies, but were anyway, and were crammed with barbecues, bicycles, and a host of other odds and ends.

From her pocket, Elspeth fished out her set of keys, which included one for the main door to the building, one for the door to the apartment, and a mail key. Having keys of her own still held a certain novelty, since she'd only been given them upon turning twelve several months before. And though she rarely went anywhere without at least one of her parents, the keys were symbolic of the fact that she now could if she wanted to.

She held the door open for her mother, and in they went. The interior of the building smelled exactly as you might expect just by looking at it, though perhaps a bit more on the cabbagey side thanks to an old German couple who had moved in next door to the Pules.

And when Elspeth unlocked the door to apartment 207 and she and her mother walked in, they found it to be more cabbagey than usual and especially quiet. Elspeth's father was currently at the other corner of the country, in Florida, attending the annual convention of Worldwide Hearing Aid Traders (also known as WHAT?), where he was due to receive a special award for twenty years of dedicated service.

"What's the matter, dear?" asked Delores. It was a question she had posed frequently to her daughter in recent months: a question that Elspeth had answered in identical fashion each time.

"Nothing. Everything is just fine."

But that's exactly what was the matter. Everything was just fine, which is just dandy if *just fine* is what you strive to be. And though there was a time when Elspeth considered *just fine* to be a perfectly adequate way of feeling, that had all changed now that she'd discovered a world so full of life and so ripe for adventure.

To feel fine was akin to feeling nothing at all as she did now, walking into the small apartment where everything was just as drab and predictable as when she had left it two and a half hours before. There was the coffee table that still featured a small bit of Elspeth's golden hair—stuck between the wooden frame and the glass top—as a result of Elspeth passing out and smacking her head on it.

And though the collision had left a good-sized lump on her forehead that remained for weeks, the coffee table had absolutely nothing to say about the encounter and simply went about its business, resting lifelessly in front of the couch, which apparently had no opinion whatsoever as to people sitting upon it.

Yes, everything seemed to be just as it always was. And it continued to seem that way until Elspeth walked into her bedroom and heard the squishing sound and felt the cold water seep in through the sides of her old "sneakers."

The sound and the sensation startled her, but not to the extent that one might think. Though it hadn't happened in quite a while, this was not the first time a puddle of water had appeared on her bedroom floor.

Once thought to be the result of a plumbing problem originating in the apartment above, Elspeth had since solved the mystery of the recurring puddle (which may or may not be the title of a Nancy Drew book Elspeth had once read). As it turns out, every magical kingdom that has a way in must also have a way out, and the way out of New Winkieland just happened to be at the bottom of an abandoned well.

The passageway had been discovered by none other than Jack and Jill, who, upon finding it, had used it on a regular basis to enter the Deadlands for a chance to look upon their precious daughter as she slept, each time leaving a sizable splash of water on the bedroom floor until the carpet became discolored and mildewed.

"I need you to try on these galoshes to see if they still fit," said Delores, appearing in Elspeth's doorway and holding a pair of what most people born in the last century would call boots.

"Great. Here we go again," Delores scoffed, when she saw that her daughter was standing in the middle of a puddle in the middle of her bedroom. "I thought we had this problem all taken care of. Well, I'll have to go find Mr. Droughns and tell him the leak has returned."

"Sure," said Elspeth, distracted by the knowledge that her biological mother and father had been in her room quite recently. Immediately, Elspeth began to worry. After all, this was the first time Jack and Jill had come to visit her in midday. Before now, it was always between midnight and early dawn. So why were they suddenly willing to risk being seen in the light of day? After all, if Delores had walked in on them she would have immediately called the police, who, most likely, would have had a very hard time believing any explanation Elspeth might provide.

"Yes, Officers. It's all very simple. You see, these are my real parents, Jack and Jill. You know, the ones who went up the hill to fetch a pail of water? Anyway, they did not break into the apartment. They arrived here quite legally from the magical kingdom of New Winkieland by way of a secret passage at the bottom of a well."

"I see. Well, thank you, young lady. That certainly explains everything. Have a good day."

Delores went off to find Mr. Droughns, the building superintendent, and Elspeth plopped down upon her bed. She picked up her plastic fashion doll, the one her parents had bought for her to replace the one she'd lost. She had yet to give it a name. What was the point? It was just a doll. As Elspeth looked into its unflinching eyes and ran her fingers down its long auburn hair, more than ever she missed Farrah, who would never visit her in the Deadlands for fear that she might turn back into a lifeless plastic toy like the one Elspeth now held.

She let out a deep sigh, and that sigh quickly turned to a scream when she felt a light tapping upon her ankle.

She jumped to her feet, causing the doll to fly from her vanishing lap and tumble to the floor very near the puddle. She spun around quickly to find, poking out from beneath the bed, a stick. And not just any stick.

"Guess who?" said the skinny, gray stick with a broad smile.

"Gene," gasped Elspeth. "What are you doing here?"

"You'll never guess in a million years."

I*t's raining, it's pouring,*
the Deadlands is boring.
Sat on my bed, a stick then said,
"I come with news and a warning."

That Gene was here in the Deadlands, still alive and as gabby as ever, gave Elspeth hope. Perhaps Farrah, too, could one day return for a visit without reverting to a lifeless state. Then again, Gene was originally from New Winkieland and had never been anything but alive and insufferably chatty.

And despite having the ability to speak, a walking stick in New Winkieland is no different than a walking stick in the Deadlands. Neither can actually walk, which means that Gene had to have gotten where he was with some help. Sure enough, there soon came a muffled grunt from under the bed.

"Pardon me. Would you mind?"

A hand emerged from the darkness. Elspeth reached down, took the hand, and tugged. She leaned back and pulled on it until a tall, thin man slid out from beneath the bed. The man was Georgie Porgie, also known as King William's chancellor and Chief Secretary of Puddin' and Pie.

"Georgie," Elspeth beamed. "What a surprise."

Georgie took Gene in his other hand, jammed the stick into the carpet like an astronaut planting a flag on the surface of the moon, and, with a grunt, pushed his lanky frame to its feet.

"Hey, easy!" protested Gene. "I'm a stick, not a handrail."

"Sorry," said Georgie, using his stickless hand to brush off the front of his puffy white shirt. Apparently Delores had been far too busy in recent weeks preparing taxes and looking for back-to-school bargains to find time to vacuum under Elspeth's bed because Georgie was positively covered in dust. In fact, clinging to his thin, yellow mustache were a couple of those bunnies of the dust variety.

"You've got something right there," said Elspeth, touching the part of her face that might feature a mustache if she had been able to grow one and had been inclined to do so.

Georgie quickly wiped the small clumps of dust from his face. With a look of disgust, he shook them from his hand. They floated peacefully to the floor like snowflakes, except that, unlike snowflakes, scientists cannot say with absolute certainty that no two dust bunnies are alike.

"How long have you been hiding under there?" asked Elspeth.

"Not sure," said Georgie. "My watch stopped working when I jumped into the well." He held his wrist to his ear to see if anything had changed since he last checked his waterlogged watch.

"And why are you here?" Elspeth urged. "Is something wrong?"

"Is something wrong?" said Gene. "That would be the understatement of the century."

Georgie glared down at Gene. "Do you mind? The king has entrusted me with the dissemination of this news, which should be delivered with tact and decorum, two things you seem to be completely without."

"Ha!" scoffed Gene. "I have more tact in my left knot-hole than you have in your entire body."

"Well, that's classy," said Georgie.

"I am one slick stick," Gene said proudly.

"What is it?" Elspeth persisted. "Is it Jack? Is he okay?"

That Elspeth would make such an assumption was not surprising. After all Jack was a large man with little regard for his own well being when it came to diet and exercise. His idea of health food was a hot dog in a whole wheat bun or bacon grease that had been freshly squeezed.

"He's fine," said Georgie, bringing Elspeth a measure of relief that would not last long. "I've come here on official royal business."

"*You've* come here?" Gene said with a deliberate clearing of his throat. "Seriously. Sometimes I wonder why I even bother."

"Okay," Georgie reluctantly agreed. "*We've* come here on official royal business. It's about Queen Farrah."

"Farrah?" Elspeth repeated. "Is there something the matter with her?"

Farrah was more to Elspeth than just the queen of New Winkieland. She had, for years, been Elspeth's favorite toy and closest confidante. It was only upon leaving the Deadlands behind that the former fashion doll had become sentient: a walking, talking, living, breathing miniature person. Not long after her arrival, her beauty and charm had captured the heart of the similarly tiny Wee Willie Winkie, also known as King William the Umpteenth.

"I'm afraid," said Georgie, "that Her Majesty has been kidnapped."

"What?" Elspeth gasped. The news was indeed alarming. "Kidnapped? By whom?"

"By Mary Mary," Georgie replied.

Elspeth had only ever heard of two people with a double first name. One of them was a boy named John John who used to be in her class but was now being home-schooled. "You mean Mary Mary Quite Contrary?"

"Contrary indeed," Gene spat. "That's the nicest thing anyone has ever said about her, I can guarantee you that. More like Mary Mary incredibly scary. Or Mary Mary better be wary. Or Mary Mary she's got a big fat hairy . . ."

"Okay, you've painted quite a vivid picture," Georgie interrupted. "She is quite hideous to be sure."

"And she smells awful," said Gene. "Seriously, would it kill her to take a bath once in a while?"

Elspeth had become accustomed to hearing about nursery rhyme characters who were not quite what she had always known them to be. Old King Cole turned out to be the evil King Krool and anything but a merry old soul. Little Bo-Peep was not so little and hadn't lost her sheep but had had them stolen away from her and eaten by Krool himself. And the Owl and the Pussycat's beautiful pea-green boat had been the target of a torpedo attack, which resulted in making a widower of Fergus, the poor old owl.

And now Mary Mary Quite Contrary apparently had things on her mind other than tending to her garden of silver bells and cockleshells. "But why would she want to kidnap Queen Farrah?"

"Money. Why else?" said Gene. "The king found one of the queen's shoes, along with a ransom note demanding one million sixpence."

"So you mean six million pence, then," said Elspeth.

"No," said Gene. "Read my wooden lips. One million sixpence."

GERRY SWALLOW is the author of the Magnificent Tales of Misadventure series, along with *A Whole Nother Story*—which received a starred review from *Kirkus Reviews* and was an Al Roker *Today Show* pick—and its sequels, *Another Whole Nother Story* and *No Other Story*, written under the pseudonym Dr. Cuthbert Soup. He began his career as a stand-up comic, making numerous appearances on NBC's *Tonight Show*. He then turned his attention to writing movies, including the blockbuster hit *Ice Age: The Meltdown*.

gerryswallow.com